George Wise

History of the Seventeenth Virginia infantry, C.S.A

George Wise

History of the Seventeenth Virginia infantry, C.S.A

ISBN/EAN: 9783741191237

Manufactured in Europe, USA, Canada, Australia, Japa

Cover: Foto ©Andreas Hilbeck / pixelio.de

Manufactured and distributed by brebook publishing software
(www.brebook.com)

George Wise

History of the Seventeenth Virginia infantry, C.S.A

Alexandria, May 18th, 1870.

Mr. Geo. Wise, Dear Sir:—

We take pleasure in vouching for the correctness of facts and incidents (as far as our memory serves us,) compiled in your History of the Seventeenth Virginia Infantry during the late war, the matter having been carefully compiled, as we know, from official reports, and diaries kept by members of the Regiment.

Wishing you much success from its publication,

We are yours truly,

Signed:

M. D. Corse,
Late Brig. Gen. C. S. A.

Morton Marye,
Late Col. 17th Va., Infantry, C. S. A.

Arthur Herbert,
Late Col. 17th Va., Infantry, C. S. A.

PREFACE.

T is that the friends of the Seventeenth Virginia Regiment may have a reliable chronicle of many of the ups and downs through which it passed during the four years' War, that the ensuing pages have been laid open for publication.

Upon its imperfections in a literary point of view I shall not comment, but of those so far more competent to such work, I ask that the intentions of the heart may be remembered, and their criticisms tempered with mercy.

The Regimental Muster Roll attached is as comprehensive as it has been practicable to make it, though still incomplete, which is a source of regret, for the desire is to omit none who deserve mention. How many familiar faces arise before the mind's eye associated with scenes of unfailing interest as we review that catalogue! A smile involuntarily comes as we glance upon some name inseparably associated with a merry-hearted, fun-loving temperament; at the next perhaps, the heart is bowed in sadness that but the name and memory alone remain of one so gifted in all the attributes of noble manhood.

HISTORY

Seventeenth Virginia Infantry, C. S. A.

ALEXANDRIA.

THE autumn of 1860 found the good old city of Alexandria, Va., enjoying its usual business prosperity and a characteristic hopefulness of "a better time coming." Soon the great tide of disquiet, arising from political differences between the Northern and Southern sections of our country, cast its waves upon our shores, producing in the minds of our little community emotions as varied as they are indescribable.

Frequent meetings were held, where the signs of the times were discussed and sentiments expressed for or against the probabilities of a disunion of the States. The city volunteer companies: "Alexandria Riflemen" and "Mount Vernon Guards," revived the "drill" and added many members to their respective corps. On the 6th December, the "Old Dominion

Rifles," composed of the "bone and sinew" of the remaining youth of our city, was organized, and every exertion made to render it, as it subsequently became, the honored helpmeet of its senior military confréres.

Our well-known and well-loved townsman, M. D. Corse, was elected captain. This high-toned, courteous gentleman, having served through the United States war with Mexico, was considered eminently fitted for the position.

All that could be done to prepare for the emergency was executed with promptness and energy. The "John Brown Raid," so well known to history, had left its impression on the minds of our quiet people; the volunteer companies of the city had tasted of "camp life" during their sojourn at Harper's Ferry in October, and, returning, gave their influence to the stirring events then transpiring. Much was to be accomplished, and citizen and soldier lent their aid to the work of military organizations.

Early in February, 1861, the Alexandria Battalion having been organized, Captain Corse was elected its major, and First Lieut. A. Herbert succeeded to the command of the "Old Dominion Rifles." The quota of troops furnished by old Alexandria to the Battalion was composed of the following companies : Alexandria Riflemen, Captain Morton Marye; Old Dominion Rifles, Captain A. Herbert; Mount Vernon Guards, Captain S. H. Devaughn; Alexandria Artillery, Captain D. Kemper.

The 22d of February was properly commemorated

by the general turnout of citizens, soldiers and fire companies, in honor to the " Father of his Country." Much enthusiasm was evinced; addresses suitable to the occasion were delivered by Messrs. K. Kemper, H. Snowden and others to a large concourse of attentive listeners.

The fall of Fort Sumter, and the stirring events rapidly transpiring in the South, having occasioned great excitement and alarm, it was deemed expedient, (in order to allay somewhat these feelings in the people, and to strengthen the tone of military power for the protection of life and property,) to call out a guard. On the 18th April, 1861, the Battalion met at its armory and the first guard was detailed. This step was hailed by all with satisfaction. On the 23d, a picket detail in charge of Lieut. W. H. Fowle, Jr., of the Old Dominion Rifles, was sent out upon the Washington and Alexandria turnpike.

Leaving the city after dark, the detachment proceeded to the Little Bridge, and, posting the reserve at that point, continued the line along the pike to the intersection of the two roads south of the Long Bridge.

The post at this point was occupied by Sergeant K. and Corporal W. of Lieut. Fowle's company, and was the only infantry post ever stationed by the Confederates so near to Washington city.

Yankee infantry, with several pieces of artillery, being stationed on the Long Bridge, the order was given the Southern pickets to watch them closely and report their movements.

Great excitement prevailed throughout the country, and volunteer troops were everywhere enrolling, preparatory to the organization of a new confederation, in which the Southern States might hope to preserve their institutions from further interference, and guard against encroachment upon their rights, by Northern fanatics and politicians. The election of Abraham Lincoln, as the candidate of the ultra Abolition party, hastened the severance of the tie between the South and a people whose objects, aims andprinciples were so utterly antagonistic to their own.

Virginia convened her statesmen in the Capitol at Richmond to determine upon the course most consistent with her principles and dignity, as the "Old Mother State," whilst her soldiery strained every nerve to be ready for the worst.

Alexandria and the roads leading therefrom were daily and nightly patroled, and every available means used to prevent surprise from the Federal troops stationed at Washington.

A telegram received the latter part of April, from the commander at Culpeper C. H., to send the "Battery up at once," was, through a mistake of the operator, construed into "Battalion;" so off the companies were hurried to the depot in a heavy, driving rain storm, and, in due time, reached their destination, where the mistake was soon rectified and we returned to our old headquarters.

Early in May the Old Dominion Rifles, having been ordered to take charge of commissary stores in the hospitable town of Warrenton, passed two weeks there, upon duty, most agreeably, when they were recalled to Alexandria. A good deal of excitement arose about this time from the sudden appearing of the gunboat "Pawnee," which anchored in front of Alexandria, with ports open, and guns bearing upon the town.

Her purpose could only be conjectured, and the emotions produced thereby were anything but pleasurable.

The 23d of May arrived; the polls were opened, and an almost unanimous vote for secession was taken—night closed upon the city—the citizens, deep in slumber, dreamed not of what the morrow would bring—the sound of the sentinel's tread and the oft-repeated cry of "All's well," were the sole interruptions to the calm of the midnight hour.

Morrill, the sentinel on duty at Cazenove's wharf, keeping a sharp watch upon the movements of the "Pawnee," caught the sound of creaking oars, and, through the faint glimmer of the dawning day, beheld the outlines of a boat coming quietly towards him. The challenge, "Who comes there?" is thrice repeated, and the sharp report of the sentinel's rifle awakes the neighboring housetop pigeons, and gives the alarm to the soldiers on guard; a volley from the boat, aimed at the sentinel, drowned the rifle's echo, but did no further damage.

A flag of truce from the enemy was received by Colonel Terrett, then in command of the city, and, after consultation with the civil authorities, terms were agreed upon for its surrender; a specified time being

promised for the withdrawal of the Confederate troops.
Long, however, before the expiration of said time, the
enemy's forces were landing upon the wharves. Orders
were at once issued for our companies to assemble at
the Lyceum Hall, the point previously designated as
our "rendezvous."

The Battalion assembled, and there being no time for
farewells to the numerous friends, most of whom were
asleep in their beds, we marched out Duke street and
took the Little River Turnpike westward, the enemy,
at the same time, entering the city from transports lying
at the wharves, and by column from the Washington
and Alexandria Turnpike, down which they had
marched during the night.

Through an oversight, the "Old Dominion Rifles"
failed to receive the order to march, and came near
sharing the fate of Captain Ball's Cavalry, who, acting
as rear guard to our forces, were captured, and, after
some months' close imprisonment, paroled as prisoners
of war. Captain Herbert, hearing musketry below,
called his men into line and started at once for the
point from whence the sounds proceeded. The Battalion was marching out Duke as the company reached
the intersection of King and West streets, where, the
Major recognizing it, a halt was ordered, and the Old
Dominions soon joined the column.

Among the Federal troops, who entered Alexandria
at an early hour, was a regiment of Zouaves under the
command of Colonel Ellsworth; this officer, with a
portion of his command, proceeded to the Marshall

House to remove therefrom the "Stars and Bars" of the new Confederacy, which were floating above it on the morning breeze. After taking from the staff the, to them, obnoxious flag, they turned to retrace their steps, the Colonel, in advance, bearing in his arms his trophy; as they reached the foot of the attic steps, they were met by Jackson, the proprietor of the hotel and owner of their booty. Aroused from sleep by the announcement of the enemy's presence, he had dressed hastily, and hurried, armed with a double-barrelled shot gun, to the rescue of the beloved flag he had sworn to protect at all hazards. In the foeman's grasp he found it; an instant later and Colonel Ellsworth fell bleeding in death. Jackson, seizing in his grasp the new-born banner, folded it around his person, ere he sank lifeless from the balls and bayonets of the dying Colonel's companions. Thus, within the space of a few seconds, the souls of two brave men were hurried into eternity; one actuated by ambition, the other a defender of the ensign adopted by his country.

Let us again join the retreating Battalion, which, on reaching the tollgate, a mile or more from the city, learned that a report was in circulation to the effect that a squadron of cavalry were in pursuit. Our Major immediately halted the column and gave the order to "fix bayonets;" after waiting a short time, the rumor proved false, and we again moved on.

Soon, the welcome sound of the car-whistle reached our ears, and striking for the O. and A. R. R. track, we had the pleasure of stopping the trains moving towards Alexandria. But little time was consumed in occupying the "Flats," and the Battalion was pushed back to Manassas where many friends from various quarters awaited us.

But oh! how sad the thought to many a weary heart as it turns once more to that memorable 24th of May, 1861!

The husband was seen for the last time, through the gray, misty morning, trudging under the weight of his knapsack and musket, and, with eye turned upward to the open casement, received the wife's last smile, and saw, perhaps, her eye's first tear, as a farewell never to be repeated.

The son lingered not to receive a mother's blessing, but hurried on to scenes of death and blood. Alas! many are the mounds that mark the spots where only the dust of those numerous manly forms are to be found, and many are the hearts that mourn, aye! mourn, and cannot be comforted!

Those unspoken farewells will never now be uttered; but in the

> " Beautiful land
> By the spoiler untrod,"

there will be joyful reunion for many who met for the last time on that memorable morning.

Our troops were concentrating at Manassas ; a few tents were pitched, and several companies were quartered in plank houses, built for the purpose, affording shelter, secure from the weather. Not expecting the Alexan_ dria Battalion so soon, no arrangements had been made for our comfort; and we were left to take care of ourselves. The first night was spent in the box cars standing near by, the men retiring to rest without blankets or covering, and supperless; yet not a murmur was heard from any, and the night passed in apparent comfort. All were in good spirits; we had voluntarily linked our fate with that of the young Confederacy, to share her sorrows, and go hand in hand through the coming bitter trials.

When the bright sun, on the morning of the 25th of May, first peeped through the haziness above Manassas, it shone upon the long train of motionless cars with its scores of sleeping forms and hosts of hungry, homeless soldiers, unprovided for in any respect, save that each man's cartridge box contained two rounds of ammunition. Yet many, it may be readily believed, gave no thought of what was to become of them individually.

MANASSAS.

MAY and June passed rapidly. Great activity in both the North and the South was evinced. The ranks of the opposing armies, one concentrating at Manassas, the other at Washington city, were being rapidly increased, and extensive preparations were made for the coming struggle. The streets and by-ways of the Federal Capitol were crowded with companies and regiments of the enemy, coming in to await the orders of their chieftain, while the roll of drums and lively airs of fifes fell harshly upon the Southern ear, detained, by force of circumstances, in their proximity.

The South sent forth her sons, the youth and flower of her firesides, to take up arms in defence of her rights, whilst every practicable preparation was made to present a bold front and deal a heavy blow when the hour of conflict should arrive. The forces at Manassas, at first but few in number, and many of those without the necessary arm of defence, were rapidly augmenting by daily arrivals from all parts of the South. Bustle and activity at the station were increasing, and each hour added new strength to the hearts and spirits of the soldiers present. New tents, and all the necessary paraphernalia for an army, were fully supplied; the comfort and health of the men were remembered and well cared for by those in command.

The Alexandria companies, belonging to the Alexandria Battalion, were fully equipped, and presented on parade a very creditable appearance. Guard duty, drills, details for cleaning camp, cutting wood and bringing water, were among the daily duties, upon which our boys grew fat and thriving. The gay songs and amusing incidents, so common to a soldier's life, kept us all in fine spirits, and were sources of pleasure in helping to beguile time of its monotony.

Several companies from the Battalion were sent on duty to the stations below, and were watching the enemy during a part of May and June.

On the 10th day of June, 1861, the 17th Virginia Regiment was organized, being composed of the following companies:

Alexandria Riflemen, Co. A, Capt. M. Marye; Warren Rifles, Co. B, Capt. R. H. Simpson; Loudoun Guards, Co. C, Capt. C. B. Tebbs; Fairfax Rifles, Co. D, Capt. W. H. Dulany; Mount Vernon Guards, Co. E, Capt. S. H. Devaughn; Prince William Rifles, Co. F, Capt. G. S. Hamilton; Emmett Guards, Co. G, Capt. Jas. E. Towson; Old Dominion Rifles, Co. H, Capt. A. Herbert; O'Connel Guards, Co. I, Capt. S. W. Prestman; Warrenton Rifles, Co. K, Capt. B. H. Shackelford; Colonel, M. D. Corse; Lt. Colonel, Wm. Munford; and Major, Geo. W. Brent, who had been commissioned by the Governor of Virginia, were assigned the command of the regiment; M. M. Lewis, M. D., was appointed Surgeon; H. Snowden, M. D., Assistant Surgeon; Lieut. A. J. Humphreys, Co. A, Adjutant, and W. W. Athey, Co. C, Sergeant Major.

Companies G and I formed after the beginning of hostilities, and were composed of Irish citizens from Alexandria, Va. The Alexandria Riflemen, the Old Dominion Rifles, and the Mount Vernon Guards, were, as we have before stated, volunteer companies, formed in Alexandria, Va., prior to the crisis. The other five companies were volunteer organizations bearing the names of their respective origin.

The Warrenton Rifles lost its first captain, John Q. Marr, in a skirmish at Fairfax C. H., on the 1st day of June, and B. H. Shackelford was elected as his successor. This company, under Captain John Q. Marr, was stationed at Fairfax C. H., to act in conjunction with the Rappahannock and Prince William Cavalry, in defence of that town. On the morning of June 1st, before daylight, a force of Federal cavalry made a rapid descent upon them, hoping, by the rapidity of the movement, to find the Confederates off their guard. In this, however, they were mistaken; in passing through the town at the rate described, firing to the right and left indiscriminately, they aroused the sleeping inhabitants, and by the time they had halted beyond and prepared for a return charge, the Rifles were ready to meet them. During the advance, Captain Marr had moved off a short distance, for the purpose of securing a position for his company; his voice was not heard thereafter, and from what information could be gathered, it is judged that he fell from the first fire of the enemy. In the meantime, General Ewell, who was severely wounded, and Ex-Gov. Wm. Smith, both of whom happened to be passing the night in the town, had taken charge of the Rifles, to all of whom they were well known, and deploying them along the main street in the Court House lot, met and repulsed the second charge of the enemy. Two other attempts were made to force a passage, neither of which, from the determination of our brave Fauquier boys, proved effectual. After the departure of the enemy, it was found that the beloved Marr had fallen.

The Regiment was attached to the 4th Virginia Brigade, commanded by General J. T. Longstreet, and was generally known as the "Alexandria Regiment."

The camp at Manassas Junction was much enlarged by the daily arrival of additional troops; it received the name of "Camp Pickens," in honor of the brave General Pickens, of S. C.

General G. T. Beauregard arrived at Manassas on the 1st day of June, and was placed in command of the army; the month passed in making the position as impregnable as possible. The work, in charge of Colonel Williamson, his chief of engineers, progressed rapidly; large earthworks and field fortifications, with wings and covers of rifle pits, and infantry works, sprang up on all sides. Details from the different regiments in camp were daily employed in digging and ditching. Many of the troops, who were reared in all the luxury of affluence, rendered themselves valuable in their active wielding of spade and axe.

Company C (Loudoun Guards) was deprived of its

he having received a commission as Lieutenant Colonel, and assigned to the 8th Virginia Regiment. Geo. R. Head, 1st Lieutenant, was then promoted to the captaincy of the Company.

For several days before the 18th of July, it was generally known that the enemy were moving against us; and every effort was made by the General in command to prepare his troops for battle; extra details were made, the works around Manassas strengthened, and the 16th and 17th of July were busy, truly busy days, in the fullest signification of the term.

Couriers were flying in every direction, delivering orders; and on the last named day, the infantry, including the 17th Va. Regiment, marched to their respective places, in line, on the banks of Bull Run.

The men were in excellent spirits, and impatiently awaited the coming of the foe. The morning of the 18th of July opened beautifully upon the Confederate line of infantry and artillery, stretched along the west bank of Bull Run.

About one o'clock the enemy advanced and attacked Longstreet's Brigade, stationed at Blackburn's Ford.

Extracts, from the report, as made by our Colonel, will give the part sustained by our Regiment, and show the valor and veteran bearing of the raw soldiers on their first battle field.

"In pursuance of orders, the rifle Companies B and H, commanded by Captains Simpson and Herbert, were deployed as skirmishers along the right bank of Bull Run, above Blackburn's Ford, whilst Companies A and G, commanded by Captains Marye and Towson, were posted at the Ford. Companies E and K, under Captains Devaughn and Shackelford, were detached and posted lower down the run, on the right of the First Virginia Regiment."

"About one o'clock P. M. the enemy appeared in considerable force on the opposite bank, and opened a severe and continuous fire upon the First and Seventeenth Regiments. At this moment, the remaining companies of the Regiment were marched to the run, and responded briskly and gallantly to the enemy's fire. Company A, Captain Marye, was then ordered to cross the run, and deploy as skirmishers on the opposite bank; Company C, Captain Head, and Company F, Captain Hamilton, were subsequently ordered to cross also, and sustain this movement. The three companies promptly executed these orders, and after bravely driving the enemy through the woods, back to their main body, returned, bringing their own wounded and seven prisoners. Some fifteen or more of the enemy were killed and many wounded."

"It affords me much gratification to remark upon the coolness and bravery manifested by both officers and men under my command."

"Particularly I must speak of the gallant conduct of Lieut. Col. Munford, Maj. Brent, Adjutant Humphreys, Captain Marye and Captain Head, who were actively and fearlessly employed during the engagement at the points where the fire was hottest."

"I must also mention Surgeon Lewis and assistant

Surgeon Snowden, who were untiring in their efforts to relieve the wounded, regardless of their personal safety. I regret to add that Captains Dulany and Prestman were severely wounded whilst at the head of their companies. Captain Shackelford, commanding Company K, and Lieut. Javins, of Company E, were slightly wounded. Private Thomas R. Sangster, Company A was killed, and four privates severely, and six slightly wounded."

List of killed and wounded in the battle of Blackburn's Ford, July 18th, 1861.

Company A—Killed, Private T. R. Sangster; wounded, A. D. Warfield, slightly.

Company B—None.

Company C—Wounded, Ed. Donnelly, flesh wound; C. G. Edwards, dangerously; J. W. Sexton, lost leg.

Company D—Wounded, Capt. Wm. H. Dulany, dangerously; Privates W. H. Steele, Thos. Beake and B. Thomas, slightly.

Company E—Wounded, Lieut. C. Javins, slightly; Privates Jas. A. Proctor and Geo. W. Tyles, slightly.

Company F—None.

Company G—Wounded, Private Wm. McKeown, slightly.

Company H—Wounded, Private John Withers, slightly.

Company I—Wounded, Capt. S. W. Prestman, dangerously; Private Dennis Murphy, lost arm.

Company K—Wounded, Capt. B. H. Shackelford, slightly; Private A. G. Sinclair, badly.

Friday, 19th, and part of Saturday, passed without change, the Regiment being held in reserve during the time. On Saturday, the 20th, they again occupied the line near Blackburn's Ford. On Sunday, the 21st of July, 1861, the first great battle in our struggle was fought, and, though our Regiment was not actively engaged, it faithfully performed its duty, and was under heavy artillery fire a greater part of the day.

A lovelier Sabbath morning never shone than that of the 21st July, 1861. The enemy's movements foretold another conflict, but more sanguinary and important in its results. Their artillery opened at an early hour from the different points along their line, while their main forces were massing on our extreme left, preparatory to a heavy assault upon our flank. Crossing at Sudley Mills, they bore down upon the South Carolina troops stationed near the Stone Bridge for the protection of our flank, and, hurling with terrific force a large body of troops against them, succeeded in forcing back our line at that point.

Reinforcements were sent to the rescue of the brave Bee and his men, and for hours the battle raged. Success varied: first one and then the other was forced back, until the few Southern troops, fighting against such fearful odds, became exhausted.

At this critical moment, the cry: " The Valley Boys have come," arose, and spread like wildfire and with marvelous effect; our men by desperate exertion held their position until Johnston's army came in to the rescue.

Fresh and ready for the "fray," they rushed onward, carrying all before them. Yells of triumph from the wounded, as well as from the uninjured, rent the air, sending a thrill of joy to the hearts of the approaching army. After the severest fighting of the day, our foes were driven from hill and dale. Peal after peal of victorious shouts followed in their wake, quickening their flight.

Our artillery made dreadful havoc among their retreating columns; the Alexandria Artillery, commanded by Capt. Kemper, was not behind in the race towards Washington city. The unerring aim of his gunners filled many a narrow home, now marked by a green-topped mound.

The rout was perfect; men, horses, wagons and artillery were one mass of moving lumber, all bound for a haven secure from the bullets of the "Rebels," from the scenes of warfare. Company H, commanded by Capt. Herbert, had been ordered across the Ford in the early part of the day, and was under a heavy fire of canister and grape. A large party of the enemy attempted to capture this Company by stealth, but failed and were driven back with heavy loss. The Company had one killed, viz: Dennis McDermot; and two wounded, viz: Corporal Jas. E. Grimes, and Private J. P. Riley.

Darkness ended the pursuit, and many of our army bivouaced upon the battle field.

On Thursday, after the battle, the dead of the enemy in the vicinity of the Stone Bridge and Henry

House lay uncovered on the field, and the sight was heart-rending. At the point where the Federal battery, known as the "Ricketts' Battery," had fought, and bled, and died, numbers of bodies, both of man and beasts, were still in the position in which they fell, and, as may be readily imagined, the effluvia arising from their decomposition was so great as to render it almost impossible to remain in the locality. The battle, at this point, must have been very severe, for as many as seven dead bodies were lying across each other just as they had fallen on Sunday.

The Confederate losses in the battle of the first Manassas, amounted to about 1,200 in killed and wounded; the enemy lost nearly 5,000, including 1,700 prisoners. We captured 82 pieces of artillery and a vast number of small arms; also, wagons, ambulances, tents, and numerous pieces of different kinds of army munitions and outfit.

During the battle, on the 18th of July, at Blackburn's Ford, when the fire of the enemy was hottest and damaging, the 1st Virginia Regiment, held in reserve, General Longstreet commanded Captain Marye, to take his company and "Clear those scoundrels out," and as the riflemen plunged into the stream with a shout, General Longstreet took off his hat, and, rising in his stirrups, called for "three cheers for the Alexandria Riflemen"—which compliment was acknowledged by a touch of the hat by Captain Marye.

The following incident, which occurred as given by the principal actor, Warfield, of this company, in his own words, we insert, believing it will be of interest to our readers:

"The order was promptly obeyed; the company crossed the Ford with a yell; upon reaching the opposite bank, Captain Marye ordered the company to deploy as skirmishers and advance. About 150 yards from the stream we came upon the skirmishers of the 1st Massachusetts Regiment, stationed behind trees, bushes, &c. At once attacking them, we had a very nice time, killing 16 of them and taking some 20 prisoners; we were all tangled up together, and the only way to distinguish one from another was by the U. S. on the Yankee breast-plates."

"In the conflict, I ordered a Yankee to surrender, but he refused. I grabbed him by the collar, my gun being empty and his loaded; he cut my head with the barrel of his gun. Being in too close quarters to use our arms, we clinched, and in the struggle rolled down the hill into a spring branch, Yank on top and myself in the mud and water, *face down*. I was only relieved from my disagreeable position by E., of the Loudoun Guards, who came up at the time and gave Yank his bayonet in left side; at this, Yank hallowed 'Good God, Capt. Hall, come here,' but I told him that his hide had gone up and that Capt. Hall could do him no good. I then took him to Gen. Longstreet, who, after finding out who he was, said to me: 'Well done, old fellow; this is the first prisoner, go back and get another,' which command I respectfully declined, as things were waxing warm just about that time."

We also insert the following letter, as copied from a Richmond paper, feeling assured that it will interest many of our readers:

"A Graphic Picture."

" We have been permitted to copy the following extracts from a letter written by a young officer who greatly distinguished himself at the battle of Manassas.

" Should his modesty take offence at the publication of his frank expressions of feeling and unreserved narration of events, our apology is found in the fact that the original was placed at our disposal by the courtesy of those to whom it was addressed. The style is singularly copious, and the descriptive passages especially fine; and the more to be admired when we reflect that the letter was written, *a la* Pope, upon fugitive scraps of paper, and *currénte calamo.*"

The Night before the Battle.

Saturday night was spent in watching. The enemy's bugles, his drums, the rumble of his baggage trains and artillery; not only these, but their very words of command being distinctly audible in the silent night.

The next morning, partly refreshed, we were ordered over the ford, (Bull Run,) as scouts in that direction. I was creeping over the field when the enemy threw a shell at my party, which exploded just in advance of ns. Here we passed a body, one of the Massachusetts slain, (shot the day before,) blackened and ghastly.

After a few hours we were ordered to our reserve, and, without breakfast, to deploy as skirmishers. The first reserve had been left in charge of Willie Fowle. I led the second further on, while the Captain placed himself in the skirt of the wood, having established a line of sentries. Here he watched the enemy's batteries, and would report their movements to the General. Becoming anxious about him, I left my reserve under Zimmerman, and advanced to the spot. The Captain said: "Don, I am awfully sleepy, and will just take a little nap, if you will watch those fellows there." I cheerfully acquiesced, and relieved Jordan, one of our men, who was the actual look-out at the fence. Here I lay on my face, my time pleasantly occupied with the proceedings at the batteries, the ceaseless explosions of the guns and the rattle of musketry from the great fight below, being in strange constrast with the quiet scenery of mountain and valleys.

Showing how Yankee Sportsmen Flushed Game and Themselves took Wing.

I unclasped my sword-belt and yielded myself to the seductions of the scene, and was startled from my almost reverie by the cry of Lovelace, one of our men, posted on the right: "Lookout Lieutenant! Here they are!" Looking around I saw their skirmishers within about thirty yards, with their pieces at a ready, and advancing, just as sportsmen approach a covey of partridges. I shouted to the Captain, and we dashed into the woods. I then asked him if we should fight them? He said, "He reckoned we had." I then yelled to the boys, "Come on, Old Dominions! now's your chance! now's the chance you've waited for!"

This shout of mine was heard by our forces on the other side of the run. The boys say I said, "Isn't this glorious!" but I don't remember. On came the boys. I led them, pointed out the Yankees, and we drove them out of the woods and completely put them to flight. As we drove them into the field, the enemy's battery, about four hundred yards off, opened on us with grape and canister, and we ordered a retreat; not, however, before our men returned it, firing right at the guns, wounding, as I have since learned from a prisoner, several of their men.

THE "IRON DICE" RATTLE.

We were exposed nearly half a mile without support. The enemy had our range completely, and we were in great peril, the balls whizzing and humming all around us.

Fowle, who had advanced his reserve and behaved with great coolness, says the line of skirmishers extended a long way and intended to cut us off; but we gave a yell, and, as I have said, drove them home.

Arthur was too slow in retreat even after he had given the order. I had to turn back twice to look for

3*

him.   How the balls rattled!   Every man would
sometimes have to get behind a tree to escape the
"dreadful storm."

A Soldier's Grave.

McDermot, one of our men, was killed by a grape-
shot. On yesterday I buried him. He had lain out
all night, and our eyes filled with woman's tears as we
covered him with his blanket, and left him to sleep
on the field where he had fallen. Hurdle put a head
and foot mark at his grave, with the inscription in
pencil:

"Dennis McDermot, of the Old Dominion Rifles,
of Alexandria, Va., died in battle, July 21, 1861; a
gallant soldier and a good man."

The Retreat of the "Grand Army."

What a glorious day Sunday was for the South!
When the rout of the enemy came down the long line
of Bull Run, (Yankee's Run? Eds.) up went a shout!
Oh! how grand it was! Imagine the quiet woods
through which the watching bayonets glittered silently,
suddenly alive with triumphant hurrahs! From right
to left, and left to right, for seven miles they were
repeated! Then came the order to advance, and as
we left the woods and gained the high and open
grounds, the grandest spectacle I ever saw met my
eyes. Company after company, regiment after regi-

ment, brigade after brigade, army after army of our troops appeared. We halted to enjoy the sight, and as our glorious artillery and dashing cavalry spurred by in pursuit, shout after shout rent the air. General Longstreet, our Brigade Commander, rode along our line with his staff, and thousands of men flung their caps in the air, or swung them on their bayonets. Col. Corse, our gallant little Colonel, got his meed of hurrahs; and *an old negro who rode by with his gun, got no small salute.* And then the sunset came in a perfect glory of light sifted through the leaves.

The following extract, from a letter to the " Baltimore Exchange," dated, Alexandria, Va., July 29th, 1861, speaks nobly of a well-deserving but deceased comrade:

" In this battle one of Alexandria's bravest sons fell, and in his fall this whole community is sunk in sadness. Thomas Sangster, son of Mr. Edward Sangster, lately the sheriff of this county, fell pierced by a ball. He was generally known, and, by all who knew him, beloved. For an entire absence from anything like fear he was remarkable from a child. He was as kind as brave. He died in a noble cause, and his memory is enshrined, along with all who fell there, in the hearts of a brave and generous nation."

Now, let us go back to the Regiment. The nights of the 21st and 22d of July, were spent by us near the battle field; and on the 23d we marched to Centreville and went into camp: whilst there we performed picket duty below, besides all the ordinary camp duties. The Regiment remained thus until the 12th day of August, when it moved to Fairfax Court House and went into camp—most of the army having preceded it to that point.

· Whilst near Centreville, the following beautifully written order was issued and read to the troops:

HEADQUARTERS ARMY OF THE POTOMAC,
MANASSAS, July 25th, 1861.

Soldiers of the Confederate States :

One week ago a countless host of men organized into an army, with all the appointments which modern art and practised skill could devise, invaded the soil of Virginia. Their people sounded their approach with triumphant displays of anticipated victory. Their Generals came in almost royal state; their great Ministers, Senators and women came to witness the immolation of this army, and the subjugation of our people—and to celebrate these with wild revelry.

It is with the profoundest emotions of gratitude to an over-ruling God, whose hand is manifest in protecting our homes and our liberties, that we, your Generals commanding, are enabled, in the name of our whole country, to thank you for that patriotic courage, that heroic gallantry, that daring exhibited by you in the action of the 18th and 21st of July, by which the hosts of the enemy were scattered, and a signal and glorious victory obtained.

The two affairs of the 18th and 21st were but the sustained and continued effort of your patriotism against the constantly recurring columns of an enemy fully treble your numbers, and this effort was crowned on the evening of the 21st with a victory so complete that the invaders were driven disgracefully from the field and made to fly in disorderly rout back to their entrenchments, a distance of over thirty miles. They left upon the field nearly every piece of their artillery, a large portion of their arms, equipments, baggage, stores, etc , etc , and almost every one of their wounded and dead, amounting, together with the prisoners, to many thousands—and thus the Northern hosts were driven from Virginia.

Soldiers: We congratulate you on an event which ensures the liberty of our Country. We congratulate every man of you whose glorious privilege it was to participate in this triumph of courage and truth—to fight in the battle of Manassas. You have created an epoch of Liberty, and unborn nations will rise up and call you "blessed."

Continue this noble devotion, looking always to the protection of a just God, and before Time grows much older we will be hailed as the Deliverers of a nation of Ten Millions of people.

Comrades, our brothers who have fallen have earned undying renown on earth ; and their blood shed in our holy cause is a precious and acceptable sacrifice to the Father of Truth and Right.

Their graves are beside the tomb of Washington,—their spirits have joined his in eternal communion. We will hold the soil in which the dust of Washington is mingled with the dust of our brothers. We drop one tear on their laurels, and move on to avenge them.

Soldiers ! We congratulate you on glorious, triumphant and complete victory. We thank you for doing your whole duty in the service of your Country.

Official :

Signed,   J. E. Johnston, Gen. C. S. A.

              G. T. Beauregard, Gen C. S. A.

Fr. S. Armstead, A. A. A. G.

"Extract from a Letter."

" The conduct of the Alexandria boys in both battles is spoken of in the highest terms ; and the charge of the Alexandria Riflemen, led on by Captain Morton Marye, in the Thursday's fight, is said to have been one of the most gallant and splendid military manœuvres ever witnessed. Most nobly did that little band of as true hearts as ever fluttered, advance upon the foe, and bearing down all before them, lead the way to a quick and glorious triumph. The old Dominion Rifles, not a whit behind their fathers and brothers, (who were in the foremost company) in courage, descipline and all that goes to make a true soldier, were in the thickest of this hard-fought battle."

FALLS CHURCH, UPTON'S AND MUNSON'S HILLS.

UPON our arrival in the vicinity of Fairfax Court House the Regiment went into camp, east of, and below the village, on the right bank of the Alexandria turnpike, upon a good location, with plenty of wood and water.

Not many days after its arrival Company H was sent on picket duty to Falls Church, a small village about nine miles east of Fairfax Court House and about the same distance from Alexandria, Va. This Company was the first Infantry stationed at this post, and had the pleasure of extending the lines to Taylor's Tavern and Rocky Ridge, points about half a mile distant from the village.

Fort, a Texan scout, with club feet, but indomitable energy and bravery, in command of ten men of Company H, met the enemy about 150 strong, near Taylor's tavern and, after expending one or two rounds of ammunition, drove the entire column from that locality, and picketed posts beyond, which were held until our evacuation of the line some months after.

Numbers of amusing incidents, various hair-breadth escapes, occurred to those on duty in that vicinity : and the minds of many on perusing these pages will revert to the early morning fights between the pickets of the enemy and themselves, over the little peach

orchard and the rich gardens below Taylor's tavern,
and to Farley's narrow escape in the woods near, when
he met two of the "blue jackets," and came near losing
his life by a pistol shot discharged by one of them.

Early in September the lines below were extended
to Mason's, Munson's and Upton's hills, where the
points were guarded by a few companies from the
army lying around the Court House. The men in
camp were employed in regular drills, guard duty, &c. ;
but found plenty of time for frolic and impromptu
tours between the hours of duty.

The bright smiles and kind words of patriotic en-
couragement from our sweet lady friends of that neighborhood, whom many of us visited whenever opportunity permitted, proved an invaluable antidote to
the weariness and ennui which might otherwise have
arisen from the labor and monotony of camp life.

The lines in front had been strengthened by earthworks and rifle pits ; a strong line of redoubts encircled
the top of Munson's hill, and *heavy wooden guns* were
mounted ready for action. The enemy did not trouble
us at that point, thinking probably the apparent Fort
was heavily armed and strongly garrisoned. At Upton's. hill the pickets were generally busy at target
practice, *at each other*, and, for many weeks the pop,
pop, pop of their firearms was of daily occurrence ;
though there was seldom any one seriously hurt, sometimes a lucky fellow received a wound and was sent
home rejoicing on a thirty days' furlough.

The enemy wasted numberless charges of powder

and ball at target practice near Arlington Heights, while we were in that vicinity, until finally their noise became annoying.

Lieut. Forrest, of Company H, bade adieu to the Regiment on the 15th of September, to join General Trimble's Staff at Evansport, by which the Command lost a good officer, a courteous gentleman, and a social companion.

The total strength of the Regiment on the 1st day September, 1861, is shown by the following figures:

Present for duty, 665; present and unfit for duty, 80; total in camp, 745.

Absent on detached service, 33; absent with leave, 4; absent without leave, 11; absent sick and wounded, 101; total absent, 149. Total on rolls at said date including officers and men, 894.

On the 24th September, the Regiment was ordered to take with them three days' cooked rations, and to march to Falls Church. That night was spent in the village. On the following day, the Colonel received orders to prepare for a march, equipped for fighting. In company with Kershaw's South Carolina Regiment, and three pieces of the Washington Artillery, the Seventeenth Virginia proceeded up the Alexandria and Leesburg turnpike, and after passing the railroad station, one mile above the village, threw out skirmishers to the right. Arriving at the intersection of the turnpike and the road leading to Georgetown, they were halted and informed that a column of the enemy was at Lewinsville, and the object of their expedition was to dislodge it.

This village was only about two miles distant, so that in a very short time we attained an eminence overlooking it, and also the Yankee line drawn up, as if ready for combat.

Our infantry were below the brow of the hill, hidden from the enemy; in a few seconds, the artillery had unlimbered and moved to the front. After one or two shots our forces moved forward in line of battle to the village, (the Yankees, having to use their own expressive term, skeedaddled at our first fire,) from which point the artillery again opened upon the retreating column.

The enemy replied from a battery at Langley, some half mile distant; and their first shot, a 24 pounder, passed over our heads and exploded in our rear; the second proved a truer aim, killing one of Kershaw's men and wounding another. Being under full range of their fire, Colonel Corse, (in command,) ordered the line to fall back, which was done in good order, the troops passing over five lines of oak paled fencing, which fell before them like chaff before a tempest.

Making a circuit we overhauled our retreating foes and opened fire on them from Langley; night put a stop to our operations.

In the excitement of the chase none of the officers noted particularly the direction they were making, and there was but one man in the Regiment who would undertake to guide us through the darkness to Falls

He took the head of the line and all passed very quietly until we reached a farm house; at that point a din arose occasioned by ducks and chickens evidently in distress, and it is presumable that many dined the next day upon more delicate soup than was furnished by army rations.

On coming in sight of Falls Church, about nine o'clock P. M., our hearts were gladdened by the camp fires of about 20,000 Confederate soldiers, sent by Gen. B. to support us in case of need.

Whilst on duty at Falls Church, the troops fared well from the excellent vegetables flourishing in the deserted gardens around them. There was more or less gaiety according to the weather, and spirit of the men. Sham battles were often indulged in, and the time, generally, passed rapidly.

On the night of the 27th of September, about nine o'clock P. M., the long roll sounded on all sides through the village; the troops hastily turned out from their quarters, and fell into line on the turnpike. After midnight, the column moved towards Fairfax Court House. They were halted at Mills' Cross Roads, about three miles west, and slept on their arms the remainder of the night. About eight o'clock the next morning, our Regiment was ordered to return to the village. After our arrival within a few hundred yards thereof, we were gentlemen of elegant leisure until about five o'clock P. M., when orders arrived for us to remove the telegraph wires from the village, westward; this was accomplished with hard labor, as the roads were deep and muddy, and the wires were to be rolled up as we marched. Upon reaching Chichester's gate, we were met by Gen. J. E. B. Stuart, who thanking the men through our Colonel, told us to return to camp at Fairfax Court House and enjoy that rest so needed by us all. On the 3d of October, "Camp Harrison" around the Court House, was the scene of a brilliant turn out of the army in honor of the presence of our President and Commander-in-chief, Jefferson Davis, who was there for the purpose of reviewing his troops, and great enthusiasm was evinced by them.

On the 11th of October, our Regiment and one company of the Washington Artillery, were sent on a scouting expedition in the direction of Anandale, but failing to find the enemy, reported to be in that vicinity, we returned to camp late in the day, tired and pretty well used up.

On the 12th of October, the Brigade to which our Regiment was attached, drilled for the last time under the command of Gen. J. T. Longstreet, and, as that officer bade adieu to the body of men so long known to him as true and brave soldiers, unbroken silence was observed along the line for a brief moment, and then, as if the earth had opened with volcanic eruptions, a loud and long peal of heart-felt cheers sounded from a thousand throats, and drowned the words of farewell from a chieftain so beloved and honored for his bravery.

In relinguishing command of our Brigade the following complimentary order was addressed to us :

HEADQUARTERS FOURTH BRIGADE, FIRST CORPS, }
A. P., FAIRFAX C. H., October 13th. }

General Order No. 17 :

In relinguishing the command of the Fourth Brigade, First Corps Army of the Potomac, the Commanding General expresses his sincere thanks to the officers and soldiers of the command, for the kindly patience, the soldierly fortitude, and cheerful obedience which they have invariably exhibited during the many hardships and privations of a long and trying campaign.

The command of a brigade, second to none, is well worthy the boast of any General, and even regret may well be felt at promotion which removes it a step at least from him.

By command of Maj. Gen. Longstreet.

G. MOXLEY SORREL,
Capt. and A. A. G.

The 14th of October found the Regiment on its way to Mills' Cross Roads, where it had been ordered on picket duty. The men were all in fine spirits, and gay songs from a hundred throats in unison, made the march a merry one. Upon reaching the line, the Regiment was drawn up, details made and the pickets relieved. During our brief stay on this occasion, our ears not unfrequently tingled with the rolling of an army of drums, apparently beaten for the benefit of the Confederates; it seemed as if all the drum corps from the Federal army had congregated at that point, each trying to rival others in noisy demonstrations.

Late on the evening of the 16th of October, the picket lines were abandoned by the infantry, and our Regiment begun a tiresome march that continued until midnight, and brought us to Centreville.

Fairfax Court House, for many months, a gay,

4*

pleasant village, presented a most deserted appearance as we passed through it, late at night; only a few cavalry were to be seen, the army having some hours previously, left for Centreville. Many of the citizens, for fear of being within the enemy's lines, left home with the troops.

The Seventh Virginia Regiment, during the hurry of moving, had a number of their tents burnt by an accidental fire, many of the men losing their clothing.

Arriving at Centreville about midnight the boys threw their tired frames upon the ground and slept soundly. Early the following morning everybody was astir. The different regiments marched off to the grounds allotted for camping, pitched their tents and made themselves comfortable. Our camp was located on the hill to the west and south of the village. This home upon the hills will never be forgotten by the survivors of our Regiment, associated as it is in our minds with a pleasant winter's amusements.

Ere the sun slumbered in the west, the hills and valleys around the little village of Centreville, were occupied by Regimental and Brigade camps. As the darkness increased, the skies above were lighted with the glimmer of a thousand camp fires; the lively song of the happy soldier, as he was attending to the duties of the camp fire, could be heard upon every hill and in every vale. All went merrily as a marriage bell.

Just here we present you a memento of the stirring scenes and trying times in picketing at Falls Church and vicinity.

"FALLS CHURCH, October 5th, 1861.

-"*Editor National Republican :*

"Enclosed, I send you a correct copy of a letter found by me, pinned on a gate near Falls Church. The letter is something of a curiosity : so I send it for publication. The direction on the outside is to 'Yankee' care of 'Luck.'

"Yours, &c.

"W. H. G.

"35th Regiment N. Y. S. V."

[COPY OF LETTER.]

"*Dear Yankees :*

"Having been resident denizens of Falls Church for sometime, we to-day, reluctantly evacuate, not because you intimidate by your presence, but only in obedience to military dictation.

"We leave you a fire to cook potatoes, also to warm by, as the nights are now uncomfortable on account of their chilling influence. Mr. J. T. Petty, an inhabitant of Washington, but a 'Secesh' in the rebel army, joins compliments with me upon this propitious occasion.

"Signed,

"JOHNSTON,

"Company B, 17th Regiment, Va. Volunteers."

"P. S.—We are members of the 'Bloody Seventeenth'—the well merited sobriquet of our Regiment gained in the battle of Bull Run."

The army of Northern Virginia soon made Centreville what Fairfax Court House had been, and the fields around were converted into drill grounds for thousands of Confederate soldiers.

Engineers were soon at work; forts, breastworks, rifle-pits and batteries, marked the high points around. Regular details from every regiment in the army were daily made for ditching and digging, and the adjacent country for miles became alive with men. The "big balloon" of the enemy appeared often in the direction of the Court House, and, no doubt, its occupants took the Southern army for a large body of "Sappers and Miners," as men and officers, for days and weeks were in the "ditch."

On the 22d October two brigades from our army were sent to support the small force at Leesburg, the enemy having advanced the day before in large num- bers, and, although they had been badly beaten in the battle of "Ball's Bluff," it was deemed prudent to send reinforcements in case of another advance.

The weather during October was cold and frosty, but the men found ample means to while the hours between drills and guard duty. Games of "foot-ball" and "bandy" were often zealously indulged in.

On the 30th October, the Virginia troops were ordered out, and a flag bearing the State crest and her motto: "Sic Semper Tyrranis," was presented to each regiment by Governor John Letcher. When the turn of our Regiment came to receive the flag, the Governor said: "I present this flag in the name of the Commonwealth of Virginia; take it, and when you go into Alexandria, drive out the invaders of our soil."

Colonel Corse, in his usual good humored manner replied as follows:

"Governor, I accept this flag from our beloved old Mother, and tender the thanks of the Regiment I

have the honor to command ; with confidence I place
it in their hands and promise you that it shall be
planted on the high places around Alexandria, or the
blood of the Seventeenth shall flow freely in the
attempt."

The following day passed pleasantly to all : a grand
review in honor of the distinguished guest was ordered,
and many happy hearts grew happier with the pre-
vailing enthusiasm.

November was ushered in like a "roaring lion,"
bringing grief and destruction in its wake to many a
well-kept camp ground. On the night of the first, a
most terrific storm of wind, rain and hail commenced
from the northwest; the howling tempest and pelting
rain blended in a continuous roar throughout the night.

When the morning of the 2d began to send its
pale rays across the hills, our camp presented a most
lamentable spectacle. Only two tents were standing
out of about one hundred and fifty; the men were
huddled together in groups endeavoring to keep warm ;
the fires having been extinguished could add nothing
to their comfort and the poor fellows, wet, supperless,
and without the fragment of a chance for breakfast,
presented a most wretched appearance indeed. Tents,
blankets, and all the paraphernalia of a soldier's outfit
were scattered right and left over the camp ground.

Our brave and ever faithful Colonel, like a man in
a dream, was seen standing near the remains of his
once comfortable tent, lamenting his lost breakfast, in
his shirt sleeves, regardless of the rain, and reminding

one of a person invited to a feast, who couldn't go. Poor fellow! he looked the personification of "Patience on a monument, smiling at Grief."

The storm continued until afternoon when the wind changed, and it cleared up piercingly cold.

On the 3d, our Regiment picketed near Fairfax Court House ; whilst there, two of the officers were put under arrest for allowing a lady to pass the outpost, losing their swords for a few hours.

Brigadier General Clark, of Mississippi, was assigned the command of our Brigade on the 4th of November, in place of General J. T. Longstreet, promoted. On the 8th, Brigadier General Ewell succeeded General Clark in the command, the latter having been ordered to the Western army. The Brigade at the said time was composed of the 1st, 7th 11th, and 17th Virginia Regiments.

On the 6th, we returned from picket duty and resumed the routine of camp life. On the 8th, Company H, voted unanimously to enlist for the war. Their example was soon followed by the remainder of the Regiment. Jackson's Brigade left our neigborhood the same day for the Valley, and their camp ground was occupied by a South Carolina Brigade. Seven prisoners were sent in by the cavalry, who were always on the allert to "gobble up" stray parties too far from home.

On the 18th, a part of the Regiment picketed near Stuart's camp, and spent a most jovial time. A number of the men took their meals at Mrs. Stewart's, several miles above the Court House, where they were highly pleased with the good fare set for their enjoyment.

During the winter months, whilst at Centerville, the men were allowed twenty-four or forty-eight hours passes, with which to visit their friends and acquaintances, indulge in a frolic, or in whatever they might choose for the time specified. It produced the good effect of keeping the troops contented and obedient.

On the 28th, battle-flags were presented to General Longstreet's Division. The presentation addresses to each regiment were enthusiastically received by the men. Senator H. W. Thomas, gave a supper to Company B. on the 29th, and on the following day a grand review of General Longstreet's Division took place, which passed off quietly, reflecting credit upon both troops and Commander.

December's severely cold nights made dreadful havoc with the soldiers toes on the out posts, where for six long hours without fire or aught to shield from Jack Frost's intrusion, they trod their lonely beat, dreaming of home and friends far away.

Only the experience can know the real state of a man's mind when on such duty, especially if in hourly expectation of the enemy's approach. They alone can understand the watchfulness and care necessary to protect the line as well as the body of the sentinel. Eyes and ears must be ever ready to catch the faintest sound, and the musket must be in place for instant use in the event of an alarm.

On the 6th December, our Regiment picketed at post No. 5. Whilst on duty there, Companys A, G, and H, were sent on a foraging expedition, and after marching down the Alexandria turnpike as far as Gooding's, the column halted, had details made and the wagons filled with corn from the fields adjacent. The detachment then returned without experiencing any remarkable adventure.

We were relieved on the 9th by the Fifth South Carolina Regiment, and returned to camp. On our arrival we received information that two of the "Tiger Rifles," of Wheat's Battalion, were to be shot for attempting the life of one of their Lieutenants. The execution took place not very far from our camp, and was witnessed by some of our men.

During the month of December, orders were issued for the troops to put up winter quarters.

The companies having wagons and horses put them in requisition for hauling the materials for building. The frame work of dilapidated and deserted dwellings was taken to camp, where we lost no time in erecting good substantial houses, with all the conveniences for cooking, sleeping, &c. we could contrive. On the 11th, Major Barbour, Quartermaster of the army, gave a grand entertaiment at his quarters in Centerville, to the Generals in command ; among those present, were Johnston, Stuart, Longstreet and Van Dorn. Egg-nog, apple-toddy, mixed and plain liquors of various kinds, with refreshments and substantials, were spread to tempt the appetite and gratify the tastes of all. The party continued their festivities until near the dawn of day. On the 13th, Longstreet had his Division drill—(he was the only General who drilled by division.)

The evolutions of at least fifteen thousand men, enmasse, was a grand sight. Thousands of the army met as spectators, and no doubt, considered themselves well repaid for coming.

On the 17th, the left wing of our Regiment went on picket at Post No. 4, and returned to camp on the 20th. On the same day, as a foraging party consisting of four regiments with an escort of Stuart's Cavalry were approaching Drainsville, Loudoun County—they were entrapped by a large body of the enemy in ambush, and, after a short and bloody battle, forced to fall back leaving their dead and wounded on the field. The weather was bitterly cold, and the suffering of the wounded intense, as they were left lying on frozen ground throughout the night.

The 11th Virginia Regiment, one of our Brigade, lost fifty men in killed, wounded and missing. As the affair was supposed to be the result of carelessness on the part of some one in command, it was more than ordinarily deplored.

Two days after a number of the dead were brought into Centerville for burial. It was indeed a heart-rending sight: frozen stiff, there was no relaxation of muscle to change the posture in which the agonies of death were endured; some lay doubled up, others with their rigid fingers clutched in their clothing or around their acoutrements.

The following beautifully conceived letter of friendship and regard, was written by the brave Samuel Garland, Jr., Colonel commanding the 11th Virginia volunteers—the gallant "Old Eleventh,"—and read to our Regiment on dress parade.

"CAMP OF THE 11TH VIRGINIA VOLUNTEERS, }
1ST BRIGADE, 2D DIVISION, }
December, 23d, 1861. }

"COL. M. D. CORSE,
      Commanding 17th Virginia Volunteers,

"DEAR SIR :—I desire to express, on my own behalf, and on behalf of the officers and men of the 11th Virginia Volunteers, our grateful appeciation of the soldierly friendship, which induced your command to unite in paying the last tribute of respect to those of our gallant comrades, whom we buried on yesterday.

"Such evidences of mutual regard cannot fail to have the effect of increasing the spirit and efficiency of both commands. Rest assured that we shall share together the hardships of the tented field, watching with eager interest the fortunes of the gallant 17th until the day shall come, when their flag shall wave once more in the streets of Alexandria.

"That our acknowledgment of the act of friendship referred to may be communicated to your command, I request that you will direct your Adjutant to read this note at your evening parade.

     "I remain, Colonel, with high regard,

       "Your friend and obedient servant,

    (Signed)   "SAMUEL GARLAND, JR.,
               "Col. 11th Va. Vols."

The 23d of December, 1861, was a severe day to the soldiers of the army of Northern Virginia. Snow, rain and hail fell in torrents, and as a preventive of colds—rations of whisky were issued to the men.

The "Seventeenth," so long without a copious supply of "Pine top," hailed the liquor with delight, and ere the faint beams of twilight's silent hour had retired, about two-thirds of Longstreet's "Bloody Seventeenth"—were certainly not frozen.

Almost every tent and house, both of officers and men, had its canteen swinging near; in many, upon the floor or "bunk," were to be seen four or more soldiers engaged in the fascinating game of "Bluff." When the cry of "Lights out" ran from mouth to mouth along the line of sentinels, the camp became shrouded in darkness—but suppose we step into a tent and see if the lights are really "out." Lifting the heavy "fly" upon the inside of which an oilcloth is pinned, we enter. Looking around we notice Capt's ——— and ———, Lieut's * * * and o o o (whom many of our readers would recognize without the aid of a magnifier) and others, seated comfortably upon a blanket; each mouth adorned with a pipe from which clouds of smoke are emanating, while their minds are all intent upon the cards before them; the light is well shaded, so as to be invisible on the outside, as the game goes on under the whispers of the players. Corn or coffee grains are spread around, each representing a specified amount, not greater than a dollar.

From the players, who are steeped in tobacco smoke and "fire-water," we catch the sentences: "I'll raise you two"—"I'll go five better"—"Can't see it"—"Three Queens"—&c., &c. Thus was the game of "Bluff" often played in our camp, and seldom was it

finished until the early morning reveillé startled the
players from their sport.

The 24th was a continuation of the preceding day,
and many fights, fisticuffs and scuffles, all brought on
by whisky, occured, but, as is generally the case, very
few were hurt. Two of our officers, allowing full
scope to their imbibing capacities, had passed the day
quietly together, but towards night the canteen of one
failed to furnish him even the agreeable fragrance of
" Pine top;" this not proving congenial with his
inclinations, he helped himself from the canteen of his
friend. The owner thereof appearing at the moment
the destitute one was slacking his thirst at his expense,
and not fancying the disappearance of his "fire-water"
except through one channel, insisted upon stopping
the leak. From words they came to blows, until they
knocked each other into the Company street, when
the Colonel soon appeared and put them under arrest.

The following morning they were much surprised
to hear of the fight, and rather mortified to feel that
they had lost their swords, but it was soon arranged
and they were released, becoming firmer friends for the
future.

The 25th (Xmas,) was a keenly cold day, and was
rendered far from agreeable under foot by a previous
fall of snow and hail. A few broken noses and a little
blood unnecessarily spilled were all that disturbed the
monotony of our every day life.

Many of the soldiers at Centerville, during the winter of 1861—received gifts from their distant homes to

replenish their larders; but those of our Regiment were not so lucky, as our homes were in the hands of the enemy. Silently we watched the wagons, loaded with Xmas boxes, pass our camp for more fortunate men; silently we saw the fat turkey stripped of his flesh in the hands of others; when suffering, we tried to bear it heroically, though no gentle hand was near to soothe the aching brow; we were refugees from home, the first in the struggle—but no laughter was more unrestrained, more merrily heart-felt than that of the 17th Va.; and no sweeter songs than those of Smith, Bradley and the Kidwells, were heard upon the midnight air.

The New Year was hailed by us all with sundry congratulations—toasts, songs, and general hilarity—these formed the programme of the day.

A "home gathering" of some description was given by the captains throughout the Regiment, in and around their tents, thus drawing the hearts of their men more closely to themselves; whilst officers and men worked as a unit in our common cause: A cause for which much that had formed life's dearest pleasures had been sacrificed without a murmur, and with the determined spirit to yield up life itself, if necessary, in upholding and defending it.

The day passed with incredible swiftness, and forms an era in our soldier life not to be forgotten by any who were present.

During the latter part of the winter, many of our men received thirty days furlough, renounced camp life pro tem, some for a trip to Richmond, others to Lynchburg, and a few to visit distant friends.

On the 7th of March, 1862, that portion of the army of Northern Virginia stationed near Leesburg, under the command of Gen. Hill, began its evacuation, and marched via the Plains and Warrenton to the vicinity of Culpeper Court House.

On the 9th, those at Centerville composing the main army, broke camp and fell back slowly towards Culpeper, passing through Warrenton. Thousands of pounds of bacon, flour and other army stores were burned, indeed, there was a general destruction of whatever could not be made transportable.

Our Regiment, in company with Longstreet's Division passed through Warrenton on the 11th, the men in high spirits; the boy's making the welkin ring with their merry songs. Most of the army reached the neighborhood of Orange Court House on the 17th of March, 1862. Our Regiment encamped on Taylor's farm about one and a half miles south-west of the village. The rains had been heavy, hence the ground was in bad condition for camping. Many of the men were unfitted for duty from sickness occasioned by fatigue and exposure during the inclement weather while falling back. On the 26th, our camp was removed a short distance to a more comfortable location, and the companies resumed the drill and parades.

While in this camp, Col. A. P. Hill was promoted to Brig. Gen., and assigned the command of our Brigade, vice Gen. Ewell, promoted.

On the 17th of March, Maj. G. W. Brent, whose social companionship had quickened the dragging hours of many a dreary march, was detached from our Regiment by order of Gen. Beauregard, and assigned to duty as Inspector General of the army of the West. The severing of a tie, that for nearly a year had given so much pleasure to all, was a source of deep regret; but like true soldiers, we were aware that duty must forestall pleasure.

Subsequently, he was assigned to duty as Adjutant General, and retained the position until the close of the war, having served as such under, Gen.'s Beauregard, Bragg, Hardee and Johnston. His career was one of hardships and excessive toils; he participated in the battles of Shiloh, Farmington, Richmond and Perryville, in Kentucky, Murfreesborough, Chickamauga, Chattanooga, and was present in several battles around Petersburg.

THE PENINSULA.

ABOUT the 6th of April the army of Northern Virginia left Orange Court House, taking the route towards Fredericksburg. Our Regiment proceeded by the road to Louisa Court House, and during the march was subjected to the discomforts of a severe snow storm which, together with previous rains, made the roads almost impassable.

The men bore their trials with veteran fortitude, and, with few exceptions, presented themselves in due time at the end of the day's march.

After bivouacing near Louisa for two days, where rations of *good whisky* were issued, the march was resumed and continued to within a few miles of Richmond.

On the 14th, the camp near Richmond was abandoned. The Regiment moved through the city, took transports on the James River, and passed down to King's Mill, where a landing was made. On the 17th, the trenches around Yorktown were reached, where Gen. McClellan was concentrating his army prior to the movement against Richmond.

Gen. Magruder was in charge of the Confederate forces at this point until the army arrived, when Gen. Jos. E. Johnston was assigned the command. About two weeks were spent in the trenches, during which the men suffered severely. We were daily annoyed by artillery and sharp-shooters, from which our Regiment

lost one man killed and had several wounded, viz:
Sergt. J. W. Ivors, Co. G, severely wounded, from
the effects of which he died; Private A. F. Skidmore,
Co. E, killed; Privates Lyman Coons, Co. D, and
H. Biggs, Co. E, wounded.

On the 26th of April, the Regiment was re-organ-
ized in accordance with a recent law of Congress. Col.
M. D. Corse was re-elected Colonel. Capt. M. Marye
was elected Lieutenant Colonel; Capt. A. Herbert,
Major.

Lieut. A. J. Humphreys was elected Captain of Company A, vice, Marye, promoted; Capt. R. H. Simpson
was re-elected Captain of Co. B; Capt. Geo. R. Head
was re-elected Captain of Co. C; but resigning on the
28th, Lieut. W. B. Lynch was elected in his stead;
Lieut. J. T. Burke was elected Captain of Co. D;
Lieut. James M. Steuart was elected Captain of Co.
E; Lieut. Grayson Tyler was elected Captain of Co.
F; Lieut. R. F. Knox was elected Captain of Co. G;
Lieut. W. H. Fowle, Jr., was promoted to the Cap-
taincy of Co. H, vice A. Herbert, promoted; Lieut.
Raymond Fairfax was elected Captain of Co. I, and
Lieut. J. D. Kirby was elected Captain of Co. K.

On the 3d of May, a retreat becoming necessary, the
army was quietly withdrawn under the Generalship of
Jos. E. Johnston, the enemy not being aware of the
movement until the following morning. Williamsburg was reached on the morning of the 4th, after a
severe night march, over roads in truly deplorable condition from recent heavy rains. The men spent the

day in the town; in the afternoon, our Regiment was ordered into line of battle near by, where we slept on our arms.

Early on the morning of the 5th the enemy advanced, and our batteries opened upon them. About 10 o'clock our Infantry moved to the front, and engaged the Federals in a most desperate fight, which lasted throughout the day. The rain poured without intermission, but the men fought stubbornly; gradually but surely we gained ground. It was a hotly contested field on which the blood of many a brave heart flowed freely, for the troops in both armies fought with irreproachable valor.

The following extracts from the official reports of Brigadier General Hill and Colonel M. D. Corse will show the part so nobly sustained by the Seventeenth Virginia Regiment:

General Hill says:

"Colonel Corse, calm and equable as a May morning, bore himself like a true soldier throughout.

"Lieutenant Colonel Marye and Major Herbert were brave, active and energetic in the discharge of their duties.

"Among those who, by the fortunes of war, were most prominently brought forward and noticed are Captain R. H. Simpson; Cadet J. Herbert Bryant, Acting Adjutant; Color Sergeant Mahlon G. Hatcher, and Color Corporal Henry N. Bradley. This Regiment mourns the loss of three gallant officers—Capt. Humphreys, Lieuts. Addison and Carter."

Colonel Corse says :

"My field officers, Lieutenant Col. Morton Marye, and Major Arthur Herbert are entitled to my highest admiration for their gallantry and great activity in inspiring the men with confidence and encouraging them forward. My Acting Adjutant, Cadet J. Herbert Bryant, displayed great zeal and courage, moving from one end of the line to the other, cheering the men on. Capt. Robert H. Simpson of Company B, won my praise for his perfect coolness and self-possession, keeping his company well in line, and directing their fire with telling effect.

Capt. Wm. B. Lynch, Company C; Capt. J. T. Burke, Company D; Capt. James M. Steuart, Company E; Capt. Grayson Tyler, Company F; Capt. Robert F. Knox, Company G; Capt. Wm. H. Fowle, Company H; Capt. James D. Kirby, Company K; and Lieut. Thomas O'Shea commanding Company I, did their duty faithfully and well. Never was a Regimental Commander more zealously supported by his company officers. When subaltern officers universally behaved so well, I cannot mention one individual without doing injustice to the others. Among the non-commissioned officers and men, I witnessed innumerable instances of distinguished courage, many refusing to leave the field, though suffering from painful wounds. Capt. A. J. Huphreys commanding Company A, my late Adjutant, and one nearest my person during the past year, fell about one o'clock mortally wounded, bravely leading his company. Of him, I must say a more gallant or better soldier never led men to battle. Lieut. John F. Addison of Company G, fell dead about the same time. His remarkable activity and intrepidity came frequently under my notice during the action. Lieut. W. L. Carter was killed early in the day cheering his men on. He was a steady, determined soldier. These officers were amongst the most beloved in the Regiment, and their loss is deeply mourned. Color Sergeant Mahlon G. Hatcher was severely wounded in the arm, while courageously bearing the colors to the front. Color Corporal H. N. Bradley was badly wounded in the face, while steadily moving forward in his place."

The enemy having been at last driven at every point, the battle proved a victory to our forces; they remained that night upon the field and commenced their retreat from Williamsburg on the following morning. Many of our wounded, who were unable to move, were left in Williamsburg and fell into the hands of the enemy. Our march was slow and toilsome; on the 9th, we reached the Christian Farm, near the Long Bridge, where we rested several days.

The hardships of those memorable three days march, were not equalled during the war, though the men of the army bore them unmurmuringly. The enemy hugged close upon the rear for some distance, but having had a taste of the fangs of the "bull dog warrior," who defended and protected the rear of the army, they preferred not giving him another opportunity to bite, contenting themselves with watching at a safe distance.

From Long Bridge we fell back to a camp near Richmond, and for several weeks did picket duty at Deep Bottom, on the James; there the line of skirmishers had a fight with a gunboat and had one man wounded.

The loss of the Seventeenth Virginia, in the battle of Williamsburg, amounted to about sixty-five men and officers killed and wounded—about thirty per cent. of the number engaged. Our camp was again moved, and we settled near the city of Richmond.

General McClellan, in command of the Army of the Potomac, had moved his forces nearer Richmond and fixed his lines, bordering the Chickahominy river, upon grounds of his own choosing. The men of the army, under General Johnston, were busy strengthening the works around the "City of Seven Hills," and in recruiting and filling up their decimated ranks.

Richmond was filled with people from all parts of the country, of every grade, from the earnest sympathizers in our cause to the Shylocks, who came like vultures to seize upon any prey within range of their tender mercies, whether citizen or soldier, widow or orphan; and it is to this class of people, whether native or imported, may be justly attributed the downfall of the Southern Confederacy; to them rightfully belongs the opprobrium which fraud and extortion should ever bring upon their votaries! It is needless to say, these people remained in civil life, pursuing what ever avocations would best accomplish their ends.

6

While we were recruiting strength to defend our Capitol, Gen'l McClellan was weaving, as he believed, a powerful net in which to entrap and crush us at one blow; but it proved a mightier task than even his great military genius had imagined. Fever and ague, malignant fevers, and disease of every description, occasioned by the miasma arising from the surrounding swamps, mowed down his men by thousands. Mired in mud that precluded the use of wheels, he could only rest on his oars until a more propitious season, a delay which afforded us ample time to mass a considerable force in his front. As the time approached for us to make a bold stroke, stringent orders were issued and great care taken to keep the men from straying off. The roads leading to and from Richmond were guarded, and a Major General's pass required to effect an entrance thereto, while her streets were lined with armed men fully empowered to enforce these regulations; *running the blockade* at that time was far from child's play. Our Regiment (Seventeenth Virginia) was a fair sample, we may judge, of our confréres in arms generally, and of it it may be truthfully told that no opportunity was allowed to pass unimproved which would bring us within range of the bright eyes and gentle words of our lady friends. The gauntlet was run regardless of distance or danger, for where was the Soldier Boy in those days—for whose coming no fair one watched in our beautiful "Modern Rome," so renowned for the loveliness and nobleness of her daughters?

Partial list of casualties in the Seventeenth Virginia Regiment, at the battle of Williamsburg, May 5th, 1862.

Field and Staff—Color Sergeant M. G. Hatcher, wounded.

Company A—Killed, Capt. A. J. Humphreys; Privates, F. H. Abbott and E. V. Fairfax. Wounded, Lieut. John Addison, Sergeants J. H. McVeigh, Jr., and S. B. Paul; the former badly; Privates R. C. Johnston, E. T. Taliaferro, T. B. Turner, C. H. McKnight, J. N. Swann, and H. S. Hite; the last two died of their wounds.

Company B—Killed, Privates, Peyton Scroggin and John W. Chrisman; wounded, Lieut. Wm. Richardson, mortally, and Sergt. W. A. Rust, badly.

Company C—Killed, Privates Jas. H. Sibbett and Chas. E. Wright; wounded, Privates R. Burke and John L. A. Murphy; the latter died of his wounds.

Company D—Killed, none; wounded, Privates S. D. Mills, D. A. Marks and J. Cook.

Company E—Killed, Privates Thos. Padgett and Jos. Penn; wounded, Corp. S. S. Coleman, severely.

Company F—Killed, Lieut. W. L. Carter and Private B. Grayson. Wounded, Privates F. Ebhardt, A. J. Carter and M. R. Newman.

Company G—Killed, Lieut. John F. Addison and Private John Murfee.

Company H—Killed, Privates Clinton Ballenger and P. Lannon. Wounded, Sergt. James E. Grimes;

Corp. E. G. Barbour, both died of wounds; Color Corporal H. N. Bradley; Private H. S. Pitts.

Company I—None reported.

Company K—Killed, Private Richard Payne; wounded, Privates James A. Singleton, J. O. Pemberton and Wm. M. Spillman, the last two, badly.

THE BATTLES AROUND RICHMOND.

WHEN night closed in on the 30th May, 1862, blindingly vivid lightning and loud crashes of thunder betokened the approach of a storm, which soon burst forth in terrific fury. Wind and rain penetrated everwhere; the camps were soon deluged and the men subjected to great inconvenience, for the darkness was impenetrable except when the heavens were illumined with electric flashes. Thus it continued until midnight; as it abated the men were endeavoring to quiet themselves down for at least a short nap, when a courier rode hastily to the Colonel's quarters, the long roll beat and the cry of "Turn out! turn out!" resounded on all sides.

The order to prepare two days rations was issued, and the men instructed to be ready to march at a moment's notice. As day dawned the drum sounded, and the Brigade falling into line moved noiselessly away. Passing around the suburbs of the city, we struck the Williamsburg road. Small streams swollen into rivers by the storm, had to be forded by the troops.

When about five miles from R. the Brigade halted, then moved into an open field on the left of the road, and awaited orders. About ten minutes to one o'clock the first gun was heard in our front, and the battle of "Seven Pines" or "Fair Oaks" was opened. Not many minutes elapsed ere the sounds of rapid firing

6*

from the pickets rolled towards us, then gradually the
roar of heavy musketry and the air filled with the
din of strife and carnage.

During this time the Brigade moved forward and
took its position to the right and in rear of the fighting. The battle continued during the entire afternoon.
About four o'clock P. M. the order for our Brigade
to move to the front was received, and, following
Kemper, we double quicked, marching at the rate of
seven miles an hour. It was the last march of many
a noble soldier. The distance was more than a mile to
the battle field, and as we filed to the right at Barker's
house, our left flank was exposed to one of the heaviest
assaults of lead and canister that we had ever passed
through. The order to charge was given, and the
men moved briskly to their work. The following
extracts, as copied from the official report of the Colonel commading the Seventeenth Virginia, will show
the part sustained by it in this battle.

"At 4 o'clock P. M., I moved my Regiment by the
left flank, following the Eleventh in double-quick
time for one and a half miles down the Williamsburg
road, passing for five hundred yards under a heavy artillery and infantry fire, to a wood pile to the left of
the Barker House, where we halted for a few minutes
to close up the ranks and permit the men to recover
breath; the Eleventh was soon put in motion. I followed by the left flank, filing to the right in front of
the redoubt and rear of the Barker House and the
enemy's camp, and the open space beyond, encounter-

ing a galling infantry fire from the enemy stationed in the edge of the woods, and meeting numbers of our own troops falling back, which prevented me from presenting a compact line to the enemy. After advancing some distance, I received an order to fall back and re-form behind the trenches, which was done in tolerably good order, which position we held until near nightfall, holding the enemy in check until they were driven from their position."

"The Regiment was then re-formed with the Brigade, and moved forward through the enemy's camp and occupied the woods beyond, from which they had been driven. About 9 o'clock P. M. we were withdrawn, and bivouaced a mile to the right and rear of the position occupied by the Brigade in the afternoon."

"In the advance into the enemy's camp, Color Corporal Morrill was struck down, wounded in three places, and rose upon his elbow to cheer the men forward. The colors were caught by Capt. Raymond Fairfax, Company I, and handed to Color Corporal Diggs, who instantly fell wounded; they were then taken by Private Harper, Company E, who retained them until the close of the day. Sergeant Major Francis fell mortally wounded some distance in advance of the Regiment; he was a gallant soldier and most estimable gentleman. Sergeant Busey, Company F, was killed while gallantly charging the enemy far in advance of the Regiment. Lieut. Wm. Gray was killed whilst bravely cheering his men on. His conduct has been remarkable for heroism on every occasion in which he has been under fire. Capt. Knox, Company G, Capt. Fowle, Company H, and Capt. Burke, Company D, were wounded whilst leading their companies. Lieut. Adie was wounded whilst gallantly doing his duty. Lieut. Thos. V. Fitzhugh received a wound, whilst passing through a shower of lead, in the voluntary act of carrying an order to Colonel Moore, of the —— Alabama Regiment; Major Herbert was wounded whilst passing through a sheet of fire to take charge, by your order, of some companies of Col. Moore's Regiment, to the right and rear of our position, having volunteered for the service, Col. Moore having previously fallen desperately wounded; Col. Marye acted with his usual gallantry."

"It gives me great pleasure to say that I was well and bravely sustained by my company officers. I could record many instances of distinguished courage among the non-commissioned officers and men, but for fear of leaving out some who are really deserving, I shall merely say, that with very few exceptions they all did their duty faithfully and well."

While holding the line beyond the enemy's camp, after nightfall, the men stood in water from one to three feet deep, surrounded on all sides by the dead and dying. It was a soul-harrowing position. On our return to the rear we passed through the camps, where many secured blankets and "grub," — two invaluable acquisitions to cold and hungry men. The loss of our Regiment in this battle was very heavy, over 70 having fallen killed and wounded in a few

Partial list of casualties in the Seventeenth Virginia Regiment at the battle of Seven Pines, May 31st, 1862:

Field and Staff—Killed, Sergeant Major J. F. Francis; wounded, Major A. Herbert.

Company A—Wounded, Sergt. W. E. II. Clagett, severely; Privates A. C. Fairfax, severely, R. W. Avery and M. L. Price, slightly.

Company B—Killed, Private E. Broy; wounded, Private Stephen Carder, who died from his wounds.

Company C—Wounded, Privates C. H. Bradfield and D. Wallace.

Company D—Wounded, Capt. J. T. Burke, Sergt. R. Steel, and Private C. Cornwell; Killed, Privates Thos. W. Lynn and C. R. Pettett.

Company E — Killed, Private Jas. E. Molair; wounded, Lieut. Wm. Simpson; Privates R. Roland, G. Kreig, A. W. Hicks, D. Bruin and R. Allison. ·

Company F—Killed, Sergeants E. Bascy and Wm. R. Smith; Privates J. D. Brady and E. W. Burgess. Wounded, Lieut. S. Harrison, Corp. Jesse S. Rogers; Privates E. W. Clowe, M. F. Davis, R. Watson and Chas. Cogan.

Company G—Killed, Lieut. Wm. E. Gray; Privates P. Doyle and P. Harrington. Wounded, Capt. R. F. Knox.

Company H—Killed, Privates W. J. Higdon, W. H. Lunt, John S. Murray and Rodic Whittington. Wounded, Captain W. H. Fowle, Jr., severely, Lieut. Thos. V. Fitzhugh, died of wound; Privates D. H.

Appich, in head, J. W. Baldwin, died of wound, E. F. Baldwin, Jas. Godwin and W. J. Hall, all severely; A. Calmus, R. Young, S. D. Smith and S. K. Sowers, slightly.

Company I—Wounded, Lieut. Geo. C. Adie and private P. Ryan.

Company K—Killed, Privates Thos. F. Kane and R. Love. Wounded, Lieut. A. M. Brodie, severely; Color Corp. C. W. Diggs, severely; Privates John E. Fisher and Henry Payne.

In the height of the battle, when the fire was hottest, the voice of a wounded officer, Capt. Knox, Company G, was heard in our front, calling for some one to move him out of range of the enemy's fire; immediately, Lieut. Kell, Company H; Lieut. Powers, Company G; Privates Harrigan, Company G, and Ashby, Company A, all of the Seventeenth sprang forward over the parapet and seizing him in their arms bore him to a place of safety.

About nine o'clock on Sunday morning, July 1st, we were again ordered to the front, and took position in support of Stuart's Horse Artillery, stationed in the captured fort, near the Barker House. The battle was again opened to the left of the Williamsburg road in our front soon after our arrival, and for several hours we witnessed, (without engaging in it,) the grandeur of an Infantry combat, about three hundred yards distant. Several lines of the enemy, making charge after charge without effect, finally gave it up and withdrew, leaving us victors and possessors

Watkins of Company H, and Hunter of Company A, were particularly conspicious in the heat of the first day's fight, for bravery and unearing aim. Guns were loaded by the boys around them, and the two standing upon the embankment, fired as rapidly as they could take the guns ; the colors of a regiment in front were cut down three times in succession.

Sunday morning, while the bullets were cutting the air, and the shells of the enemy were spluttering around, several of the boys performed the last sad offices for the dead of Company H, who fell in the battle the day before. A grave was dug in the circle of the fort, and the remains of the gallant dead, Higdon, Lunt, Murray and Whittington were laid side by side therein, with their blankets folded carefully about them. The last named had joined the Company but a few hours previous, and in the flower of youth was cut down, without even a sight of the enemy that slew him. As soldiers they met their death in the path of duty and were awarded a soldier's grave—a burial in the midst of strife.

Sadly were the duties performed, and the tears that again start forth in the review of these pages, bespeak in strong, deep language, a memory, that words are too feeble to portray.

The gifted, loved and noble Morrill, (the one who fired the first gun on the morning of the 24th of May, 1861,) as brave a man as ever entered battle, fell on Saturday, proudly waving in the enemy's face the battle-torn banner of the Seventeenth Virginia Regiment. As he fell, courageous and true to the last, his memory will ever be enshrined in the hearts of those who knew him.

About noon, the Brigade moved position to the extreme right of our line, and, after throwing up rifle pits, awaited further orders.

This battle, in which the Confederates lost over 5,000 men, was one of the hottest of the war. Gen. Johnston was severely wounded in the shoulder and sent to Richmond. The command of the army was then given to Gen. R. E. Lee.

On Monday night, June 2d, the troops were withdrawn, and our Regiment returned to its camp. Several days after, our camping-ground was moved to a point on the left of the Williamsburg road and about two miles from the city.

While in this camp, very little of interest beyond the usual routine occurred, and the 25th of June soon dawned.

At this time, orders were issued for the troops to prepare to march; this being done, we awaited further orders, which were received on the following morning. Our Regiment formed and moved out from camp in company with the Brigade. Numbers of troops were moving in different directions, and brigade after brigade was passed as we marched partly around and halted on the suburbs of the city, near the Mechanicsville turnpike.

We remained in this position until late in the day. About four o'clock in the afternoon, the guns of General Hill were heard in our front, as he moved his Division against the enemy who were strongly posted around the village of Mechanicsville, three miles distant from us. The battle was continued until late at night before the enemy gave way, and many on both sides were killed and wounded.

About dark we moved forward, and halted on the narrow causeway crossing the Chickahominy Swamps, where the night was spent, the men and officers sleeping on the gravel road.

While we were all sound asleep, and no doubt many dreaming of what the morrow would bring, a horse broke loose from his halter, and knocking down several stacks of arms, caused quite a commotion in our midst; the cry of "Look out! Yankees!" &c., &c., broke frightfully upon the ear. Many being half awake, must have thought the enemy were really upon us, for, like frogs chased by bad boys, they went into the adjacent ditches headforemost. About fifty were completely drenched, and looked not quite so self-possessed as usual when the cause was discovered.

Early on Friday morning, (27th,) we crossed the river and moved slowly forward in direction of the battle then in progress. Before our arrival, General Hill had driven the foe before him after a sharp conflict, and was following close upon his heels. We passed many of the dead and wounded of both armies in our march. The Federal troops had fired the stores, camps, and surplus baggage; clouds of smoke filled the air before us as we advanced.   The enemy had in readiness for our reception a strong line of works well manned in the vicinity of Gaines's Mill, against which our army was put in position ready to drive them out. Their line was so well chosen and so strong, that time, perseverance, and superior generalship were required to dislodge them.

Longstreet, with the Hills in his front, opened battle upon the well organized and equipped troops of General McClellan's army, about noon.

Brisk cannonading was continued and good show made in the enemy's front.   In the afternoon, a single gun was heard far in the enemy's rear, then another and another, until the forest around resounded with echo upon echo of artillery reports.

Soon the truth, like lightning, flashed upon us and was carried down the line, that "Stonewall Jackson" had arrived, and the guns heard were his.   Now, kind reader, imagine the result!   A yell of joy broke forth, such as may well have struck terror to the hearts of the enemy, and the lines, as if by magic, moved forward to the charge.

Over hill and vale, field and morass, swept the Confederates, until the entire line of the Federals was carried by the bayonet.

The enemy, like a wounded lion at bay, fought with desperation, doing all in his power to keep back the advancing, victorious army of General Lee.

The intrepid McClellan, by far the best General in the Federal army, had found his match in General R. E. Lee, while the flank movement of "Stonewall Jackson" (peace to his noble ashes!) completely out-witted the "Mogul" of the Chickahominy, and caused him to seek safety in flight. Our Regiment was not engaged in this fight, being held in reserve, consequently it lost none of its men.

The number of killed and wounded on both sides was great; the fields and woods for miles were filled with the dead and dying. We spent the night on the battle-field, part of the Regiment doing picket duty in the Chickahominy swamps. During the first night, as many as forty of the wounded enemy died in our midst, and numbers during Saturday; most of the day mentioned was employed in removing the wounded and burying the dead. Just after the battle ended on Friday night, companies H and K took charge of 1,400 prisoners and escorted them to General Lee's quarters; after guarding them during the night these companies were relieved by cavalry and returned to the Regiment. Many of us saw General Lee take his breakfast in the saddle, about daylight on the following morning, before the cavalry relieved us.

Coming out of the house in which he had passed the night, a slice of bread and ham in his hand, he mounted his "charger" and calling out to his aids, he said: "Come, boys, it is time for us to be off," and, suiting his actions to his words, he galloped away, followed by his staff.

General McClellan's army had taken the direction of the Seven Pines battle-field, having crossed the Chickahominy via the " Grapevine " and " McClellan " bridges. A division had been sent to cut off his retreat, but failed, and he was allowed to proceed towards the James River.

On Sunday morning, our Brigade crossed at " Grape-vine " bridge, and followed the enemy at a rapid pace; the day was very sultry, and numbers of the men fell by the wayside from exhaustion. Reaching the vicinity of the enemy, on Frazier's farm, on Monday morning, June 30th, 1862, the Brigade was formed into line and arrangements made for battle. Our position was on the right, and our Regiment was on the extreme right of the line.

In the afternoon, about 4 o'clock, we were ordered to charge a battery on the opposite hill, near the Frazier's farm mansion, and the troops moved forward briskly to the work. The guns of the enemy were abandoned, and we had possession of that portion of the field for a short time; but a terrific fire from the front and an enfilading fire from both flanks caused us to fall back; the Brigade having been unsupported, a retreat was compulsory. The vastly superior numbers of the enemy enabled them to almost surround us, causing the Brigade a severe loss in killed, wounded and missing.

The following extracts from official reports will show the part sustained by this Regiment.

Col. M. D. Corse says:

"Capt. Simpson's Company (B) and Capt. Kirby's Company (K) were sent forward as skirmishers, with orders to advance about two hundred and fifty yards, and, if they met the enemy, to engage them. The Regiment remained in position until about 4 o'clock, when I received an order to advance with the other regiments of the Brigade, which was done with spirit and enthusiasm. After moving forward about fifteen hundred yards, a great part of the way through dense woods, the ground covered with thick undergrowth, fallen timber and swamps, which rendered it totally impracticable to keep a compact alignment, we encountered the enemy's infantry in large force, with a battery in position playing upon us with grape and canister for some minutes, when the left of the line of the Brigade commenced to fall back, and an order for similar movement was sent along the line; from whom it originated I cannot tell. Soon after, the enemy appeared in large force on our right and left flanks; the men stubbornly stood their ground until greatly outnumbered, and, seeing no support on either flank, I rallied a few men on the colors and slowly fell back, making repeated stands facing the enemy, and finally reached the position occupied before the advance was made. The right companies of my Regiment came upon the enemy in an open field and drove them from a breastwork made of some fencing and earth; my left companies were in the woods, engaging the enemy in

"The only field officer I had with me, Lieut. Col. Marye, behaved with distinguished gallantry, and all the company officers, as far as I could observe, did their duty bravely and well. The non-commissioned officers and men lost none of their reputation for valor won at ' Bull Run,' ' Williamsburg,' and ' Seven Pines.' "   *   *   *   *   *   *   *

Brig. Gen. Kemper says :

"This Brigade left its camp on the Williamsburg road about dawn on the morning of Thursday, the 26th ultimo, numbering fourteen hundred and thirty-three muskets, and provided with three days' rations, which were carried by the men in their haversacks. The Division being marched left in front during the late operations on the north side of the Chickahominy, the First Brigade brought up the rear of its line, and was not ordered into any of the actions which occurred prior to Monday, 30th ultimo. It was held in reserve, however, in immediate proximity to the battle-fields of the 26th and 27th ultimo, as well as that of the 1st inst., in readiness to be thrown into action at a moment's notice."

" Upon the 30th ultimo, the Division was halted in the vicinty of the enemy, on the road leading through Frazier's farm, and under the orders of Brigadier General R. H. Anderson, commanding the Division, I formed my command in line of battle on the right and nearly perpendicular to the road; one regiment of the Second Brigade being posted in line between my left and the road. My command constituted the

extreme right of our general line of battle, and was
posted upon the rear edge of a dense body of timber;
the Seventeenth Virginia Regiment (Colonel M. D.
Corse,) occupying the right; the Twenty-fourth Virginia Regiment, (Lieut. Colonel Hairston commanding,) the left; the First Virginia, (Capt. Norton commanding,) the centre; the Eleventh Virginia, (Capt.
O'cy commanding,) the right centre, and the Seventh
Virginia, (Colonel W. T. Patton,) the left centre.
Soon after getting into position, I received orders
from Major General Longstreet, to use the utmost
care in guarding against any movement of the enemy
upon my right, and I at once caused Colonel Corse, of
the right regiment, to change front to rear on his
left company, so that his regiment formed an obtuse
angle with the line of the Brigade, and fronted obliquely to the right. I also caused two companies of
this regiment to move forward from Corse's new
front, as skirmisers, under command of Capt. Simpson.
After advancing several hundred yards, these skirmishers were halted upon the rear edge of an open field, a
good view of which was commanded from their position.
I also posted Rogers Battery of four pieces upon an
open eminence, near the right of my line, and in
supporting distance of Corse's Regiment; the position
being such as to command an extensive field upon my
right. About five o'clock, P. M., an order being
received from Major General Longstreet to advance
my line, I immediately, in person, ordered Colonel
Corse to change his front forward so as to bring the

right of his Regiment up to the Brigade line, and
sent my staff along the line towards the left, so as to
ensure the simultaneous advance of the entire line.
The Brigade advanced in line of battle steadily and
in good order, notwithstanding the unevenness of the
ground, which, in places, was almost precipitous, the
entangled undergrowth which filled the woods, and
the firing of one of the enemy's batteries located
directly in front, which rapidly threw shell and round
shot over and almost in the midst of my command.
The advance continued to be conducted in good order,
until very soon coming upon the pickets of the enemy,
and driving them in, the men seemed to be possessed
with the idea that they were upon the enemy's main line,
and, in an instant, the whole Brigade charged forward
in double-quick time, and with loud cheers.   Nothing
could have been more chivalrously done, and nothing
could have been more unfortunate, as the cheering of
the men only served to direct the fire of the enemy's
batteries; and the movement in double-quick time
through dense woods, over rough ground, encumbered
with matted undergrowth, and crossed by a swamp,
had the effect of producing more or less confusion,
and breaking the continuity of the line, which, however, was preserved as well as it possibly could have
been under the circumstances.   But a single idea
seemed to control the minds of the men, which was to
reach the enemy's line by the most direct route, and
in the shortest time; and no earthly power could have
availed to arrest or restrain the impetuosity with

which they rushed towards the foe, for my orders previously given, with great care and emphasis, to the assembled field officers of the Brigade, forbade any movement in double-quick time over such ground, when the enemy were not in view."

"The obstructions were such as to make it impossible for any officer to see more than a few files of his men at one view, and it was apparent that any effort to halt and re-form the entire Brigade would be futile, and would only serve to produce increased confusion. But whatever the error of the men in advancing too rapidly, in disregard of previous orders to the contrary, it was an error upon the side of bravery. After advancing in this way probably ten or twelve hundred yards, crossing two bodies of woods, and a small intermediate field, the line suddenly emerged into another field, facing a battery of the enemy, consisting of not less than eight pieces, distant but a few hundred yards, while the enemy's infantry were found protected by an imperfectly and hastily-constructed breastwork, and a house near by. At the same time, it became apparent that another battery of the enemy was posted a considerable distance to our left. These two batteries and the enemy's infantry poured an incessant fire of shell, grape, canister and lead upon my line, and did much execution. Still there was no perceptible faltering in the advance of these brave men, who rushed across the open field, pouring a well-directed fire into the enemy, driving him from his breastworks and the battery in our front. The guns of the battery were abandoned to us for the time being, and my command was in virtual possession of the chosen position of the enemy. A more impetuous and desperate charge was never made than that of my small command against the sheltered and greatly superior forces of the enemy. The ground which they gained from the enemy is marked by the graves of some of my veterans, who were buried where they fell; and those graves marked with the names of the occupants, situated at and near the position of the enemy, show the points at which they dashed against the strongholds of the retreating foe. It is proper to be stated here that the left of my line was entirely unsupported, and greatly to my surprise and disappointment, for I had supposed that the movement of my Brigade was a part of a general advance of our entire lines. Up to this time no firing was heard upon my left, except the firing of the enemy, which was directed upon my line with telling effect."

" Afterwards, at a late hour, I found the right regiment of the Second Brigade (on the right of which I had originally formed) standing fast at or near the position they had occupied in the beginning, and near the line from which my advance was begun. I was informed that this regiment had remained from the first in that position, having received no subsequent orders to move forward. I trust I shall not be understood as alleging or intimating any delinquency upon the part of the Second Brigade, and I certainly do not undertake to say at what time that Brigade, commanded by Colonel Jenkins, advanced; but, if its advance was simultaneous with my own, it must have happened that the lines of advance of the two brigades were so divergent as to leave a wide interval between the right of the one and the left of the other. Whatever were the operations of the Second Brigade, they were doubtless in keeping with its proud character in the past and that of its gallant commander. All that I undertake to state positively in this connection is, that the right regiment of the Second Brigade did not advance for a long time after my Brigade had been moved forward, and that at the time when my command had obtained virtual possession of the enemy's position, no Confederate troops were anywhere visible except my own. It now became evident that the position sought to be held by my command was wholly untenable by them unless largely and immediately reinforced. The inferior numbers which had alarmed the enemy, and driven him from his breastworks and batteries soon became apparent to him, and he at once proceeded to make use of his advantage. While greatly superior numbers hung upon our front, considerable bodies of the enemy were thrown upon both flanks of my command, which was now in imminent danger of being wholly captured or destroyed. Already they were capturing officers and men at different points of my line, principally upon my right. No reinforcements appeared, and the dire alternative of withdrawing from the position, although of obvious and inevitable necessity, was reluctantly submitted to."

"Owing to the difficulties offered by the wilderness through which the Brigade had advanced, the task of reassembling and reforming the regiments was attended with much trouble. I sent out details as speedily as possible to direct officers and men where to reform, and as soon as this task was accomplished, imperfectly it is true, but as effectually as was possible at so late an hour of the day, I repaired to General Longstreet's headquarters as soon as I could find them, and, under instructions there received, it now being night, I proceeded to select a suitable position on the road in the rear, at which stragglers could be arrested, and such of my men as had not then come in could be re-collected."

"I should have mentioned before, that soon after my command was overpowered, and before all of it had fallen back, General Branch's Brigade was found coming up, and General Branch was shown by me into the position which my gallant men had vainly sought to hold against overwhelming odds, and immediately afterwards the Third Brigade of this Division, Colonel Hunton commanding, took position on Branch's right. If it had been possible for these brigades to have advanced simultaneously with my own, the victory of the day would have been achieved on the right of our line with comparatively little difficulty, and at an early hour. When my line emerged into the open field in front of the enemy's batteries, the Seventh Virginia, commanded by Colonel W. T. Patton, gallantly assisted by Lieutenant Colonel Flowree and Major Swindler, was in good order, considering the difficulties of the ground over which it had passed, and this Regiment and the First Virginia, nobly sustained by such portions of the other regiments as had come up, made the first daring charge which drove the enemy from his position. Several companies of the Seventeenh Virginia were unavoidably delayed for some time by the almost impassable nature of the swamp at the point at which they crossed."

"Praise is due to Colonel Corse, Seventeenth Virginia, and to Lieutenant Colonel Hairston, Twenty-fourth Virginia, as well as to Colonel W. T. Patton, Seventh Virginia, (who acted with eminent gallantry,) for discharging their duties with the utmost fidelity and bravery."

"The same praise is accorded to Captain K. Otey, commanding Eleventh Virginia; Captain Norton, commanding First Virginia; Lieutenant Colonel Marye and Captain Simpson, of the Seventeenth Virginia, fell into the hands of the enemy while discharging their duties with conspicuous gallantry. I am satisfied all the field officers did well. I especially commend the good conduct of Captain W. T. Fry, my A. A. General, and Mr. A. Camp Beckham, who acted as my volunteer aid-de-camp."

"Among those reported to me as deserving especial notice for gallantry on the field, are Captain Joel Blanchard, Company D, and Lieutenant W. W. Gooding, Company K, Seventh Virginia, who were both killed; Lieutenant W. E. Harrison, Company A, Sergeant Major Tausill and Color Sergeant Mays, both wounded, and both of whom had distinguished themselves in the battles of Williamsburg and Seven Pines; First Sergeant William Apperson, Company C, who was killed, and Private George Watson, Company F, who has also repeatedly distinguished himself for bravery, all of the Seventh Virginia Regiment."

"Captain James Mitchell, Company C, and Lieut. Logan Robins, Company B, First Virginia Regiment, both of whom were wounded; Lieut. W. R. Abbott, Company E, and Lieutenant E. S. Dix, Company K, Eleventh Virginia, both of whom were killed; Lieut. Calfee, Company G, of the Twenty-fourth Virginia, who was killed within a few paces of the enemy's battery, and Captains Bently and Nowlin, of the same regiment. I doubt not there are many others, omitted in the reports, who equally distinguished themselves. The list of killed and wounded are made up of the very best officers and men of which my command could boast.."   *   *   *   *   *   *   *

Major General Longstreet says:

* * * * * "Troops were thrown forward as rapidly as possible to the support of the attacking columns. Owing to the nature of the ground that concert of action, so essential to complete success, could not be obtained, particularly attacking such odds against us and in position. The enemy, however, was driven back slowly and steadily, contesting the ground inch by inch. He succeeded in getting some of his batteries off the field, and by holding his last position

till dark, in withdrawing his forces under the cover of night. The troops sustained their reputation for coolness, courage, determination and devotion so well earned on many hotly contested fields. Branche's Brigade of Major General A. P. Hill's Division did not render the prompt support to our right which was expected, and it is believed that several of our officers and men were taken prisoners in consequence. The other brigades of this Division were prompt, and advanced to the attack with an alacrity worthy of their gallant leader. They recovered and secured the captured batteries, from some of which the troops of my Division had been compelled to retire for want of prompt support. The odds against us on this field were probably greater than on any other." * * *

"I would also mention, as distinguished among others for gallantry and skill, Brigadier Generals R. H. Anderson, Kemper, Wilcox, Pryor and Featherstone, (the latter severely wounded,) and Colonels Jenkins, Corse, Strange, Patton, Perry, severely wounded; Lieutenant Colonel Marye, Lieutenant Colonel Coppens, Lieutenant Colonel Royston, and Major Caldwell, the two latter wounded." * * * * * *

General Lee says:

* * * * * "Huger reported that his progress was obstructed; but about four P. M., firing was heard in the direction of the Charles City road, which was supposed to indicate his approach. Longstreet immediately opened with one of his batteries to give notice of his presence. This brought on the engagement, but

Huger not coming up, and Jackson having been unable to force the passage of White Oak Swamp, Longstreet and Hill were without the expected support. The superiority of numbers and advantage of position were on the side of the enemy. The battle raged furiously until nine P. M. By that time the enemy had been driven with great slaughter from every position but one, which he maintained until he was enabled· to withdraw under cover of darkness. At the close of the struggle nearly the entire field remained in our possession, covered with the enemy's dead and wounded. Many prisoners, including a General of division, were captured, and several batteries, with some thousands of small arms taken. Could the other commands have co-operated in the action, the result would have proved most disastrous to the enemy."   *   *   *   *   *   *   *

The loss sustained by our Regiment was heavy, having three officers and fourteen men killed, two officers and twenty-one men wounded, and thirteen officers and sixty men missing.

The crowning effort of the six days was made by both armies on Tuesday, July 1st, and the bloody battle of " Malvern Hill " was fought. The two armies rested within a short distance of each other, panting from the exhausting struggles of the past week. The hill, occupied by the enemy, bristled with at least three hundred pieces of artillery, supported by about sixty thousand bayonets. Below and partly around this mountain of iron and steel, the army of

General Lee was posted, awaiting quietly the order to strike the last great blow. General Lee, in his report, speaks of the enemy's position in the following words : "On this position, of great natural strength, he had concentrated his powerful artillery, supported by masses of infantry, partially protected by earthworks. His left rested near Crew's house, and his right near Binford's. Immediately in his front the ground was open, varying in width from a quarter to half a mile, and sloping gradually from the crest, was completely swept by the fire of his infantry and artillery. To reach this open ground our troops had to advance through a broken and thickly wooded country, traversed, nearly throughout its whole extent, by a swamp passable but at few places, and difficult at those. The whole was within range of the batteries on the heights and the gunboats in the river, under whose incessant fire our movements had to be executed."   *   *   *   *   *   *   *

Generals Longstreet, Jackson, the Hills, McLaws and others were there. Ere long the earth around fairly trembled from the heaviest cannonading ever before heard upon this Continent, and the infantry were ordered forward to the charge. The lateness of the hour in which the advance was made, the unevenness and extreme difficulty of the ground, ignorance of the country by subaltern officers and other causes, prevented that concert of action, so necessary for the attacking columns, and not a great deal was accomplished before the darkness of night put a stop to our movements. During the time that the troops were engaged the battle was terrific, and the two monsters grappled hand to hand upon the hill-top, neither side gaining much advantage.

Night had closed upon the combatants side by side when the conflict had ended. The troops of both armies, now exhausted, lay perfectly quiet, the well in sleep, the wounded in the agonies of death.

When the following morning dawned upon the field of blood and carnage, the enemy had withdrawn, leaving his killed and wounded in our possession.

The neighboring farm houses were turned into hospitals for the wounded of both armies. Federal and Confederate surgeons united their efforts to supply their wants and relieve their sufferings.

Our Regiment was not actively engaged; its position being on the right of the line, it received no attack, nor was it ordered to advance. From that field we followed General McClellan's retreating army to Harrison's Bend, on the James River, where we remained several days. On the 7th of July, we returned to our old camp near Richmond, whence we had marched on the 26th day of June. On the 10th, our encampment was removed near "Darbytown," on the James, where we spent a pleasant month, during which the men rested, and the decimated ranks again filled. Such of the sick and wounded as were able returned and the spirit of the men was unbroken.

Partial list of casualties in the Seventeenth Virginia Regiment at the battle of Frazier's Farm.

Field and Staff—Lieutenant Colonel M. Marye,

Company A—Killed, Privates R. C. Johnson, D. McLee, John S. Hart, and T. A. Partlow. Wounded, Captain W. W. Smith; Privates V. W. Ashby, T. L. Chase, and H. B. Eaches, the latter severely and left in the hands of enemy; missing, Lieutenant C. W. Green, Corporal William Perry, Privates Wm. Harmon, A. Hunter, W. J. Paul, R. C. Paul, and J. H. L. Sangster.

Company B—Captain R. H. Simpson, captured; Privates P. C. Darr, and J. W. Steele, killed.

Company C—Killed, Lieutenant G. T. Lamden, and Private James M. Wallace.

Company D—Missing, Lieutenant W. A. Barcs, and Privates Newcomb and D. A. Marks.

Company E—Killed, Corporal G. T. Warfield, Privates A. Wools and Joseph Bushby; wounded, Sergeant J. Proctor, Corporal S. S. Coleman, Privates F. Fields, F. Emmerson, E. Warren, and Thomas Hudson.

Company F—Killed, Lieutenant J. N. Hullfish, Privates J. R. Burgess and F. G. Hixson; wounded, Privates J. D. Rollins, M. W. Galliher, and J. W. Cornwell.

Company G—

Company H—Killed, Privates C. K. Burgess and H. Fewell; wounded, Privates V. Brent, severely, and H. S. Pitts, the latter left in the hands of the enemy.

Company I—Killed, Lieutenant George C. Adie.

Company K—

FROM RICHMOND TO THE POTOMAC.

ON the 10th of August, 1862, we broke camp on the Darbytown road, six miles below Richmond, and by daylight were on the march for the city, which we reached in time for the Gordonsville train. That afternoon the Regiment arrived safely in the village of hard boiled eggs and chicken bones, and bivouaced in the neighbouring woods for the night, during which we had full benefit of a soaking rain. The following morning, after marching a short distance in the direction of Orange Court House, an order was received causing a "Right about-face" movement, and we retraced our steps, passed through the village, and encamped two miles southwest of it.

In this encampment several days were passed pleasantly by us all; the monotony of camp life being relieved by numerous bathing and fishing excursions. On the 16th of August, we marched in direction of Orange Court House, and owing to the extreme heat we were ordered to halt during the middle of the day. The whole army was moving in the direction of Fredericksburg. We passed that night in an old encampment, near Taylors's farm, and were greatly refreshed for the next day's operations.

We marched on Sunday (17th,) down the Plank road and again on Monday, until near the Rapidan river; here Lieut. Colonel Marye returned to us and took command, having been exchanged, after his incarceration in Fort Warren. On Tuesday (19th,) we stopped near Raccoon Ford, and on Wednesday crossed the stream, marched a short distance theredown, and taking a southeasterly direction, moved towards the Rappahannock.

While approaching Kelly's Ford, the following day (21st,) the enemy opened on the head of the column from a field battery, but were soon persuaded to desist from such amusement by one or two rounds from our artillery, and the command proceeded.

The night of the 21st was passed near Stevensburg, where the command rested on the following day. During the afternoon of the 23d, we arrived at Brandy Station, O. and A. R. R., encamped on a hill near by and spent the night. On the following day, a heavy artillery duel occurred at Rappahannock Station. Several brigades of the Division, including our own, were sent forward and formed in line of battle on the plains west of the station. There was some picket firing, but towards evening the enemy were driven off, and we proceeded up the river, bivouacing for the night near the small village of Jeffersonton.

On the 25th we arrived in the neigborhood of Waterloo, on the Warrenton and Little Washington turnpike, where we spent the night. After nightfall, while we were eating and smoking quietly around the camp-fires, several shells landed in our midst, creating much amusement, as they did no damage. We remained here until late the following day, when we marched via Amesville to Hinson's Ford, which we stum-

blingly crossed in the dismal darkness of that night,
clambered up the opposite hill, rocky and rough though
it was, and succeeded in finding a suitable place for
bivouac in a wheat field on the left of the road leading to Orlean, and near the top of the ascent.

On the 27th, we continued the marched; about
noon, as we came in sight of the town of Salem, it was
ascertained to be occupied by Federal cavalry, which
rendered a halt necessary. Generals Lee, Longstreet
and Staff rode forward to the head of the corps to
reconnoitre, and while in this position, (rumor says,)
they had a narrow escape from capture, a column of
the enemy's cavalry passing within a short distance
of them without noticing them.

Salem having been vacated, our Corps moved on
after nightfall until midnight when they halted near
the Plains. General Lee's Headquarters were established at the hospitable mansion of Mr. J. W.
Foster, above and below which his men were bivouaced for miles.

The Federals having possession of Thoroughfare
Gap, in the Bull Run mountains, it was deemed expedient to drive them out before joining Jackson's army,
then at or near Groveton, some miles east of the small
range of mountains. The Gap was narrow and held
by a large force. A brigade was detached from our
Corps, with orders to cross the mountain at Hopewell
Gap, and after reaching a flanking position from which
they could fire with telling effect, to open upon the
enemy. This was accomplished and resulted in the

enemy's retirement from the Gap, leaving about fifty dead, and consuming almost the entire day, hence it was late in the afternoon when one portion of the Corps passed through. General Jackson had cut the enemy's line of communications at Manassas, burnt his stores, trains, and baggage, played the mischief generally, and had quietly fallen back upon Groveton, where he awaited the coming of Longstreet. His guns could be plainly heard as he defended his position against the forces under General Pope.

Having marched hundreds of miles and fought numerous battles, his men were greatly exhausted when General Longstreet's forces reached him on Friday, the 29th of August. The delay at the Gap allowed General Pope time to concentrate his army and meet General Lee on ground of his (Pope's) own choosing.

Our Regiment passed through the Gap on the morning of the 29th, coming in sight of Gen. Jackson's army and the enemy at a passage of arms, a mile or more distant, in the valley below. Our timely arrival ended the battle. Gen. Longstreet's corps formed in line on the right of Gen. Jackson's in crescent shape, extending around the enemy to the M. G. R. R. on the right of the turnpike.

The march from the Gap was indescribably severe, the weather being exceedingly warm and water not obtainable, except in ditches or stagnant pools on the sides of the road; these were eagerly drained by the half-famished men, with their heat and green slimy skim, regardless of the animated nature which at other times would have been so revolting to them.

Our Regiment was sent to the extreme right of the line, where it took position under a heavy shelling from one of the enemy's batteries, posted near the Junction.

C. Fadely of Company E, had his arm broken by a piece of shell, and was sent to the rear; one other of the Regiment (whose name we cannot now recall,) was wounded.

We moved position several times during the night, but not to any distance.

The morning of the 30th of August, 1862, dawned upon the First Manassas battle-field, again lined with troops and artillery ready for action. Not a sound arose to disturb the quiet of the early morning.

Corn-fields and gardens in the locality suffered terribly, no rations having been issued to us for several days previous; these were our only resources against the ravages of hunger. The fields around were dotted with half-starved Confeds., who were plucking the daily rations of corn to be distributed, three ears to the man. The morning was passed in preparing and eating the food thus obtained; many a poor fellow, as he feasted upon the delicious grain, little imagined it to be his last repast upon this earth.

Ere long came distant rumbling of artillery, and all eyes were turned in direction of the enemy's line, whence the noise proceeded, Clouds of dust arose in our front, and, as they drew nearer, the stillness was harshly broken by a cannon shot, followed by the bursting of a shell over the centre of our line, a notice that the battle was about to begin.

Gen. Jackson's Corps met the assault of the enemy on its centre and left; charge upon charge was made upon its position, only to be repulsed with the indefatigable energy and unwavering promptness for which the "Stonewall" was so justly famed. A part of our Corps was moved to the front, and the enemy received from its veterans a heavy blow that sent them reeling back upon their reserves.

The battle was continued all the afternoon. About five o'clock our Division, commanded by Gen. Kemper, formed and hurried to the scene of carnage. Our Brigade was commanded by Col. Corse and our Regiment by Lieut. Col. Marye. We moved in upon the enemy's extreme left, and striking them near the "Chinn House," where, after a short but decisive engagement, they fell back, closely followed by the Confederates until about nine o'clock P. M., when the chase was relinquished.

"The gallantry and skill of Col. Corse in the management of his command, won for him the admiration of all who witnessed the conduct of his Brigade upon the field. He was wounded while leading his men and had his horse shot under him."

"Lieut. Col. Marye, who, while bravely leading his Regiment, was wounded by a minnie ball. He lost his left leg, the ball penetrating the knee joint, compelling amputation. His loss from the active duties

of the field was seriously felt by his Regiment; while
a brave and gallant officer, he was an accomplished,
courteous and high-toned gentleman, who held the
confidence and esteem of his comrades in arms." (The
above is copied from the writings of Capt. Wm. B.
Lynch, commanding Company C, Seventeenth Virginia Regiment.)

The following extracts from the official report of
Major Herbert, commanding the Regiment after the
fall of Lieut. Col. Marye, will show the part sustained
by it in the second battle of Manassas:

"Leaving our bivouac at Thoroughfare Gap on the
morning of 29th, we soon came in sound of the guns,
and a short distance below Gainesville in sight of our
batteries, then replying rapidly to those of the enemy;
were soon sent with our Brigade and took position on
the extreme right of our lines. In taking this position
we had to cross an open field in full view of the
enemy's batteries, which opened upon us with a hot
fire of shell, under which our line advanced steadily
and coolly; our casualties were two men wounded.
We were afterwards moved with our Brigade some
three-quarters of a mile to the left, where we remained
under arms and bivouaced for the night.

"On morning of 30th again under arms in same
position, and remained so until about four o'clock in
the evening, when orders arrived for our Brigade to
forward in the direction of the Chinn House; some
one-half mile this side our Brigade was formed in line
of battle, the Seventeenth occupying the right, Col.

Marye, commanding; when near the Chinn House came under heavy fire, shell and musketry, the enemy's batteries and line of battle being in full view on the hill beyond. Our line advanced firmly under the enemy's fire, and not until the men commenced firing and advancing did any irregularity occur, though many were shot down in this part of the engagement. It was here that Lieut. Col. Marye received his wound and fell nobly doing his duty. The well known bravery and good conduct of this officer needs no eulogy. Our Color Sergeant being struck down, the colors were hardly allowed to touch the earth before they were seized by Corporal Harper of the Color Guard, and by him carried steadily and bravely to the front during the remainder of the fight. Though somewhat scattered, our Regiment assisted in capturing the enemy's guns and driving him from that portion of the field."

Private Coleman, Company E, taking from the enemy's Color Bearer the national colors of one of his regiments, handed them to Colonel Corse, who waving them in front of the Brigade added life and renewed vigor to our men. Officers and men with rare exceptions, behaved well and were conspicuous for their coolness. I beg leave to mention Lieut. Gardner, Acting Adjutant of the Regiment, Lieut. Perry, in command of Company A, Lieut. Turner, commanding Company C, Lieut. Wallace, commanding Company F, Lieut. Tubman, commanding Company E, Sergeant Lovelace, Company H, killed on the field.

Privates Harper and Manly, Company G, Corporal
Ryan, Company I, and many others whose names
cannot be learned at this late day owing to absence
from wounds and death of officers."   *   *   *   *

The following is from General Longstreet's official
report:

*   *   *   "Early on the 29th, the columns were
united, and the advance to join General Jackson was
resumed. The noise of battle was heard before we
reached Gainesville. The march was quickened to
the extent of our capacity. The exitement of battle
seemed to give new life and strength to our jaded men,
and the head of my column soon reached a position in
rear of the enemy's left flank, and within easy cannon
shot. On approaching the field, some of Brig. Gen.
Hood's batteries were ordered into position, and his
Division was deployed on the right and left of the
turnpike, at right angles with it, and supported by
Brigadier General Evan's Brigade."   *   *   *   *

*   *   *   "Three brigades under General Wilcox,
were thrown forward to the support of the left, and
three others under General Kemper, to the support of
the right of these commands. General D. R. Jones'
Division was placed upon the Manassas Gap Railroad
to the right and in echelon with regard to the three
last brigades. Colonel Walton placed his batteries
in a commanding position between my line and that
of General Jackson, and engaged the enemy for several
hours, in a severe and successful artillery duel. At a
late hour in the day, Major General Stuart reported

the approach of the enemy in heavy columns against
my extreme right. I withdrew General Wilcox, with
his three brigades, from the left and placed his command in position to support Jones in case of an attack
against my right. After some few shots, the enemy
withdrew his forces, moving them around towards his
front, and about four o'clock in the afternoon, began
to press forward against General Jackson's position.
Wilcox's brigades were moved to their former position, and Hood's two brigades, supported by Evans,
were quickly pressed forward to the attack. At the
same time Wilcox's three brigades made a like advance, as also Hunton's brigade, of Kemper's command." * * * * * * * *
* * * "After withdrawing from the attack,
my troops were placed in the line first occupied and
in the original order." * * * * *
* * * "From an eminence near by, one
portion of the enemy's masses attacking General Jackson were immediately within my view and in easy
range of batteries in that position. It gave me an
advantage that I had not expected to have, and I
made hast to use it. Two batteries were ordered for
the purpose and one placed in position immediately
and opened. Just as this fire began, I received a
message from the commanding General, informing me
of General Jackson's condition and his wants. As it
was evident that the attack against General Jackson
could not be continued ten minutes under the fire
of these batteries, I made no movement with my

troops.   Before the second battery could be placed in position, the enemy began to retire, and in less than ten minutes the ranks were broken and that portion of his army put to flight.   A fair opportunity was offered me and the intended diversion was changed into an attack.   My whole line was rushed forward at a charge.   The troops sprang to their work, and moved forward with all the steadiness and firmness that characterise war-worn veterans.   The batteries continuing their play upon the confused masses, completed the work of this portion of the enemy's line, and my attack was, therefore, made against the forces in my front."   *   *   *   *   *   *   *

*   *   *   " The battle continued until ten o'clock at night, when utter darkness put a stop to our progress.   The enemy made his escape across Bull Run before daylight.   Three batteries, a large number of prisoners, many stands of regimental colors, and twelve thousand stands of arms, besides some wagons, ambulances, &c., were taken."   *   *   *   *   *

General Lee, in his official report, says :

*   *   *   " Longstreet took position on the right of Jackson, Hood's two brigades, supported by Evans being deployed across the turnpike and at right angles to it.   These troops were supported on the left by three brigades under General Wilcox, and by a like force on the right under General Kemper.   D. R. Jones' Division formed the extreme right of the line resting on the Manassas Gap Railroad."   *   *   *

*   *   *   *   " About three P. M., the enemy

having massed his troops in front of General Jackson, advanced against his position in strong force. His front line pushed forward until engaged at close quarters by Jackson's troops, when its progress was checked, and a fierce and bloody struggle ensued. A second and third line, of great strength, moved up to support the first, but in doing so, came within easy range of a position a little in advance of Longstreet's left. He immediately ordered up two batteries, and two others being thrown forward about the same time by Colonel S. D. Lee, under their well directed and destructive fire the supporting lines were broken and fell back in confusion. Their repeated efforts to rally were unavailing, and Jackson's troops being thus relieved from the pressure of overwhelming numbers began to press steadily forward, driving the enemy before them. He retreated in confusion, suffering severely from our artillery, which advanced as he retired. Gen. Longstreet, anticipating the order for a general advance, now threw his whole command against the Federal centre and left. Hood's two brigades, followed by Evans, led the attack. Gen. R. H. Anderson's Division came gallantly to the support of Hood, while the three brigades under Wilcox moved forward on his left, and those of Kemper on his right. Gen. D. R. Jones advanced on the extreme right, and the whole line swept steadily on, driving the enemy with great carnage from each successive position, until ten P. M., when darkness put an end to the battle and the pursuit."　　*　　*　　*　　*　　*　　*　　*

As we went into the fight and just after passing the "Chinn House," many of us witnessed the charge of one of Gen. D. R. Jones' brigades to our right; they moved forward slowly but in perfect line. It was indeed a heart-thrilling sight those men presented marching so coolly into the jaws of death.

A charge by one of Gen. Stuart's brigades of cavalry was made soon after. The column of horsemen, moving like the wind, soon disappeared behind the woods to our extreme right, leaving but an impression upon the minds of the infantry of what cavalry fighting was.

This battle took place upon the first Manassas battlefield, the lines being reversed, we holding and fighting from the position, from which the enemy were driven in the first engagement.

The rout was complete, and as in the first Manassas battle, the enemy retreated by way of Sudley Mills and the Stone Bridge, leaving knapsacks, guns, wagons and every conceivable article pertaining to an army in quantities along the roads. Their dead, wounded, many prisoners, and a number of guns, fell into our hands.

Our Regiment brought from the field five stands of colors. The Brigade captured about sixteen stands of colors and four pieces of artillery, with the remaining horses attached, most of them having been killed by our heavy fire. After the battle we bivouaced on the field near the "Chinn House," where the night was passed. The dead were buried by details for that purpose from the Division, while the wounded were brought in and cared for.

Colonel Corse received a wound in the leg and had his horse shot, but did not leave the field. Lieut. Colonel Marye was removed from the field in the midst of the battle, and several of the men were wounded whilst bearing him to the rear.

Early the following morning, (Sunday 31st), our Division marched forward, took the Sudley Mills road, crossing at the ford, and went into bivouac for the night on the opposite bank of Bull Run. Our breakfast that morning consisted of beef, sliced off by us as we hurriedly passed the smoking carcass, slaughtered by the enemy a short time previous. Rations issued to us on Sunday evening at Sudley, consisted of two crackers and about one quarter of a pound of bacon to each man. On Monday the march was continued; as we neared Chantilly, (a long name for a small Postoffice,) a heavy thunder storm overtook us soaking every man to the skin.

Having scarcely tasted food since the morning previous it is unnecessary to say we were getting hungry, but we comforted ourselves with the hope of being soon overtaken by the wagons, which to our minds, then seemed as desirable as anything that could happen.

A fight occurred just before our arrival in the valley below Chantilly, in which Generals Phil. Kearney, (one of the best and bravest men in the Federal Army,) and —— ——, (name forgotten) lost

their lives. We moved into a meadow on the right
of the turnpike and prepared for a good nights' rest,
but alas! for human hopes! We kindled fires and
were in the act of drying our wet garments, when the
order came to move the Brigade to the front. Passing
to a piece of woodland not far off on our right, the
Brigade entered, single file, and posted sentinels from
the rear as we moved through the impenetrable darkness; our Regiment being in advance had the longest
march and after going about a mile we halted and
took position as a reserve, supposing ourselves about
fifty yards in rear of our pickets. Imagine our aston-
ishment, as the tedious, dragging night at last gave
way to the coming morning, to find ourselves facing
our line and between it and the enemy. Front to
rear was soon ordered and we had the satisfaction of
hearing that our foe had left us during the night.
Fires were soon blazing in our midst to the no small
enjoyment of our rather forlorn looking band, who
refreshed themselves for at least an hour chewing the
substance from sassafras twigs.

Returning to the meadow where the fires had been
vainly kindled the evening previous, the unwelcome
tidings, " The wagons had'nt come," greeted us on all
sides, so we raised our " flies " and sought forgetfulness
in slumber,

In the afternoon, a wagon load of provisions arrived,
as a present to the members of Company C, from the
ladies of their native place, the good old town of Leesburg. The unloading of bread, hams, cakes, pickles

and other delicious edibles was a sight productive of indescribable feeling to men who had not tasted food for forty-eight hours. Company C, composed of noble, generous spirits were not long in extending to the Regiment a whole-souled invitation to partake with them of their luxuries; a second invitation was not necessary, as we most promptly accepted and joined them in the feast.

And such a feast! Who could forget it? There was even *old wine* to wash our dinner down! Now judge if it was not a feast? Can any one wonder that under the circumstances we review it as one of the happiest eras in our soldier life?

The next morning, (September 3d,) we took up the line of march northward, passing by "Frying Pan Church," and on until we came to the A. L. and H. R. R. (at Guilford Station); marching thereon in direction of Leesburg for a short distance, the head of the column filed to the right, striking the Alexandria and Leesburg turnpike south of Broad Run, and passed down the road until near Drainsville where we passed the night quietly.

On the afternoon of the fourth, we again passed over a part of the route traveled the day before, and about night halted near Mr. Robert Harper's farm, two miles south of Leesburg. The next day (5th,) the troops commenced crossing the Potomac river at the different fords above Leesburg.

Our Corps marched through the town the same day and passed the night in the vicinity of the "Big

Spring." On Saturday (6th,) we crossed the river at Noland's Ferry and marched as far as Monocacy river, crossing that stream and bivouacing beyond. Our army was much reduced from battle, straggling and sickness, while many of the men, for want of shoes, were ordered to remain on the Virginia shore.

For the first time the borders of the enemy's territory were crossed, and strict orders issued by General Lee for the protection of private property. So far as destruction of grain and fruit was concerned, it would have been almost an impossibility to have prevented starving men from helping themselves whenever an opportunity presented itself; our own State having been stripped of its standing corn for the sustenance of both armies, it was not to be supposed that Pennsylvania would suffer less.

Partial list of casualties in the Seventeenth Virginia Regiment at the battle of second Manassas :

Field and Staff—Wounded, Col. M. D. Corse, Lieut. Col. Morton Marye, and Color Sergeant Robt. Steele.

Company A — Wounded, Lieut. John Addison, Corp. Wm. Perry, Privates A. Hunter, J. S. Mason, C. A. Smith, and J. H. L. Sangster, the latter mortally.

Company B—Wounded, Capt. R. H. Simpson ; Private S. F. Spengler, mortally. Killed, Privates C. J. Steed and J. W. Simpson.

Company C—Wounded, Private D. Dove, mortally.

Company D—Wounded, Privates P. Haward, J. Sewall, J. D. Newman, R. Beach and W. S. Ford.

Company E—Lieut. Simpson, wounded.
Company F—None reported.
Company G—Wounded, Private D. Manly.
Company H—Killed, Sergeant W. A. Lovelace and Private F. Ballengen; wounded, Lieut. W. F. Gardner, Asst. Adjt., severely, Sergt. W. H. Boyer.
Company I—
Company K—Wounded, Private E. Fletcher.

THE MARYLAND CAMPAIGN.

ON the 7th of September, 1862, the bivouac on Monocacy river was broken up, and our Regiment marched to Buckeyestown, and, after a short rest, again took up the line of march and halted near Monocacy Junction, B. & O. R. R., where the men (who were so disposed,) enjoyed a good bath in the river. On the 9th, the railroad bridge was blown up by our forces, and one poor fellow, (whose name we cannot now recall,) not a member of our Regiment, was killed whilst bathing near the bridge by a fragment of iron from it.

On the 10th, the line of march was resumed, and we passed through Frederick City and Middletown, bivouacing some two miles beyond the latter place. As we were passing through the last-mentioned place, several ladies appeared on the street with cockades of ribbon, red, white and blue, upon their breasts; one of our men, C——, of Company E, stepped up to them, and very politely touching his hat, said: "If you will take the advice of a fool, you will return into the house and take off those colors; some d——d fool may come along and insult you." The advice had its effect, for they at once withdrew.

On the 11th, we left our bivouac beyond Middletown at 5 A. M., and marched through Boonsboro', halting for the night about five miles from Hagerstown. On the 12th, we started at 7 A. M. and traveled until

:wo o'clock, passing through Funkstown and Hagerstown, halting about a mile beyond the latter place, where the remainder of that and the whole of the next day (13th,) were spent.

While here, the "Pirooters" and "Pisanters" (the latter, a sobriquet given to Company H by Col. Corse,) were busy in foraging for their stomachs, and kept no record of the quantity of butter, honey, bacon, &c., brought into camp for both individual and social enjoyment.

On Sunday, (14th,) the battle of "Boonsboro," on "South Mountain," took place. Leaving camp about five o'clock A. M., we retraced our steps through Hagerstown and Boonsboro'; took the road leading to Harper's Ferry for two miles, then along the mountain side until we came out on the turnpike about a half mile from *where we started.* Marching several hundred yards further, our baggage was dispensed with, and then up the mountain side, in full view of the enemy, our column was moved.

They opened on us with shell and grape, enfilading our line, but doing very little damage. This was about four o'clock P. M. The Regiment soon after moved to the edge of a corn-field, skirmishers were thrown out, and the men formed in line of battle. While moving to this battle-field, the sad intelligence reached us of the fall of Gen. Garland, formerly Colonel of the Eleventh Virginia Volunteers—a man that was loved and honored for his gentlemanly courtesy and noble bearing by all the Brigade. The Seventeenth and the

Eleventh had been on the most friendly terms since their first encampment at Manassas, and had fought side by side on every battle-field. Brothers in arms, they felt themselves brothers in heart, and the fortunes of each were watched over and guarded by the other. Their blood had been mingled in many a hard-fought battle; their tears had blended o'er many a loved one's grave; now they sorrowed, as with one heart, for the brave Commander who had been friend and comrade to each, and the conservatory of each heart still nurtures the myrtle and cypress enwreathing his memory.

In this battle, the Seventeenth, though greatly out-numbered by the opposing forces, held their own. Major Arthur Herbert was not with the Seventeenth Virginia on this day, but commanded the Seventh Virginia Infantry, with which he passed safely through the battle.

The following is from the official report of Colonel Corse, who was slightly wounded during the engagement:

"My Regiment was placed in line of battle about four o'clock P. M., in a field to the right of the road leading to the summit of the mountain, and to the left of Crampton's Gap. In the act of taking that position, the Regiment was subjected to a very fierce shelling from a battery of the enemy, which enfiladed our line; fortunately, however, we suffered very little loss from that, having but two men slightly wounded."

"I moved the Regiment forward about a hundred

yards, by your order, towards a woods in our front and ordered Lieut. Lehew, with his company, to deploy forward as skirmishers into the woods and to engage the enemy, which were supposed to be there; very soon I heard shots from our skirmishers; your aid, Capt. Beckham, at this time delivered me an order to move my Regiment by the left flank and to connect my line with the Eleventh, occupying a corn-field, which order was obeyed; we remained in this position a few minutes, when Col. Stewart's Regiment (Fifty-sixth Virginia), Pickett's Brigade, joined my right. Immediately the brigade on our right became hotly engaged; we reserved our fire, no enemy appearing in our front."

" After the fire had continued about fifteen minutes, Col. Stewart reported to me that the troops on his right had fallen back. I also observed that they had abandoned the left of the Eleventh. I communicated my intention to Col. Stewart and Major Clement, of the Eleventh, to fall back about ten or fifteen steps behind a fence, which was simultaneously done by the three regiments in good order. We held this position until long after dark, under a severe fire of musketry obliquely on our right flank and in front, until nearly every cartridge was exhausted. Shortly after the enemy had ceased firing, about half-past seven o'clock P. M., I received your order to withdraw my Regiment, which was done in good order, and halted to rest on the Boonsboro' and Frederick Town road, with the other regiments of your Brigade."

" In this engagement I was particularly struck with

the determined courage of officers and men ; they held
their ground manfully against a largely superior number, as far as I could judge, from the heavy fire of the
enemy upon our right and front. Those who deserve
particular mention for distinguished gallantry and
activity were Capt. J. T. Burke, of Company D, Lieut.
Thos. Perry, of Company A, Lieut. Turner, of Company B, Color Corporal Murphy, of Company C, Color
Corporal Harper, of Company E, who won my highest
admiration for their cool bravery."

The following is from the official report of General
J. T. Longstreet:

· * * * " We succeeded in repulsing the repeated
and powerful attacks of the enemy, and in holding
our position till night put an end to the battle. It
was short but very fierce. Some of our most gallant
officers and men fell in this struggle, among them the
brave Colonel J. B. Strange, of the Nineteenth Virginia Regiment."

After the battle was over our Regiment returned to
where their baggage had been left, resting until all
the wounded from the field had been brought in and
cared for. We then took up the line of march, passing back through Boonsboro' and taking the road to
Harper's Ferry. On the morning of the 15th, after
a weary night's march, we halted near the small town
of Kistersville and were allowed time to cook and eat
breakfast, after which we again started, marched to
Sharpsburg and took our position in line of battle
southeast of the town. Soon after sun-rise on the fol-

lowing morning (16th,) the enemy commenced shelling, our batteries replying slowly; near noon a battery of eight pieces on our left opened, and a most terrific artillery duel commenced. Our batteries being situated in front of Sharpsburg, the shots from the enemy passed over our heads, bursted and fell in the town, from the effects of which many of the houses suffered terribly.

At midnight, four men from the Regiment (Hough, Company A, Lewis, Company E, Sherwood, Company F, and a member of Company D, whose name we have forgotten,) were detailed and sent back to cook; after getting flour from the provision train, two miles to the rear, they returned to Sharpsburg to *borrow utensils* in which to bake bread—our wagons having taken the wrong road and left us destitute. Most of the citizens had deserted their homes, and there was some difficulty in borrowing from the few who remained, consequently, it was nearly daylight when they met to commence operations, having obtained *one skillet* and an old oven *with the bottom half out.* They were genuine men, not easily baffled; they persevered, but had hardly made up one batch of dough when the guns of the enemy opened again, and the shells falling about them compelled a change of position. Two shells bursted in the yard in which they were cooking, about ten yards in front of them; two more struck the house behind which they were standing, and a fifth struck the adjoining house, bursted inside and set it on fire.

They retreated and sought refuge in the cellar, but even that proved unsafe—a shell came down through

two floors into their midst and buried itself in the
ground, fortunately without bursting, else all would
inevitably have been killed. From cellar to yard again
they flew, where, the enemy's fire having abated, they
continued their cooking. About four o'clock in the
· afternoon, Hough and Lewis started for the Regiment
with a batch of biscuits, and just after their return
from delivering them the battle opened fiercely along
the line. The "Report" of the "Captain" of the
squad closes thus: "The cooks were now *ordered* to
retreat out of town, which they did 'in good order,'
but making very good time."

The ranks of the Seventeenth Regiment had been
greatly reduced by the hard marches, desperate battles
and the excessive toils of the preceding thirty days.
The small number carried into the battle of Sharpsburg, as will be shown by extracts from official sources
further on in the succeeding pages, was diminished yet
more, until but a handful of that once numerous, fearless body of troops, now rallied around their battle
stained banner. The battle was severe upon our
Regiment, for nearly all that went into the fight
were either killed, wounded or captured. "The
gallantry of the command, (wrote an officer of our
Regiment,) was never more conspicuous than in those
engagements."

The following is from the report of Colonel Corse,
who was wounded and fell into the hands of the
enemy, but was afterwards rescued by Toombs'
Brigade.

"About four o'clock P. M., the enemy was reported to be advancing; we moved forward with the First and Eleventh regiments of the Brigade (the Seventh and Twenty-fourth being detached to operate on some other part of the field) to the top of the hill to a fence, and immediately engaged the enemy at a distance of fifty or sixty yards, at the same time under fire from their batteries on the hills beyond."

"My Regiment being the extreme right of the line then engaging the enemy, came directly opposite the colors of the regiment to which it was opposed, consequently being overlapped by them, as far as I could judge, at least a hundred yards. Regardless of the great odds against them, the men courageously stood their ground, until overwhelmed by superior numbers, were forced to retire."

"I have to state here, General, that we put into the fight but forty-six enlisted men and nine officers, out of this number seven officers and twenty-four men were killed and wounded and ten taken prisoners."

"It was here that Captain J. T. Burke and Lieut. Littleton fell, two of the bravest and most valuable officers of my command. Color Corporal Harper also fell fighting heroically at his post, these brave men I think deserve particular mention. I received a wound in the foot which prevented me from retiring with our line and was left in the hands of the enemy for a short time, but was soon rescued by General Toombs' Brigade and a portion of yours, who drove the enemy back beyond the line we had occupied in the morning."

"I saw Major Herbert come up with a portion of the men of the First, Eleventh and Seventeenth regiments of your Brigade on the left of General Toombs' line, cheering the men on with his accustomed cool and determined valor. Lieut. W. W. Athey, Company C, captured a regimental color of the 103d New York Regiment, presented to them by the city council of New York City, which I herewith forward to you; my wound being painful I rode to the surgeon to have it examined, leaving the command to Major Herbert."

The following is from General Longstreet's official report, he says:

*   *   *   "Before it was entirely dark, the hundred thousand men that had been threatening our destruction for twelve hours, had melted away into a few stragglers."   *   *   *   *   *   *   *

*   *   *   "The name of every officer, non-commissioned officer and private, who has shared in the toils and privations of this campaign, should be mentioned. In one month, these troops had marched over two hundred miles, upon little more than half rations, and fought nine battles and skirmishes, killed, wounded and captured nearly as many men as we had in our ranks, besides taking arms and other munitions of war in large quantities. I would that I could do justice to all of these gallant officers and men in this report. As that is impossible, I shall only mention those most prominently distinguished. These were   *   *   *   * Brig. Gen. Kemper, at Manassas plains, Boonsboro' and Sharpsburg.   *   *   *   * Colonels Hunton,

Corse, Stuart, Stevens, Hately, (severely wounded,) and Walker (commanding Jenkins' Brigade, after the latter was wounded,) at Manassas plains, Boonsboro' and Sharpsburg. * * * * Lieut. Colonels Skinner and Marye, at Manassas plains, where they were both severely wounded."

The remainder of the Regiment spent the night near the battle field about half a mile out of town. The next day was passed in apparent quiet, with nothing occurring to disturb the men but an occasional "whiz" from some sharp-shooter's passing bullet.

The Regiment returned to their old position on the line and held it during the day.

About nine o'clock on the night of the 18th, we again took up the line of march in direction of Shepherdstown; crossing the canal and river about half a mile below the town, we found the water very cold and about waist deep, but it brought us once more to Virginia soil.

After crossing the river a very amusing scene occurred. Major Herbert had received orders to follow Drayton's Brigade; in the darkness and confusion arising from fording we had entirely lost sight of it and were hurrying forward to overtake it. We were to pass up a narrow ravine in front of us which would admit but one regiment four abreast at a time. At its mouth, coming from another direction we met the Fifth North Carolina and, as both could not enter, Major Herbert explained to the Major in command of the Fifth, that we had to follow Drayton, being under orders to do so

—to which from some misapprehension of the circumstances perhaps, our friend from the good old State as renowned for its patriotism as for its "Tar and Turpentine," paid no attention, but ordered his men forward. Herbert also gave the order: "Forward Seventeenth," and the head of the two columns met in the mouth of the ravine, and such a scene took place as was never before witnessed.

The repeated orders: "Forward Seventeenth;" "Forward Fifth;" and from Mitchell in rear commanding the Eleventh "Forward men, follow the old Seventeenth, and don't let them get between you"— rang out upon the midnight air. The Fifth was jammed against the sides of the steep rocky ravine, while many clambered up the hill side and clung to the roots, as we passed triumphantly through. The victory was announced with a shout from the boys and "Come along Fifth?" sent back upon the ears of our necessarily inhospitably treated friends from North Carolina.

We marched four miles from the river and rested as day was breaking. In an hour and a half we were ordered back towards the river and after returning two miles, we halted, stacked arms and awaited further orders. An attack had been made by the enemy's cavalry at the crossing, but they were beaten back. About five o'clock P. M. we left there, reached the turnpike leading to Winchester, and after marching several miles thereon, we stopped in the woods where the night and the greater part of the following day

On the afternoon of the 20th, about five o'clock, we started again taking the road to Martinsburg, halted about fifteen minutes past one o'clock A. M. within three miles of town, tired, sleepy and nearly worn-out. About nine o'clock the next morning, we forded Opequan creek halting about half a mile beyond.

The Chaplain of the First had service in the afternoon, and preached from the text: "I have fought a good fight, I have finished my course, I have kept the faith." Paul's 2d Timothy.

On the 27th, we broke camp near Opequan creek and marched all day, bivouacing near Bunker Hill. The next day, (28th,) we moved to near the Hopewell Meeting House, where we remained in camp some days, nothing taking place of much interest.

On the 6th of October, General Kemper reviewed the Brigade; on the 9th, General Longstreet had a review of the Division.

On the 13th, a review of a part of the Corps took place for the benefit of some English Lords, who were making a tour of inspection for their own gratification.

On the 16th, Gen. Pickett inspected the Division, and, on dress parade, orders were read for us to be ready to move at a moment's notice, but it amounted to nothing.

On the 20th, we changed our camp ground and pitched tents near White Hall, about two miles from Bunker Hill.

General R. E. Lee reviewed our Division on the 22d, and the day passed away quietly.

On the 28th of October, we left Bunker Hill and

took up the line of march through Winchester and beyond, about five miles on the Front Royal road where we passed the night.

The march of the 29th brought us to one mile south of Front Royal, after fording the North Fork of the Shenandoah river, and crossing the South Fork on a bridge of wagons.

On the 30th, the mountains were crossed at Chester Gap, and the road to Gaines' Cross Roads taken; passing two miles beyond the latter point the Brigade bivouaced for the night.

On the following day, (31st,) we marched within one mile of Culpeper Court House, via Little Washington and Sperryville, and encamped about half-past five P. M. The night was made so lively among some of the Regiment, by the introduction of " pine-top," that after midnight the Colonel had to turn out to quell the disturbance and restore quiet.

While in the vicinity of the Court House, where we remained some time, the drills, guard and picket duties, were resumed, and the ranks of the Division greatly augmented by the return of convalescents and stragglers. The Division received orders on several occasions to pack up ready for a move, but each time the orders were countermanded and the tents re-pitched. On the 20th of November, we marched two miles beyond the Court House in direction of Raccoon ford, but were ordered to return after a short halt; the following day, however, the right order came, and by daylight we were on the march; we crossed the Rapidan river at Raccoon ford and took the road to Fredericksburg. After a march of about twenty-two miles we encamped for the night.

On the following day, (22d,) we marched as far as Chancellorsville, where the night was passed. On the 23d, we marched to a point beyond the Telegraph Road and west of Fredericksburg, where we went into regular camp.

The army of Gen. Burnside was concentrating on Stafford Heights, opposite Fredericksburg; we were in his front to oppose his passage of the Rappahannock river.

The men of our army, notwithstanding that they had passed through battles, marches and trials of every kind, were buoyant in spirit and quite ready to meet the hosts of the Federal army upon any field.

The ravages made among our troops by death, wounds, disease and discharges, were being rapidly remedied, thus restoring the usual cheerfulness and strength to our ranks.

Our camp was beneath the green feathers of a large pine forest, and there the order for the promotion of our brave and dearly-loved Colonel to a Brigadier Generalship was read to the men on the 1st of November; his command to consist of a brigade formed expressly for him.

Many hearts were filled with sadness in losing so dear a friend. The pages of this record of facts have chronicled in brief some few of his noble acts whilst Colonel of the Seventeenth Virginia, but the history of him as an accomplished soldier, a revered commander, a beloved companion, is engraved upon the hearts of his men in characters not to be tamed into language.

The following are incomplete lists of casualties in our Regiment in the battles of Boonsboro' and Sharpsburg:

BOONSBORO'.

Field and Staff—Wounded, Adjutant J. H. Bryant, Colonel M. D. Corse.

Company A—None.

Company B—Killed, Marcus D. Darr.

Company C—Killed, Sergeant F. M. Wallace.

Company D—Wounded, Lieutenant W. A. Barnes and Private John Hickson.

Company E—Wounded, Lieutenant A. M. Tubman and Privates A. F. Rose and W. H. Underwood.

Company F—Wounded, Private R. M. Lee.

Company G—Killed, Private Daniel Dohoney; wounded, Lieutenant F. Powers.

Company H—Wounded, Lieutenant A. C. Kell.

Company I—

Company K—

SHARPSBURG.

Field and Staff—Wounded, Colonel M. D. Corse.

Company A—Wounded, Corporal W. J. Paul.

Company B—Wounded, Corporal Thos. N. Garrison, badly.

Company C—Killed, Lieut. F. B. Littleton and

Privates Luther L. Attwell and John C. Brown; wounded, Privates W. H. Hardy, badly, and —— Wallace.

Company D—Killed, Captain J. T. Burke and Sergeant J. R. Steel; wounded, Privates M. Crowley and D. McC. Chichester.

Company E—Killed, Color Corporal W. Harper and Private J. Calmus; wounded, Lieut. W. P. Mc Knight and Sergt. Jos. Gregg.

Company F—Wounded, Private W. E. Davis.

Company G—Wounded, Corporal Thomas Hays.

Company H. Killed, Private W. A. Castleman; wounded, Private W. J. Hall, shot in four places.

Company I—

Company K—

11*

FREDERICKSBURG AND THE WINTER CAMPAIGN.

UNTIL the morning of the 30th November, 1862, the encampments around Fredericksburg remained in such perfect quietude, that drills and the regular routine of camp were again resumed. At the above mentioned time, however, the guns of the enemy opened upon the town from the hills opposite and shelled it throughout the day, to the great annoyance of the inhabitants.

On the 3d of December, our camp was broken; we bade adieu to the men of our old Brigade and removed to the encampment of the new one: the Seventeenth Virginia Regiment having been assigned with the Fifteenth, Thirtieth and Thirty-Second Virginia regiments to the command of Brigadier General Corse. Upon General Corse's promotion, the Colonelcy of our Regiment devolved upon Lieut. Colonel Marye, but owing to his misfortune at the second battle of Manassas, he was physically incapacitated to assume the command. Major A. Herbert was promoted to the Lieut. Colonelcy and Capt. R. H. Simpson, of Company B, became Major of the Regiment; Lieut. Lehew, succeeded to the command of Company B.

Notwithstanding the severity of the winter, we had no cause for complaint, our rations being sufficiently good, and warm clothing having been issued to most of the men.

The enemy were working like beavers in our front strengthening their position and preparing all things for a grand move.

On the 11th of December, we were all startled by the reports of two signal guns; they were fired about half past four o'clock A. M., and immediately thereafter, orders were issued us to make ready for a march.

The Brigade formed and moved out to the road leading into the town; thence to a position in line of battle to the right and below Fredericksburg. The Division was in line upon a slope of hills forming a "horseshoe," and had strengthened their position by erecting breatworks of rails and earth, from which to fight in case of an attack being made upon them. In our rear, upon the crest of the hill, were planted a number of pieces of field artillery, with which the plains below could be swept in case of their occupancy by the Federals. Heavy cannonading was in progress above the town, caused by an attempt of the enemy to throw pontoons across the river and thereby effect a passage; but our pickets stationed along the banks of the river, fought them hard, driving them back each time the attempt was renewed; a number of Federal soldiers were reported killed. The artillery was in operation most of the day, and night closed upon the Confederates in line prepared for battle.

The morning of the 12th opened quietly, but towards nine o'clock A. M., our guns were in opera-

tion; very soon the musketry broke loose on our left
and sounds of heavy fighting reached us. A crossing
had been effected by the Federals above the town, our
forces falling back without *much resistance* and per-
mitting them a free passage.

The 13th arrived, and as yet no very heavy battle
had transpired; the morning was dark, damp and
gloomy, enveloping the plains below us in such impenetrable fog that nothing was discernable in the
direction of the river. At noon, however, the sun
appeared and rapidly absorbed the veil in its majestic
brightness. Then the lines on the right and left of
us opened with artillery and musketry. The battle
raged for hours; musketry was heard above the roar
of the artillery, and particularly on our left, the fighting was terrific.

From our position overlooking the river bottoms
for miles to our right, we had an excellent view of
the enemy's position; they crossed the open plain,
four lines deep, and made charge after charge upon the
" Rebels " posted in the edge of the woods. General
Hood was protecting our right with his brave Texans,
consequently, each effort was repulsed, and whenever
the blue curl of smoke was visible from the Texan's
line, parts of " the grand army " dropped away until
the ranks were not only thinned but completely scattered.

Towards night the battle closed; the enemy had
been repulsed at all points and fell back discomfited
upon his reserves.

" The sight in our front, and, to the right, during that

afternoon, (writes one of the Seventeenth,) was as grand as could be witnessed. The number of the Federals in sight at the time was estimated at, at least, sixty thousand, and lines upon lines moving beautifully and with perfect order in quick succession upon Hood, melted into nothingness, soon as the blue smoke curled above the Texans' position. Their officers endeavored by every means to reform their broken ranks, but all in vain, they could not be made to meet that galling fire the second time."

During the heavy fighting on the right and left, a brigade of the Yankees advanced in our front, to the right a short distance, and deployed their skirmishers. They were met by our skirmish line, who fired and fell back slowly, then halting, firing and again retreating. After drawing them into really close quarters, a section of artillery was unlimbered, moved quickly to the front, and fired upon the advancing column; at the same moment a brigade of infantry moved out in line, from under cover of the brushwood, and charged them with a yell. The Federal line broke at once, and made good speed to the rear. The loss on each side was small, having only a few killed and wounded.

Saturday night passed off quietly, and the morning of Sunday, (14th,) opened beautifully. Column after column of the enemy could be plainly seen from our elevated position passing down the river to the right, but the fighting and charging had ceased; the earnest zeal of the "Rebels" having been fully tested the day before, Gen. Burnside seemed quite satisfied. We had acted altogether on the defensive in this battle, and our victory was a complete one.

Monday passed without demonstration on either side, except occasional cannonading, the lines being about the same as on Saturday. Our men waited in readiness for whatever was to be done, though much wonderment was exhibited: "Does General Lee intend to allow Burnside to re-cross the river without molestation?" was asked on every side, and anxiously the answer was looked for.

Tuesday, being a dark, rainy morning, our artillery opened fire to ascertain the Federal whereabouts, and, being replied to from the opposite heights, it was conjectured that a crossing had been effected during the night, and so it proved to have been. Amid the darkness, Gen. Burnside's army had slipped from General Lee's grasp, and was safely landed upon the Stafford shore.

Their dead had been left in our hands unburied, and on a small lot of ground above the town, supposed to contain about one acre square, as many as eleven hundred of the enemy's dead were counted by one of our Regiment. As many as seven and eight were noticed lying one upon the other, showing that the battle at that point must have been frightfully sanguinary.

General Jackson's Corps occupied the extreme right of our line, and received the assaults of the enemy without giving a single advantage; his men could not have fought better, and the real victory should be given to him; the unexampled fortitude of his body of brave troops needs no laudation.

The position of our Corps, (Longstreet's,) in this battle was as follows: General McLaws' Division occupied the heights, behind the town; General Anderson's Division on McLaws' left, above the town, extending to Taylor's Hill, on the river; General Pickett's Division on McLaws' right; General Hood's Division was posted near Hamilton's crossing, and General Ramseur's Division between Generals Hood and Pickett filled the gap, left open in the first of the army's movements.

The following are the losses, copied from General Longstreet's Official Report:

Anderson's Division	159
McLaws' Division	858
Pickett's Division	54
Hood's Division	251
Ramseur's Division	535
Artillery	37
	1,894
Jackson's Corps lost	2,682
Making a total of	4,576

"We captured 9,000 stands of arms, 255,000 rounds of ammunition, and 1,800 sets of accoutrements."— *Col. Baldwin's Report, Chief Ord. A. N. Va.*

On the evening of Tuesday, (16th,) our Regiment was sent on picket duty on the banks of the river, below the town, and the men were all in such good spirits from the recent victory, that it was considered a pleasure rather than a duty, although the weather was intensely cold and the men suffered severely while on picket post.

On the 18th, (Thursday,) the Regiment returned to their old camp, and then removed from the bleak hills to a piece of woods about a half mile back; after pitching tents and gathering wood, large fires were built, and all hands warmed up.

The next morning, after the men had made themselves comfortable and all were congratulating themselves upon the situation of affairs, orders were received to march; the tents were struck, the baggage was packed, and the line formed; marching out upon the open hillside, we patiently awaited further orders; towards night they arrived and the *line was dismissed;* the previous day's work had to be re-performed; the cold not having abated, and there being no fires, it was a "long, long weary" day of suffering to many.

The second Christmas to us was a dull one; very few extra edibles were handed around, and only a sprinkling of liquor was to be had outside of the joyous group that encircled the table spread by the energetic and gentlemanly caterer, Mr. Jonah White, our worthy Brigade Sutler; his good things were well received and much enjoyed by his numerous friends.

On the 27th, our camp was removed to within a few

miles of Guinea Station, R. & F. R. R., where we found abundance of wood and water. Here we went into winter quarters, and the men were not very long in making themselves comfortable. The following month (January,) passed off quietly, and nothing worthy of note, outside the usual routine of daily camp life, transpired.

On the 27th of January, 1863, orders arrived for us to march, and in a heavy rain, which soon changed into snow, we filed out of camp, traveled in a northern direction, and at nightfall arrived at a point about fifteen miles above Fredericksburg. The tramp was a very severe one, as the snow laid six inches deep before it ceased to fall, and the roads were heavy with mud and water. Upon our arrival, a large forest of pines was selected as our place of bivouac; ere long the men had roaring fires burning, and were engaged in preparing for the night's rest. The wind howled above us, and the snow fell thick and fast; large pine trees were torn up by the roots, and the men were in much danger of being crushed by the falling trees and limbs. Our ordnance wagon during the night was crushed to its bed by a tree twelve inches in diameter, that was uprooted and thrown across it; fortunately, no persons were sleeping in it at the time, or they would certainly have been killed.

Several days were passed here, during which the men held themselves in readiness to move at a moment's notice; then the order arrived to return, and the line formed, and we moved back to our quarters.

What a glorious time some of the Regiment had during
that night, after our return, can only be told by themselves.   But it is a fact worth mentioning, to remind
them, that a self-constituted provost guard confiscated
several barrels of whiskey, which enabled a large portion of the boys to be " gay and lively too."

While encamped near Guinea's, the Regiment did
picket duty at times on the Rappahannock river, and
also worked on the trenches near Fredericksburg,
details being made for the latter purpose.

On the 11th of February, Colonel Herbert received
a twenty days furlough, and Major Simpson was left
in command of our Regiment.

On the 15th, our camp was broken up, and, in company with the Division, we marched, taking the direction of Richmond. The baggage was sent by the
cars, and about nine o'clock, in a hard rain storm, we
set out; after a wearisome march, we went into bivouac
at nightfall.   The next morning, a detail of one company from each regiment of the Brigade was sent
about one mile back, for the purpose of getting the
wagons out of the mud, where many of them had
remained immovable.   We then continued the march
and arrived near Hanover Junction, where we encamped.   A heavy snow storm set in during the night,
through which we marched on the following day.

February 17th, was a severe day upon both men
and teams. Company G was detailed to accompany the Brigade wagon train, to haul them out as
they became stuck in the mud.   We halted about

eleven miles from Richmond, and built large fires by which to dry our saturated clothing.

The following day, the march was resumed in a hard rain storm; we halted within five miles of Richmond where we went to rest, wet and cold; the rain continued to fall during the night, rendering it yet more chilly and disagreable. The next day about ten A.M., we were again on the march; we passed through Richmond and crossed the James River at Mayo's Bridge.

The Division marched through the city by companies in column, presenting a handsome appearance. The sidewalks were filled with ladies, and many highly palatable gifts were distributed by them to the men. We encamped some three miles below the city, and passed the following day in quietness.

On the 21st, about 10 A. M., we again started, reached Chester Station, nine miles from Petersburg, and bivouaced for the night. It was there, and on that very night, that the heavy snow storm fell in which Pickett's Division was lost for so many hours. The men had retired under their blankets and fallen asleep before the storm set in, and, when morning came, they were all invisible, being entirely covered by the snow, which laid on the ground to the depth of eight inches. Many found themselves so comfortable in this pleasant situation, the warmth of the snow being equal to many blankets, that they did not rise until mid-day.

On the 25th, a battle took place between Generals Jenkins' and Kemper's brigades; but as it was a friendly combat, in which *snow balls* were the only missiles used, no one was seriously hurt.

We remained at Chester Station in regular camp, (our tents, baggage &c., having arrived,) until the first day of March, when we bade adieu to that place and left for Petersburg; the roads were in dreadful order, rendering the march a memorably tiresome one. Arriving at the bridge over the Appomatox river, below the city, the Division formed by companies in column, marched through, passed down the City Point road some three miles, and encamped for the night.

The following day very little transpired worthy of note; our bivouac remained undisturbed, and the day passed rather quietly than otherwise. On the 3d March, Col. Herbert re-joined the Regiment, having been absent on furlough; on the 4th, we moved our camp a short distance and settled near the City Point railroad, where a permanent camp was laid out.

On the 9th, General Garnett's Brigade left for the vicinity of North Carolina.

On the 18th, we had Brigade Inspection, which passed off quietly. On the 19th, Kemper's Brigade started for North Carolina, leaving only Gen. Armstead's and ours in camp, both under command of Brigadier General Corse.

On the 20th of March, a tremendous snow storm occurred, completely blockading the roads, in consequence of which drilling &c. were temporarily suspended; it fell to the depth of twelve inches, occasioning much suffering, as the atmosphere was piercingly cold. When the light of the 21st dawned upon us, the snow had increased to fourteen inches on the level ground, and still continued falling until towards noon, when it was superseded by rain, which caused its rapid disappearance.

On the morning of the 23d, preparations were made for removal, tents were struck, baggage packed, and the Brigade took up its line of march. Passing through Prince George Court House, we took the road leading to Ivor Station, N. and P. R. R.; just before dark we halted and went into bivouac. The following day brought us a tedious march, the small streams having swollen into rapid, almost rivers; the roads in many places were so submerged that we were very frequently wading in water; soon after getting into bivouac it rained heavily, necessitating all hands to pass the night in their wet clothes.

About daylight on the 25th, we arose refreshed, and very soon after were on the move; it would puzzle one to imagine a more toilsome, disagreable march, through sand and water, than we underwent, until reaching Ivor, where we encamped in a swamp, near the Station, for the night. This neighborhood has notoriety in history, as that in which the scene of Nat. Tyler's negro insurrection was enacted, in 1831; New Jerusalem, the place of rendezvous for himself and accessories, was only a few miles off from our encampment.

On the morning of the 28th, Compaies A, E and C, were sent on picket duty to the Blackwater river; field artillery from Petersburg had arrived the day previous and was parked near the Station, ready for instant service.

On the 30th, General Pickett appeared and took command; his headquarters were located near Ivor. On the 31st, our Regiment filed out and, marching several miles from the "Swamp," encamped near Tucker's Swamp Church, pitching our tents in a piece of woods bordering on a small stream, where we resumed regular camp life. Whilst here, the men exercised their talents in the interesting and highly necessary operation of brushing up, washing, and cleansing generally, greatly to their individual benefit both in feeling and appearance.

Information soon arrived, that Longstreet's Corps was approaching our locality in anticipation of a movement to be made upon a point below. The roads were improving, rendering active operations practical. The succeeding chapter will show the destination, success and general movements of this Corps, particularly the part sustained by the Seventeenth Virginia Regiment, in the battles, skirmishes and incidents consequent upon so interesting a campaign.

The men were in fine spirits, quite ready and almost anxious to meet the enemy once more, after such prolonged rest from the excitement of battl-   T .

acquired a right good opinion of themselves from the records of former days, they were quite confident of ability now, to keep their names untarnished upon the rolé of honor. It was while encamped at Tucker's Swamp Church, that the Twenty-ninth Virginia Regiment was added to our Brigade.

SUFFOLK, AND THE MARCH TO WIN-
CHESTER.

ON the 6th of April, Lieut. Col. Herbert was assigned the command of the Twenty-ninth Virginia
Regiment, of this Brigade, and Major R. H. Simpson
left to take charge of our Regiment.

On the morning of the 9th, our camp near Tucker's
Swamp Church was broken, and the tramp commenced
towards the Blackwater river. We reached the small
village of Franklin on the 10th, after a slow, quiet
march, passing through and halting near South Quay,
where we received orders to prepare four days rations,
and be ready to move at short notice in light marching
order, baggage, tents and wagons, to be left at South
Quay.

On the following day, (11th,) the troops crossed the
river on pontoon bridges, Generals Jenkins' and Hood's
divisions at Franklin, and ours at South Quay, where
the command, consisting of infantry, artillery and
cavalry, under General J. T. Longstreet, made a rapid
march in direction of Suffolk, reaching a point about
seven miles distant therefrom before night.

About four o'clock on the morning of the 12th, we
moved forward by the various roads leading thereto,
and before noon the Corps had encircled the

the enemy were first apprised of our presence by several shots from our line, then extending in readiness for combat for ten or twelve miles around the town.

The following day, (13th,) our Regiment moved to its position in the siege, near White Marsh, holding the road and a narrow neck of land between there and the Dismal Swamp; the other part of the Brigade was posted further to the left; heavy skirmishing took place soon after the lines were occupied.

The supply train was left at South Quay, but on the above-mentioned day a portion of it moved across the river and proceeded to forage through the counties adjacent; the regimental wagons of the Commissary Department were ordered to follow the troops, and started to do so on the 14th, but the roads were in such bad condition that the train did not reach the vicinity of the army until about two o'clock the following morning, after hard labor, each wagon having taken its turn at a "stick in the mud."

On the morning of the 15th, at early light, our Regiment was attacked by a greatly superior number of the enemy, consisting of infantry, cavalry and artillery. They opened with two cannon shots, immediately after which their infantry and cavalry advanced upon our pickets, and drove them in upon our Regiment, which had not been formed, a greater part of the men having been asleep when the artillery opened. But well aware of the proper course to pursue, they immediately fell back and took position in a piece of woods some half a mile to the rear, opening a brisk fire, which retired the enemy quickly from his position, leaving three dead horses on the field, two prisoners, two horses, (alive,) five saddles and a number of small arms, in our hands. Soon after, the Fifty-seventh and Third Virginia regiments came to our relief, and our former position was reoccupied, after several well directed shots at the retreating Federals. Our loss was four wounded and four captured.

The following are the names of those wounded in this little skirmish: Privates C. O. Sipple, Company E, O. F. Hoffman and T. B. Saunders, of Company K, the latter very badly wounded.

In the afternoon our skirmishers advanced, whilst our artillery operated against the enemy, and took position a long distance in front of our line, the enemy falling back as our skirmish line moved forward.

The following day, (16th,) another attack was made upon us, and a part of our line was broken by the charge of their cavalry and driven in, but the Fifteenth and Thirtieth Virginia regiments of our Brigade advanced and dispersed the Federals in short order. The loud rattle of musketry and booming of cannon on our left the same day, was caused by the attack of a part of General Armstead's Brigade upon the enemy, and the "driving out" of the Federal pickets from a thicket, the possession of which was necessary to us for the straightening of our lines.

The troops of the Corps were posted as follows: General Pickett commanded the right, General Jenkins the center, and General Hood the left. Our Regiment was on the extreme right of the line, and we picketed in the Dismal Swamp.

On the 17th, the Twenty-ninth Virginia of our Brigade, commanded at that time by Lieut. Col. Herbert, met the enemy, (who charged them,) repulsed and drove him a considerable distance. On the 18th, their cavalry again advanced, when the firing of a few volleys caused them to retire.

The heavy cannonading above the town and to our extreme left on the 19th and 20th, proceeded from the gunboats of the Federals, and from a portion of our field artillery that had been sent down upon the river bank to harrass them.

On the 23d, the enemy again advanced in our front, threw out their skirmishers in order to engage our attention, while they set fire to a large building several hundred yards from our outposts, and then retired, but not without some loss, as our pickets report having seen them carrying several men from the field.

The next day they reappeared in front of our Regiment, engaged our pickets who fought them until each man had fired thirty rounds of ammunition, and then retired until they re-entered our lines to await an attack. The enemy at once advanced and formed in a piece of woods, of which we commanded a full view, and where our artillery opened upon them with terrible effect; so true was the aim of the efficient gunners, and so demoralizing in its influence upon the enemy, that they broke ranks, and, to use their own phrase, "skedaddled" in unmeasured haste, accelerated by deafening cheers from our soldiers. Our loss was three wounded among the artillerymen, and several horses killed. We found four of their dead on the field, and numbers of guns, haversacks, &c., &c., improvidently abandoned in their precipitate flight. On the 25th, they sent into our lines a flag of truce for the purpose of obtaining the bodies of their men left on the field the day before. The same night, we left the White Marsh road and rejoined our Brigade, stationed about three miles to the left.

The wagons were busily engaged, after our arrival here, in removing further back into the country the bacon, hay, grain, and other forage from this part of Virginia, and a portion of North Carolina had also been well visited for the same purpose.

There were heavy cannonading and musketry on the left on the 30th, but the Federals did not make the attack that we supposed they would, but satisfied themselves with watching our movevents.

The month of May, 1863, opened beautifully, and found the lines maintaining comparative quiet. On the third, orders were received to prepare to march; in the afternoon the wagons started to the rear, taking the direction of South Quay, and about 9 o'clock P. M., the main body of the army withdrew from around Suffolk, and returned to the Blackwater river by the roads marched down one month previous. The trains crossed the river at South Quay and Franklin, about midnight, and at daylight on the morning of the 4th, the troops commenced crossing.

By twelve o'clock M, all had passed over but the rear guard, which was in line on the Suffolk side and remained in position until about four P. M., when, they too, came over and the pontoon bridges were taken up. The enemy's cavalry followed us, but only captured a few stragglers; they had not forgotten the retreat from Yorktown, one year before, when we gave them such a "drubbing" for coming too near our rear.

At an early hour on the 5th, we were again in motion, and not long after starting we received the welcome tidings, through a despatch from General Lee to General Longstreet, of the victory at Chancellorsville. This announcement acted like a charm upon the men, almost annihilating all thought of physical inconvenience arising from the toils of the day's march.

About sundown we halted and bivouaced beyond the beautiful village of Jerusalem, through which we passed in a drenching rain. On the 6th, the rain continued at intervals throughout the day; after marching about twenty miles, we bivouaced, wet and tired, near the village of Littletown, and made a rather successful effort to sleep.

On the 7th, we reached a point about seven miles from Petersburg after a most wearying twenty miles march. The next day, (8th,) we passed through the city and bivouaced a mile or so beyond, when many of the men were allowed to return to the "Burg," and spend a portion of the night with their friends and acquaintances. It was a great treat, after such a prolonged campaign, to visit the dear old city so populous with kind hearts, so noted for genuine hospitality.

Leaving our bivouac about nine o'clock on the 9th of May, we marched to within about six miles of Richmond, and encamped near Falling Creek on the R. and P. R. R. Whilst here the men passed their leisure hours in fishing, boating, bathing and sight-seeing in the vicinity.

On the 11th, the sad news of the death of Lieut. Gen'l Jackson was made known to the men of our Division, causing a general depression of spirits among all classes. His death took place at the residence of Mr. Chandler, near Guinea Station, on the evening of the 10th of May, 1863: words could not express the intensity of sadness that filled all hearts for this irreparable loss. His remains were conveyed to Richmond on the evening of the 11th, and upon their arrival all business was suspended, all business places closed; his body was embalmed and remained in the Governor's Mansion until the next day, (12th,) when it was removed to be laid in state in the hall of Representatives, where until night closed in, a living stream of sorrowing hearts gathered for a gaze, (to be cherished through time,) upon the face of the unwavering Christian Hero of so many hard fought battles. On the following day, the remains were taken to Lexington, Virginia, for interment. The escort from the Capitol building to the depot, consisted of two regiments of our Division, a battery of artillery, and a detachment of cavalry; a long procession of citizens, preceded by President Davis and staff, followed the soldiery.

On the 13th, Lieut Col. Herbert returned to the Regiment and resumed command. On the 15th, orders were received to march; after striking tents and packing baggage, we moved, with the Division, to within a short distance of Manchester and encamped for the night.

The following morning we passed through Richmond and onward about twelve miles, going into bivouac about three P. M. on the Hanover Junction road. The march on the 17th was short, as we halted about 12 o'clock M. within three miles of the Junction. Here we went into regular camp and received orders to resume the company drills.

In the month of April, while the army was lying in quietude, having closed every approach to Suffolk from the Nansemond river to the Dismal Swamp— General Pickett, wishing to know the situation of the enemy in his front, applied to Capt. Wm. H. Fowle of this Regiment, (then performing picket duty with his Company on the line,) to procure him the services of a good scout for the accomplishment of this very desirable object.

Sergeant J. P. Jordan, of this Company, having been successful before upon similar errands, was summond, and the General gave him instructions to proceed in direction of Suffolk, and, if practicable, to ascertain the situation of the enemy's camp, report their strength, &c., without arousing their suspicions

or disturbing them, as he particularly wanted them
kept quiet until his plans were perfected.

Posted with the necessary instructions, and knowing
well his duty, our Sergeant after selecting three of his
companions: John T. Mills, Company H, Seventeenth
Virginia, S. C. Madison, and Wm. Gravatt, Company
F, 30th Virginia, all of distinguished bravery and
unimpeachable reliability, to accompany him, pushed
forward into the forest on his left, moving in the
direction of the Federal line.

With great caution the quartette glided stealthily
along in single file, and struck the swamp, studded
thickly with under-growth, pursuing their way until
they thought themselves near the enemy's picket line.
The Sergeant then rose to his feet and upon looking
around, he says: " I found that I had *unobserved
passed the enemy's pickets*, posted not over *fifteen paces*
on either side of me, and was a short distance in *their
rear*."

They were now really in for it; nothing but un-
shrinking nerve whilst they avoided attracting attention, surrounded as they were by enemies, could ensure
success to their undertaking.   The utmost caution
was observed; not even a twig was broken, the noise
of which could arouse suspicion, as the brave soldiers
crept on almost into the enemy's midst.

The timber here being more open, they could see distinctly, some distance in front of them, a line of the
enemy busily engaged in throwing up breastworks,
thus rendering impracticable their further advance in

direction of Suffolk. This was a movement of importance to them, and a master stroke was required by which to spirit themselves back through the line of pickets. Certain capture, and, probably death, would attend their advance; to retrace their steps in the path they came, was utterly out of the question, and, after consultation, the advice of Jordan, to work their way as near the lines as possible, without being seen, was concurred in, and they immediately commenced operations.

Proceeding cautiously, they came in sight of the pickets posted in squads of four about twenty paces apart. This was truly the climax of the "situation" and made another council necessary, as they laid themselves down together in the sheltering undergrowth; some thought escape impossible, but Jordan, ever quick-witted and prompt in facing danger, determined to make a bold effort before yielding to the pressure against them.

They were now on that part of the line which skirted the edge of the woods, and the Confederates could be seen, about four hundred yards beyond, quietly walking their posts, not dreaming of the danger of their comrades, who were watching them so anxiously from the enemy's picket line.

The active brain of our Sergeant soon concocted a plan, which he communicated to his companions, and told them to follow him; the four sprang upon the pickets, (four in number,) ordering them to surrender, which they did without waste of words, by throwing

down their arms. They then ordered their prisoners
to run for their lives, and the party, friend and foe,
dashed across the field, our boys keeping the captured
ones near them for protection. Not a shot was fired
from the enemy, and in a few minutes they were safe
in our line, each with his prisoner.

The following order was issued from Division Headquarters soon after—in proof of the appreciation of
such service—and was read to the troops on dress
parade, on the 19th May, 1863, while encamped near
Hanover Junction:

HEADQUARTERS, PICKETT'S DIVISION,
May 15th, 1863.

Special Orders No. 48:

The Major General commanding takes pleasure in expressing his
high appreciation, to his command, of the gallant and meritorious
conduct of Sergeant J. P. Jordan, Company H, Seventeenth Virginia; Private J. T. Mills, Company H, Seventeenth Virginia;
Private S. C. Madison, Company F, Thirtieth Virginia, and
William Gravatt, Company F, Thirtieth Virginia, in the late siege
of Suffolk. These gallant soldiers, being sent by their commanding
officers, when on picket duty on the new Somerton road, immediately in front of Suffolk, alone and unsustained, pierced the enemy's
line of skirmishers, penetrated to within a few yards of his main
line of battle, gained valuable information, and returned, bringing
with them four (4) prisoners and all their arms and equipments.

It is with especial pleasure that the Major General commanding
observes such acts of gallant chivalric daring among the brave men
whom he commands, and while the above-named soldiers have, in
so doing, written their own names on the roll of honor, it is hoped
that their example will incite others to deeds of a similar nature.

He desires that this order be published to each regiment and battalion of the Division on dress parade.

By order of Major General Pickett:

(Signed)　　　E. R. BAIRD, A. A. A. Gen'l.

Official: H. BRYANT, A. A. A. Gen'l.

To J. P. JORDAN, Co. H, 17th Va. Reg't.

Passing on to the latter part of May, we find the 28th was the day for the Gubernatorial, and other State officer's elections. The soldiers in camp voted for the candidates from their districts, and quite a lively canvass occurred. Our Regiment was handsomely entertained by the brief, but happy remarks of Surgeon H. Snowden, upon the questions at issue.

At this time the army of Northern Virginia was divided into three corps, commanded by Lieutenant Generals Longstreet, A. P. Hill and Ewell, each of whom it is a pleasure for us to remember, as Brigadier Generals in command of our old Brigade.

On the 2d of June, 1863, while we were preparing to attend a review of the Brigade, an order was received for the Regiment to escort a wagon train, about to visit King and Queen county for the purpose of collecting forage. We were soon in line with one company of the Fifty-seventh Virginia and a detachment of cavalry; we moved off, taking the road leading to Newtown.

After marching about ten miles, we were informed that the enemy·were advancing; the Colonel dispatched a courier to General Pickett to inform him of the report, and we pursued our way, crossing the Mattapony river and halting on its opposite bank; the cavalry were then sent forward to reconnoitre; in an hour we moved on, and, at night, bivouaced under arms on the Matococy creek.

Early the following morning, a courier arrived from General Pickett, informing Colonel Herbert that the

Division would start at four o'clock A. M. *via* the Bowling Green and Tappahannock road; we then moved forward to Newtown, where we halted and loaded the wagons with bacon and meal. The ladies of the village were very kind, sending us out boquets of flowers and delicious eatables in abundance. Some of them having expressed a desire to see a dress parade, we were marched to a neighboring field, and, with pleasure, gratified the wish. Passing on about five miles beyond, to Garnett's Mill, companies A and G were sent out as pickets.

On the morning of the 4th, two brigades of the Division arrived and bivouaced a short distance in advance of us, the residue of the Division remaining some four miles to the rear.

Early on the morning of the 5th, the Division commenced its return march to our old camp near Hanover Junction, our Regiment having been detailed as rear guard. When within a few miles of Newtown, we saw dense columns of smoke rising in our rear; a courier bearing dispatches from General Pickett arrived, but we continued the march towards Newtown. On reaching the above village, we about-faced and formed in line of battle; a section of artillery was placed in a field near, and companies A and I detached to support it.

The report was abroad that the enemy were landing about five miles off from three boats, and Company H was sent about half a mile to the front as a picket, while a detachment of cavalry, supported by two regiments of infantry, remained to support us in case the enemy advanced; the remainder of the Division moved on towards Hanover Junction. About three o'clock, we were relieved by a regiment from General Kemper's Brigade. We rejoined the Division at the Mattapony river, and passed the night at " Ruddy Mills," on said river.

The march was resumed next morning, the Seventeenth Virginia in advance, and about four P. M., we halted near Taylorsville and went into camp. On the next day, (7th,) late in the afternoon, the Regiment fell into line and moved down to the railroad bridge over the South Anna river, to which place we were sent as a guard.

The Division, except our Brigade, marched on the 8th to join the army in the neighborhood of Culpeper Court House. We put on a strong guard at the " Bridge," and throwing out pickets a short distance in front, made ready to resist any attack that might be made upon us. General Corse's Headquarters were at Taylorsville; the different regiments of his Brigade were engaged in guarding the numerous bridges in that vicinity. But we were not destined to remain long in this quiet and beautiful spot, for on the 10th, orders came for our departure, and being relieved by a part of the Twenty-seventh North Carolina Regiment, we marched to a point about half a mile beyond Hanover Junction and awaited the arrival of the rest of our Brigade. While there we received a visit from Col. Marye, which afforded much pleasure to the members of his old command, its only defect being its brevity.

About eight o'clock on the morning of the 11th, the Fifteenth and Twenty-ninth regiments having joined us, we began the march in direction of Culpeper Court House, taking the Telegraph Road as far as Mt. Carmel, and then the left hand road, passing through the village of Childsburg, where the Thirtieth Virginia joined us; we bivouaced beyond, having marched eighteen miles. The march on the following day, (12th,) was a very tiresome one, warm almost to suffocation, while the dust was most uncomfortably perceptible; we halted about fifteen minutes in every hour to rest. We bivouaced about three o'clock P. M. near Taylor's Mill, when a courier arrived, bidding us to remain until further orders.

By eleven o'clock on the 13th, orders arrived for the Brigade to return to Hanover Junction, and we moved off, arriving about night at the camp we had occupied on the night of the 11th. We marched about four o'clock A. M. on the 14th, and after a tramp of twenty-three miles, we reached Taylorsville and spent the night. The next day we took our old position at the South Anna bridge, settled down very naturally to the enjoyment of the pleasures of fishing, bathing and boating, on the river. Our duties at the bridge being light, we all passed many pleasant hours, feasted on the fruits and vegetables of the neighborhood, and had a good time generally.

On the night of the 24th, orders were received by General Corse from General Lee to report, with his Brigade, at Gordonsville; soon after, a dispatch came from General Elsey at Richmond, informing us that the enemy were landing troops at the White House. A guard of ten men, in charge of a lieutenant, was detailed to remain at the bridge while the residue of the Regiment marched to the Junction, where the Brigade was forming, and we then moved on some six miles beyond, where we were overtaken by a courier with the welcome news that the cars were coming to carry us to Gordonsville.

About ten o'clock that night we gladly availed ourselves of car transportation, arriving at Gordonsville about daylight on the 26th, and bivouaced in the woods near the village to await further developments.

On the Friday after we left the bridge, on the South Anna, the enemy appeared, and as a detail of eighty North Carolina troops had been sent to assist in its defence, the squad of ten men and a lieutenant, (formerly referred to,) were sent on a scouting expedition to *hunt up* the raiders. Not long after leaving the bridge, as they were approaching a piece of woods, they were greatly surprised at hearing an order to surrender from a body of the enemy among the trees; they made an attempt to escape, and four of the men succeeded. The Federal's then moved down upon the North Carolinians stationed at the bridge, and drawn up on either side of the railroad to receive them; before attacking, several companies of their dismounted men were sent over the river at a ford below, but not until after they had taken position in rear did our men become aware of the movement, and then it was too late; whilst attempting to cross the bridge the whole force of them fell into the hands of the enemy, whose number was estimated at about twelve hundred, while our force consisted of but eighty. A gallant fight was made, and twelve fell out of the eighty. The enemy then set fire to the bridge and soon after retired.

We return now to Gordonsville, where the Regiment was in bivouac awaiting further orders.

On the 28th, about eight o'clock in the afternoon, we were ordered back to Richmond, and embarking on the cars, at that hour, we were transported thither; arriving about daylight the succeeding morning, we encamped about three miles from the city on the north side of the James. On the following day we were again ordered to move, and about three P. M. we marched to the depot of the Central Railroad; after remaining there patiently until about nine o'clock P. M., we took the cars for Gordonsville, where we arrived after a tedious ride and many stoppages about ten o'clock the next day.

We went into camp near the village and had a pleasant, quiet time, as communications with Lynchburg and Richmond, for several days, were entirely cut off. The weather was warm, but we enjoyed our idle life and relaxation from fatiguing marches, to the utmost.

Our camp near Gordonsville was broken up on the 8th July, 1863, and the Brigade began the march to the Valley. After effecting a progress of nineteen miles the first day, we bivouaced near Madison Court

House. On the 9th, we proceeded to within six miles of Milan's Gap and encamped on the mountain side; where, in the enjoyment of delightfully cool water, a pure bracing atmosphere, and the unbroken slumber a tired soldier can so well appreciate, we were amply remunerated for the fatigues of the march. Swollen streams were forded, and a detail of twenty men from the Brigade was made to repair the roads for the passage of wagons.

About six o'clock on the morning of the 10th, we began the ascent of the Blue Ridge along the steep and winding road. It was a glorious march; all nature seeming jubilant. In the rushing mountain streams we listened to majestic music, while the forests were vocal with melody from the little throats that weary not in sounding the "Jubilate Deo." The gorgeous sunrise viewed from the mountain height, the evidence of Divine handiwork bursting upon us at every step, swelled our hearts with unutterable emotions. Arriving upon the summit each would stop and gaze with breathless admiration upon the grandeur of the scenery; the west side of the range particularly, presented a picture of unparalleled beauty; farms clad in the richness of garden spots were ranged continuously as far as the eye could reach. This portion of our State not having then experienced the ravages of war, presented itself with luxuious beauty depicted upon its every feature, from the outstanding crops to the barns and storehouses replete with its produce.

After moving on about twenty-two miles, we halted a short distance beyond Luray, the county seat of Page, and went into bivouac. The morning, (11th,) bright and early we resumed the march, and had not gone very far when a courier reported to General Corse that the Shenandoah was not fordable; the General determined, however, to make the attempt at a ford higher up, so we passed to the left of the main road, and after marching about sixteen miles, bivouaced for the night near McKay's ford, on the South Branch.

On the 12th, we continued the march, forded both branches of the river which were deepened, widened and the current greatly strengthened by recent rains, consequently, we made a march of about twelve miles only, so much time being consumed in the crossing.

On the 13th, we struck the " Valley Pike " at Middletown, taking the direction of Winchester; immediately after marching through Newtown, quite a sizable village, we passed a column of prisoners about 4,700 in number, guarded by a regiment of infantry, a detachment of cavalry and two pieces of artillery, on their way to Staunton from the battle-field of Gettysburg, where they had been captured; we passed on through Kearnstown, (noted for the battle between Generals Jackson and Shields,) forded a stream four feet deep, and arrived within a mile of Winchester about three o'clock P. M. During the last day's march it had rained without intermission, consequently, when we encamped, no one in the Regiment could boast of a dry thread in his clothing.

We remained at the camp near Winchester some days, and learned the particulars of the great battle of Gettysburg, in which the loss of our Division was unprecedentedly heavy. The army had recrossed the Potomac about the time of our arrival, when a period was allotted us for recruiting strength, washing clothes and righting up generally. Passes were granted the men to visit Winchester, of which many availed themselves. The works surrounding it had been strengthened, and every preparation made to thwart the enemy in any attempt to surprise the town.

THE BATTLE OF MANASSAS GAP; ONE MONTH IN TENNESSEE, AND WINTER OF '63 AND '64.

ON the morning of 20th July, 1863, the camp near Winchester was broken up, and our Brigade, (as the advance of the army lately returned from Maryland,) moved off in direction of the mountains. Striking the Front Royal road about three miles from Winchester, we proceeded slowly, owing to the extreme heat of the weather, and, at the end of fourteen miles, bivouaced near Cedarville. About daylight on the following morning the march was resumed, and the Brigade hurried towards the Gap in the mountains.

The north and south branches of the Shenandoah were so high that the troops had great difficulty in fording them, particularly the latter; several men were carried down by the rapidity of the current, and would certainly have been drowned, had it not been for the prompt assistance of the mounted officers, who spared no effort necessary to the rescue.

After passing through Front Royal, our Regiment was ordered to Manassas Gap, east of the town. The enemy were in force at Linden Station, on the east side of the mountains, and were advancing upon the left of our column by two roads, each leading to the town of Front Royal, one passing through the Gap of the Manassas railroad, and the other, over the mountain by the little village of "Wappen." Companies B and C were detailed by Col. Herbert to proceed out the road on the left, while the remainder of the Regiment met the enemy on the road crossing the mountain. The principal fight took place on the mountain and resulted in the enemy's defeat. The companies fought bravely at both points; at the Manassas road the enemy were held in check for the greater part of the day, and when ever they approached too near our thin line, strongly posted in the woods on the mountain side, they were severely punished.

This was a victory of great importance to our army; had the Federals succeeded in gaining possession of the Gaps at that time, we can form no conjecture as to what the results would have been, as it is well known, that they had two corps in reserve not far distant, while our handful of men, (comparatively speaking,) were battling for most of the day against ten times their number. Great credit was awarded them from the rest of the army, when the facts became known, and they were loudly eulogized on all sides. Our loss was three wounded, (one of whom afterwards died,) five officers and sixteen men captured.

During the progress of this battle, Color Coporal Robert Buchanan, Company H, seized the colors from the hands of Color Sergeant Robert Steel, who fell wounded, and had not held them many minutes before he, too, fell pierced by a ball. His wound proved fatal; after lingering many weeks in the town of Lynchburg, he died, lamented by his comrades in arms, and numerous friends and relatives as a gallant, good and courageous soldier.

Those captured, were on picket duty at the time, and having been surrounded by cavalry, it was impossible for all to escape. The cavalry force opposed to the Regiment in this battle was composed of the First and Second Regulars of the United States Army. On the cast side of the mountain, the Sixth Pennsylvania and the Fifth Regulars, with a battery, were posted, under command of General Merritt.

Lieut. Scott Roy, Company B, who was among those captured, effected his escape on the night of the 22d, thus, for the second time, outwitting his captors.

The night of the 21st of July, was passed by the Regiment on the summit of the mountain, near Chester Gap, to which point we marched after the battle. Early on the 22d, General McLaws' Division of infantry moved foward, clearing the way for the passage of the army. In the afternoon, we moved through the Gap, and after a tiresome night march, reached Gaine's Cross Roads about daylight, and there encamped. The weary men gladly threw themselves upon the grassy fields, and slept, during the few hours halt, in preference to preparing breakfast. The column was then formed, and we again moved, taking the direct route to Culpeper Court House, near which point we bivouaced for the night. The wagon trains were sent to Little Washington, and then to Culpeper, making the trip in two days.

For some days the camps near Culpeper were quiet —

going through the regular routine of duties peculiar to army life. On the night of the 30th, Lieut. Scott Roy, Company B, of this Regiment, whose escape from the enemy has been referred to, returned to the Regiment, greatly to the surprise of all, as he was generally supposed to be dragging out the weary term of a prisoner in some of the Northern strongholds. When the squadron in charge of the prisoners, captured at Manassas, halted the night of the 22d to rest and sleep, the fearlessly brave Lieut. Roy, undaunted as usual by surrounding circumstances, promptly laid his plans to circumvent the kind intentions of those having him in custody, watched his opportunity, and, after they had fallen asleep, he *rolled himself out of the circle* of slumbering guards, made choice of the finest horse in the group, and rode off without molestation, enriched by the possession of a valuable steed and a full cavalry outfit, a result which amply repaid him for the inconvenience endured in obtaining them.

While we were encamped near Culpeper, the enemy advanced, threatening an attack. Troops were moved to the Hazel river, where preparations were made to meet them, but no opportunity for battle was afforded us, the enemy preferring to remain on the defensive.

On the 3d of August, the army again changed position, taking the direction of Orange Court House. Our Regiment marched with the Division, crossed Cedar Run, passed the battle-field of Cedar Mountain at the point where the hardest fight had occurred, moved over the river near Rapidan Station, in the neighborhood of which we spent that night and the day following.

On the 5th, we moved down the river, and went into camp near Summerville ford. Nearly a month was passed in this pleasant locality; the Regiment was increased in strength and numbers by the return of the sick and wounded reinvigorated by several months absence and rest. The period was passed quietly, and without other occupation required of us than the regular camp duties, which proved highly beneficial to all, recuperating health, energy, and buoyancy of spirit for the winter's campaign.

On the 18th, orders were received allowing fifteen days furlough to two men in each hundred, by which numbers were sent home rejoicing. A great revival of religion, throughout General Lee's army, took place during its encampment on the Rapidan, which added many, from every regiment, to the Army of the Cross.

On the 8th of September, 1863, the camping grounds of Pickett's Division were left bare, and we began the march to Petersburg. The first night was passed about five miles east of Gordonsville, nothing occurring on the route worthy of noting as an incident of interest. The following day we passed through Gordonsville, and bivouaced within two miles of Louisa Court House. The march was rather a rapid one in such torid weather, consequently, many lagged, being utterly incapable of locomotion at such a gait, for so long a time.

On the 10th, we moved seventeen miles; the day

was cloudy, hence, there was not so much suffering from heat. The vicinity of Richmond was reached on the 12th, and we encamped, the men in good spirits, and glad to be so near the "City of Seven Hills." During the following day, the Division marched through the city to the depot of the R. & P. R. R., occupied the cars, and were conveyed to Petersburg, near which we went into camp. On the afternoon of the 14th, we moved down to the depot of the South-side Railroad, for Lynchburg, the trains leaving the city after night had set in. Our Brigade only embarked, the residue of the Division remaining in the vicinity of Petersburg. A very sad affair occurred prior to our leaving the depot. Two of our Regiment becoming involved in a quarrel with each other, Hirst, of Company F, a good soldier, was mortally wounded by a stab in the groin, inflicted with a small knife in the hands of the other, belonging to Company G. The latter was arrested and confined for trial in Petersburg, but finally acquitted, and returned to his company.

Arriving in Lynchburg early on the morning of the 15th, we remained until evening, when we left on the V. & T. R. R. train, and traveled all night, reaching Glade Spring the next afternoon. Several hours were passed at Wytheville, many of the Brigade taking advantage of the opportunity for a stroll through the village. Just before leaving, Hansborough, of Company K, had his hand crushed by the cars. One of the Fifteenth Virginia was also wounded; he fell from the

cars while they were in motion, thereby fracturing his
leg so severely as to render amputation necessary.

At daylight, on the 17th, we arrived at Zollicoffer,
Tenn., having halted a short time at Bristol, a town
belonging, according to State lines, equally to Tennessee
and Virginia.   The cars were unloaded, and the Brigade encamped near the village.   The ride from Petersburg to Tennessee was truly a pleasant change from
our previous tedious marches ; the scenery from either
side of the route, in passing through the rich valley of
Roanoke, was magnificent, and doubly recompensing a
lover of nature for any annoyances occasioned by the
trip.   The fair sex was well represented at each station
we passed, and our hearts gladdened by kind words
and gentle smiles, as most acceptable lunches to regale
our inner man were dispensed to us by delicate hands.
It is hard to determine which was most grateful to us.
Perhaps the memory of both nerved our arms to more
valorous deeds, but be that as it may, we shall always
think of them with pleasure.

We were all much pleased with the wild country of
East Tennessee, so different from the open fields of the
section we had just left.   Provisions were abundant,
and fruit, so much sought for in Virginia, abounded.
The grist mills in the vicinity were kept grinding in-
cessantly day and night to supply the army.   The army
was commanded by General Jones, an officer who had
spent the greater part of the war in that section of our
Confederacy.

On the 19th, it was ascertained that the enemy were

advancing in our direction from the village of Blounts-ville, and preparations were made to give them a warm reception. The Brigade was marched a short distance from camp, the regiments placed in position on the hillside, and pickets from the Twenty-ninth Virginia Regiment thrown out. The next morning, (20th,) the enemy neared our picket line, throwing out their dismounted cavalry as skirmishers. They, no doubt, expected their advance to meet with but slight resistance, but upon striking the brave men of the Twenty-ninth, they met with such sharp repulse, that they fell back discomforted. Several rounds of shell from a mountain howitzer were fired at our line, but, fortunately, did no damage. The Twenty-ninth Virginia lost two killed, and four wounded, in the skirmish. The Federals then withdrew, taking the road to Bristol, thus leaving us for a while in quiet.

On the 24th, they again approached our line, and after discharging a few shots at our pickets, which were promptly reciprocated, they retraced their route in direction of Blountsville.

A small party of the Quartermaster's Department, belonging to our Regiment, while returning from Bristol, where they had been on duty, met a squad of the Confederate Tennessee cavalry, and, as night had closed in, each mistook the other for the enemy, and the cavalry fired into the squad, scattered them into the woods, giving them a good scare, and furnishing material for a long and exciting story after their return to camp of an attack from a large body of the enemy.

This was all spoiled, however, and the participants quite crest-fallen, when enlightened, after the narration of their wonderful escape had been listened to by many, by the information that the imaginary foe was in reality a party of *our own* cavalry.

One of our Brigade officers, (Staff,) was so over-joyed at hearing the glorious news from Bragg's army, that he snatched up a gun and charged upon a *cow* standing in the road; the creature very naturally retreating, developed, to his astonished gaze, the form of a lady seated upon a stool in front of an *overturned milk pail.* The Lieutenant apologized, explained and righted matters, to the best of his ability, but could not restore the " *spilt milk.*"

On the 27th, the Regiment, in company with the Brigade, moved down to Carter's Station, ten miles below Zollicoffer, and remained there until the 30th, when it marched back, and embarked on the cars for Lynchburg. We arrived in Lynchburg on the 1st of October, without anything worthy of note having transpired; here we idled our time away until the following night; during our stay, Captain Wallace, of the Fifteenth Virginia, was severely hurt from a fall over a railroad tie, and one of the Thirtieth Virginia was killed by a negro, on the outskirts of the town.

About 11 o'clock, on the night of the 2d, we took the cars for Petersburg, arriving safely the following morning. We remained near there for several days, and on the 8th, our Regiment was detached from the Brigade, and sent by railroad to Ivor Station. P. & N.

R. R., where we went into camp, on the left of the road, opposite the Station. Colonel Herbert, at this point, was in command of the Department known as the "Blackwater line," with his Headquarters at Ivor.

Soon after our arrival there, a regular camp was laid out, and the tents pitched. Clothing was issued, and most of us put in comfortable trim for the winter. We found oysters and sweet potatoes abundant, the former could be purchased for $5.00 per gallon, and the latter for $6.00 per bushel. The remainder of our Brigade left Petersburg for Dublin, Va., on the 15th of October, General Armistead's Brigade having gone to North Carolina some days previously.

On the 21st and 22d, a number of refugees from Norfolk came into our lines, having been sent out of the city by the United States authorities; most of our tents were vacated for their accommodation, and as the trains came down but twice a week, they were necessarily compelled to remain two nights. There were many pleasant ladies in the party, and our time passed with agreeable rapidity in their society. The first night of their stay, they were serenaded by the Glee Club of the Regiment; the next night we arranged for, and enjoyed a dance in honor of their presence, in a wheelwright's shop near the Station. When the train came down on the 23d, the ladies were escorted thereto and regretfully bidden farewell; the remembrance of those truly happy hours, so replete with social pleasure, will ever be bright in the hearts of no small portion of the Seventeenth Virginia, though they never more may meet, in this life, those gentle heroines.

On the 24th, Colonel Herbert sent in a flag of truce to Suffolk, accompanied by some of our wagons in charge of the Quartermaster, for the purpose of transporting from there more refugees to some points within our lines.

Two of our companies were posted on picket at the river; above and below the infantry pickets, outposts of cavalry, were constantly kept on the alert, in case of an advance by the Federal troops. On the 3d, 4th, and 5th days of November, salt was distributed among the citizens of the adjoining counties; great numbers of them came in gladly to get it, riding in every conceivable sort of conveyance; a large majority freighted with something they hoped to sell to the soldiers. On the 9th, we received orders to march; previous to this time, Colonel Herbert, having dispatched Lieut. Roy, Company B, on a scout into the enemy's line near Suffolk, received information of their not being in very strong force at that place. In company with a detachment of cavalry and a section of artillery, we vacated our camp at Ivor, crossed the Blackwater at Broad Run Ferry, and halted about 11 o'clock P. M., near a Mr. Marshall's, where we slept on the ground without fires; it was cold napping, but as we were on a "Surprise party" expedition, we did our best to enjoy it.

The march was resumed on the 10th, and upon arriving at Windsor Station, we halted, stacked arms, and awaited the report of a party of the cavalry sent forward upon a scout; they returned not many hours after at full speed, with seven prisoners, eight fine horses, and an excellent spring wagon, all of which they had captured in Suffolk. The next morning we returned to Ivor, not having accomplished the object at which we aimed, the why and wherefore of the failure being ascertained only upon our arrival at Windsor.

Lieut. Scott Roy, who had been captured while scouting within the Federal lines, returned to camp on the 15th, having for the third time outwitted his captors. It appears, that after he was captured, some Federal officer recognized him as one who had escaped once or twice before, and to make themselves doubly sure of retaining him this time, they placed him, with his comrade, (one of Company B,) in an upper room of Fort Norfolk, and deputed a heavy guard to take care of him. Roy had advised the Federals to watch him closely, as he intended to leave them, if possible. So, after remaining several nights in the Fort, he and his companion cut through the roof of the building, and, sliding down the lightning-rod, passed the sentinel's beat in the darkness, and finding a canoe near the Fort, on the river, quickly availed of it and paddled up the Nansemond to a convenient landing, whence they came into camp.

Early in the month of January, 1864, our Regiment marched in direction of Chuckatuck, on a reconnoisance; without anything of importance transpiring, we returned the following day to camp. This move was made in consequence of a report of the arrival of two

gunboats, from which the enemy were landing a raiding party; it was incorrect, however, there was only
one gunboat, and no attempt to land.

On the 23d of January, after a long rest and quiet
winter, our Regiment took the cars, and arrived safely
in Petersburg, where several days were spent. On the
28th, we left Petersburg for Kingston, N. C., preparatory to the attack contemplated upon Newbern at that
time, and arrived on the 30th; on the evening of that
day the march to Newbern was commenced; on the 1st
of February, we arrived near the city, and opposite
Fort Anderson. This was the longest forced march
the Regiment had ever been called upon to make,
having traveled 53 miles in 27 hours. It being considered impracticable to attack the Fort at this time,
Col. Dearing, in command of the troops, ordered a
withdrawal, and after another weary march over the
sandy roads of North Carolina, the Regiment reached
its encampment, near Kingston, on the 5th of February.

The following day, (6th,) the march was commenced
to Goldsboro', where we arrived on the 7th. On the
24th, we were ordered to Lexington, N. C., to quell a
disturbance apprehended in that locality. We remained
two days and then returned to Goldsboro', leaving
Companies F and I as a guard; after a stay of about
ten days, the companies above-mentioned rejoined the
Regiment.

On the 7th of March, we moved by railroad to
Kingston, where we encamped. At that time the

Brigade marched to Deep Creek as a feint, to prevent the Yankees from reinforcing Plymouth from Newbern, while that place was besieged by General Hoke. The Regiment encamped on the Neuse river, and whilst there, a conscript member of Company G was tried by court martial at Petersburg, for desertion, sent to the Regiment at Kingston, where he was executed on Friday, April 1st, being shot in the back.

The rations at this time were rather light, consisting of $1\frac{1}{4}$ lbs. of meal and $\frac{1}{3}$ lb. of bacon per day, with an occasional ration of rice or beans. The prices of everything, at all saleable, were enormously high, as the following price-list will show: Board in Richmond, at private house, $25.00 per day; at hotel, $30.00 per day, $10.00 per meal; butter, $12.00 per lb.; sugar, $8.00; coffee, 15.00; beef, $8.00; bacon, $7.00; flour, per barrel, $300.00; corn meal, per bushel, $50.00; shoes, per pair, $100.00; boots, $350.00.

On the 3d of May, General Corse's Brigade marched from Kingston to participate in the contemplated attack upon Newbern, by General Hoke's command. Arriving in front of Newbern on the 5th, our Regiment was assigned a position in the line of battle on the east of the city, bordering upon the river. During the evening and night, we were under a terrific fire from the gunboats of the enemy, but suffered no loss. The operations in Virginia having caused the suspension of hostilities against Newbern, before an attack had been made, our Regiment was ordered back to Kingston, where it arrived on the 8th; orders were immediately issued for cooking three days rations as preparatory for the return to Virginia.

The great battle of the Wilderness commenced on the 6th, between Generals Lee and Grant; on that day, General Longstreet was severely wounded. The enemy were repulsed at all points, and a great number of them killed, wounded and captured.

On the 9th, our tents were struck, and a general packing up ensued in the Regiment to make ready for the trip to Petersburg; we then marched into town, stacked arms in the street, and there passed the night. During the night three regiments of the Brigade and the artillery, embarked on the cars for Petersburg. The following morning we left in the train, which was laden with the pontoons of the Division; between Wilmington and Weldon, a fire having broken out in the woods, had spread to the railroad and consumed or rendered useless a portion of the ties; consequently, we were delayed at that point until the damage was repaired, which prevented our reaching Weldon until about daylight. Moving down to Bellplain, we left the train, the track in advance of us having been torn up and the bridges burned by a raiding party from the enemy. We then marched about nine miles to Stony Creek Station, where we again availed of the cars and traveled for Petersburg, arriving there on the 12th, about two o'clock P. M.

We moved about three miles from the city and encamped for the night, tired and pretty well worn, from the effects of hard marching and excessive fatigue

THE BATTLES OF FLAT CREEK AND DRURY'S BLUFF.

UPON our arrival at Petersburg, on the 12th of May, 1864, we learned that Butler had landed at City Point, with about 25,000 troops, and that several fights had already taken place. There being but a handful of men present, on Butler's arrival, General Pickett had the engines on the rail roads around fired up and moved to and fro, while their whistles resounded in the most business like manner, creating the impression, that large reinforcements were at hand, thus producing the desired effect of saving the city from capture. A force of the enemy sent to Chester Station, destroyed the railroad and burned the buildings, but they were soon after driven back, until they found protection under cover of their gunboats.

On the above date, 12th, Gen'l Beauregard arrived and assumed command of the army around Petersburg. On the morning of the 13th, we were ordered to the vicinity of Amelia Court House, on the line of the Danville Railroad, to repel a Cavalry raid, which threatened destruction to the railroad bridges in that locality. In company with the Thirtieth Virginia, we availed of the cars at Petersburg, and traveled therein as far as Burkeville Junction, and thence, were moved rapidly down the road, about twenty-six miles, to the neighborhood of two large bridges, arriving about three o'clock P. M. Just before reaching the iron bridge, the Federals made their appearance, but did not attack us, as the Eighth and Thirtieth Virginia regiments were in position to receive them. Finding the force sufficient at that point, we passed on to the wooden bridges, and took our position. Three companies of the Regiment, B, C, and I, were ordered to the bridges over Flat Creek. Company B was posted above the railroad bridge, and instructed to guard the county road bridge, which had been barricaded by order of Colonel Herbert the night before; Companies C and I were put in position below the railroad bridge; the residue of the Regiment acted as a reserve ready to reinforce either point, in case of need.

About midnight, the men were called up, the scouts having reported the enemy at the Station some two miles above; soon after, we heard the pickets, across the bridge, firing. About daylight, we moved to the bridge, and had scarcely taken position behind the embankment of the railroad, when the enemy's pickets opened fire, and our pickets were driven in.

Their main force attempted to obtain possession of the bridge, guarded by Company B, under command of Capt. Lehew. They opened upon it with artillery, then charged with a detachment of cavalry, but the steadiness with which their attack was received and responded to, forced them, after severe fighting, to retire, leaving several of their dead within a few feet of the bridge. The greatful acknowledgment of the

Company's services at this time, was publicly expressed to them by the Colonel commanding. Our loss was two killed and two wounded. Company B—Privates M. Roberts and Joseph Kellar, killed; Privates Joseph Miller, in arm, and L. Reager, (who afterwards died,) wounded.

The attack below the bridge was made by a heavy line of skirmishers, who were driven back by Companies C and I, reinforced by Company E. The battle was in progress about three hours before the enemy commenced to retire, at which time the remainder of our Regiment passed, by order, over the bridge with a line of skirmishers in front, and drove them towards Amelia Court House. We found nine of their dead on the field, and as we crossed the bridge, we captured thirteen, five of whom were wounded; we came in possession also, of a number of carbines, sabres and pistols. Most of their wounded had been carried off in ambulances; from the prisoners we learned that their force consisted of four companies of cavalry, and six pieces of artillery, under command of Gen'l Kantz.

On Sunday morning, May 15th, we marched to Powhatan Station, six miles distant, and, after remaining about an hour, received a dispatch from Richmond containing orders for a return to the bridge. Fortunately, the trains had just arrived from Richmond, thus enabling us to avail of them for transportation to our old position. Soon after, another dispatch arrived, in consequence of which we made ready for transfer to Drury's Bluff.

That evening, we passed on board the Danville railroad train, and were carried by it to Richmond, where we arrived about midnight. Passing through Manchester to the Petersburg Railroad, we found the cars in readiness for us; after riding about eight miles, we left the cars, marched down the pike, and took our position in line of battle, and under fire, losing Sergeant Major Hart and several men; the Brigade occupied the extreme right of the line, our Regiment being the second from the left.

About ten o'clock on the morning of the 16th, (Monday,) the order to charge the enemy was given, and the Brigade, composed of the Fifteenth, Seventeenth, Eighteenth, Twenty-ninth and Thirthieth Virginia Regiments, commanded by General Corse, moved against the enemy in gallant style, driving them from their fortifications, killing and wounding a great number, and capturing many prisoners. It is as well to remark here, that as the Brigade was preparing to charge, General Corse received a wound across the loins, but as in previous instances, he did not allow the injury to prevent his taking the front of the line, as it moved against the enemy. The charge was made with a vigorous yell, and the enemy was forced to retire nearly a mile from his entrenchments. After the Federals were driven from our immediate front, they still held a position on the extreme right, where we were losing heavily. When the Regiment was reformed, and joined by men and officers from the rest of the Brigade, it changed front, and by a flank fire, drove them from their last position. The injury our Regiment sustained in killed and wounded was not heavy, and the wounds of many were but slight.

Casualties at Drury's Bluff Battle, May 16, 1864.

Field and Staff—Wounded, Colonel A. Herbert, slightly; Major R. H. Simpson, leg amputated—died June 9, 1864; Ensign Robert Steele, arm, severely; Sergeant Major T. G. Hart, mouth.

Company A—Wounded, Privates S. McMurran, face, and E. T. Johns.

Company B—Killed, Private John N. Brown.

Company C—Killed, Private R. Muckle; wounded, Private J. T. Brightwell, side—mortally.

Company D—Killed, Private Robert Corbett; wounded, Private S. Spindle, leg amputated.

Company E—Wounded, Privates Wm. Underwood, knee—severely; H. C. Crowder, thigh and foot; F. Fields, J. Rudd, Geo. Summers, Chas. Arrington and —— Briggs, slightly.

Company F—Wounded, Private William Baxter, severely.

Company G—Killed, Private William Haywood; wounded, Sergeant Jas. Fisher, slight; Privates T. W. Austin, face—severely; John Harrigan, abdomen—mortally; T. G. Elliott, leg; L. Loving, slight.

Company H—Killed, Corporal John T. Mills; wounded, Captain W. H. Fowle, Jr., leg—severely.

Company I—Killed, Private Jas. Whalen.

Company K—Killed, Private H. A. R. Stanfield;

wounded, Privates Henry Briggs, shoulder; G. T. Mooney, slightly.

Recapitulation.

Killed . . . . 7 } Total, 30.
Wounded . . . . 23 }

The line then moved to the breastworks of the enemy, and the men of Company A were deployed as skirmishers; the position was strengthened, and rifle pits dug for our pickets with the shovels captured from the Federals.

A quantity of sugar, coffee, "hard tack," rubber blankets, canteens, money, watches, &c., &c., were also among the spoils.

Major Robert H. Simpson, during this engagement, received a musket shot in his knee; amputation was resorted to in the hope of saving a valuable life, but without avail; he died in Richmond, June 9, 1864. "His loss was a source of deep and painful regret to the entire Regiment; a graduate of the Virginia Military Institute, he was among the first to buckle on his sword for his country. 'As Captain of Company B, Warren Rifles,' at the organization of the Regiment, he had shared all its vicissitudes and perils up to the time of his death. Being thoroughly familiar with the duties of the officer and soldier, and with a fearless and conscientious discharge of his responsibilities, in both field and camp, he combined the qualities of an estimable gentleman with a kind and agreeable companion in arms."

After this temporarily effectual defeat of the enemy, our troops held possession of the line until evening, when, in accordance with an order received about three o'clock P. M., they moved to the extreme left, a distance of about two miles, passing under a galling fire from the enemy's artillery. Immediately after arriving, our Regiment was counter-marched, and returned to its former locality, near the Petersburg turnpike, where we formed a second line of battle in rear of the first, and passed the night, the lines continuing in undisturbed quietude.

On the morning of the 17th, our forces advanced in three columns, in the second of which our Regiment was placed. We had the satisfaction of finding that our antagonists had fallen back, upon lines around Bermuda Hundreds. The Petersburg turnpike was well strewn with broken drums, guns, cartridge boxes &c., which they had thrown away in their flight. The buildings occupied for hospital purposes, contained a number of wounded, among whom were some of our own men. A line of battle was formed in the enemy's front, and about half a mile west of the Howlett House. The position of our Regiment was near the centre, and not far distant from the building occupied by Butler, as his headquarters.

Towards midnight a strong demonstration was made in our front, and several companies were sent forward to the support of our skirmishers. The firing was prolonged for about an hour, when the enemy concluded to retire; the Regiment then resumed work upon the breastworks in course of erection. Several hours after, the Federals returned with a few pieces of Light Artillery, and a heavy fire was poured upon us the remainder of the night.

Throughout the entire day of the 18th, heavy skirmishing was going on ; a small party sent out to construct a battery, was discovered and driven back. The line was inspected by General Beauregard in the afternoon, and such changes ordered as his unquestionably military genius suggested.

On the 19th, the gunboats opened on our line and continued their shelling operation at intervals during the whole day; one of our Regiment, Geo. W. Rancy, Company C, was deprived of his legs, poor fellow, by a piece of shell, whilst in front of the pickets.

General Corse's Brigade left the trenches on the James river, after night on the 19th, and marched to Richmond city, where it halted in the Capitol Square, and remained until the next morning about three o'clock A. M., when the trains on the Fredericksburg Railroad transported it to Penola Station, thirty-two miles from Richmond. About three o'clock in the afternoon of the same day, (20th,) upon which we arrived at Penola, information was received that the raiders were moving upon Chesterfield Station ; leaving two regiments to protect Penola, the remainder of the Brigade, (our Regiment included,) moved forward to intercept them. After marching about three and a half miles, we came to the road over which the enemy must necessarily pass in order to reach the

Station; here, we threw out skirmishers, formed line of battle, and awaited their approach. About dark, General Rosser's Brigade of cavalry joined us, with a batallion of artillery. They had been watching the movements of the enemy, and reported his cavalry supported by a corps of infantry. It afterwards came to light that General Corse had been endeavoring to entrap General Hancock's Corps. A mighty deed, if it could have been carried out, considering the small Brigade commanded by the former.

We rested on our arms the night of the 21st, which passed quietly. On the 22d, we moved a short distance, fronting the railroad, and again formed in line of battle, but were soon after ordered to Hanover Junction. The armies of both Generals Lee and Grant were at this time moving in direction of Richmond, General Lee, however, having the inside track.

Just before reaching the North Anna river, we overtook General Ewell's Corps, marching towards our destination; we halted until it had passed, when we fell into line of General Longstreet's Corps, then under command of General Anderson; we marched all night, halted south of the North Anna, and bivouaced. There was sharp skirmishing between the cavalry forces beyond the river, on the 23d. In the afternoon of the same day, our Division moved to the neighborhood of the Junction, and being held as a reserve, encamped in a piece of woods, but before the night was over we were ordered to the front.

General Grant's attempts at flanking General Lee,

had all proved abortive, so he had rested for a short time on the North Anna, where our army watched his every movement. Fortifications were thrown up by our forces, and preparations made for battle, but our opponents, for very good reasons, declined making an attack at that time.

On the 27th, General Grant moved on, followed by our army, which kept pace with his movements, until arriving at Cold Harbor, when the two again faced, built very strong fortifications, and rested awhile.

On the 31st, Butler having withdrawn his army from the neighborhood of Petersburg, General Beauregard's troops passed through Richmond and added their strength to the army of General Lee.

On the 3d of June, a part of our line near Cold Harbor was assaulted, and after a very bloody battle, the assaulting party was repulsed with very heavy loss in killed, wounded and prisoners; our loss was comparatively light. Our Regiment, with the brigade, was daily engaged in heavy skirmishing, equal in losses and hard fighting to many of the earlier battles of the war.

On the 7th, the line of skirmishers in front of our Regiment advanced, drove the enemy out of his first line of breastworks and made a picket line of it. Our loss was two wounded, both mortally. Private Wm. Terrett, of Company H, and Sergeant J. W. Newcomb, of Company D. Privates A. G. Embrey, Company K, and Wm. Hickson, Company B, were also killed while on this line.

The lines were strong with abatis in front; about three hundred yards in front of our Brigade, our pickets were posted, while those of the enemy were about one hundred yards distant, and his main line of battle behind strong earthworks, about seventy yards beyond them. Music from the bands of the enemy was of no unfrequent occurrence; on one occasion they struck up "Dixie," which brought forth on our side, a loud and prolonged cheer; immediately, that was succeeded by "Yankee Doodle," when a thundering groan was emitted, while the Yankees cheered lustily. Our rations whilst on this line were ample and of a superior quality to those ordinarily issued; bacon, corn meal, coffee, sugar, salt and rice or beans, were issued every day.

16*

THE SUMMER OF 1864.

On the 13th of June, our troops were in motion early, in consequence of the enemy having withdrawn from the front of General Lee's army during the previous night.   About eight o'clock the Corps moved, crossed the Chickahominy on the McClellan bridge, passed over the battle fields of Seven Pines and Frazier's Farm, and about the same hour P. M., encamped near Malvern Hill.   General Grant was evidently making for the Southside, so the main part of our army marched down within striking distance of the nearest point needed by them.

About five o'clock A. M., on the 15th, after our Division had received marching orders, they were countermanded, just as the rear brigade was moving out of camp; thereupon, we returned, resuming our old position.   The next morning, (16th,) at daylight we moved, crossed the James river on the pontoon bridge at Drury's, and marched in direction of Petersburg.   As the head of the column, passing leisurely along, reached a point some five miles from the above-mentioned city, it was fired upon by the enemy. Skirmishers were immediately thrown out, and the troops of that portion of the column formed in line of battle; they soon discovered that the enemy's troops were in possession of our breastworks; (General Beauregard having been forced to withdraw most of his troops from them, in order to defend Petersburg, leaving only a skirmish line for their protection.) General Hunton's skirmishers attacked them so vigorously, as to drive them back. Our Brigade moved down through the woods, until it reached the first line of breastworks. The Fifteenth Virginia, and some companies from the Seventh Virginia Regiment were then deployed beyond the fortifications as skirmishers, while the residue of the Brigade marched by the right-flank down the earthworks, until reaching that portion thrown up by them on the 17th ultimo; here, the pickets of the enemy appeared in front, and we exchanged fire.

By this time our skirmishers arrived, and the order to charge having been given them, they obeyed with alacrity, driving the Federals, first from their rifle-pits, and then from their line of earthworks. Our Regiment moved forward, took possession of these breastworks and threw out pickets; one-third of the men were ordered to remain up at a time, ready for duty during the night.

Just before daylight, on the following morning, the other regiments of the Brigade marched forward to our position, and the Seventeeth Virginia was ordered to the front as skirmishers. We deployed and took position in a ravine, some three hundred yards from the breastworks; we had hardly arrived, when the Federals opened on us briskly. Their fire was quickly returned, and thus, for an hour, the picket fight was continued; the enemy occupied rifle-pits and a *Church*, about four hundred yards in our front. ·

About three o'clock P. M., our Regiment was relieved and returned to the main line; just after, our artillery opened a heavy fire upon the enemy; loud musketry then commenced in front, our troops having attacked, and driven their's from a portion of our old position they had continued to hold.

On the 18th, the position of our Brigade was changed to the occupancy of that part of the line nearest the Howlett House, on the James river. Our Regiment was posted on the right, about half a mile from the river.

About four o'clock in the afternoon of the 18th, our artillery opened a rapid fire upon the enemy, which continued thirty minutes; our pickets then advanced, drove the Yankees out of their rifle-pits, and established our skirmish line in advance of our old one. We had one man wounded only, while we captured a few prisoners from them.

The fortifications on the south side at that time were defended by Pickett's Division, and became known as the "Howlett's Line;" they extended not quite three miles in length, from the James to the Appomattox rivers, and consisted of a heavy line of earthworks along the entire distance, with felled trees at intervals in front, and rifle-pits, for the protection of the pickets, still beyond. Heavy guns were mounted at the Howlett House, overlooking the river, to guard against the passage of gunboats up the stream; occasionally the guns were put in requisition, and then, heavy cannonading proceeded therefrom.

General Grant's army was on the south side of the Appomattox, next to Petersburg; his lines extended from the river, in a semi-circular shape, to a point beyond the P. & N. R. R.   General Smith's Corps, (10th,) was in front of the Howlett's Line.   On the 19th, the complimentary order of General Lee, upon the gallantry of our Division in recapturing the works on the 16th, was read to the regiments.

On the 20th, our Brigade moved further to the left, allowing space for General Davis' Brigade to take position in the line.   A very sad accident occurred in the Regiment soon after moving.   Adam Goucher, of Company I, accidently discharged his gun, the load of which, passing through his head, killed him instantly. At night, the pickets in front of our Regiment were advanced about two hundred yards without meeting with any trouble, thus securing a better position.

On the 21st, the Confederate gunboats on the James, moved a little below the Howlett House, and, in conjunction with our heavy land batteries, opened fire on the fleet of the enemy, which replied promptly, and thus the fight was kept up all the afternoon, though but little damage was done; one of the heavy land guns at Howlett's was dismounted, and one man wounded.

The following day, our scouts, who were kept in front to watch the movements of the Federals, reported a very perceptible stir among them, hence, orders were issued to prepare for action, but as it amounted to nothing, we resumed our original state of quietude.

About four o'clock on the 23d of June, our batteries opened, but received no reply; after continuing the fire for at least one hour, we desisted. There was but little picket firing, at this time, along the line. Some several days previously, a considerable force of the enemy had re-crossed the James river and entrenched themselves at Deep Bottom. Our removal further to the right, on the 24th, thinned the line, one brigade already having been sent across the James. There was artillery firing nearly all day, from which the woods in our front were set on fire, and numbers of shells that fell and had not exploded were bursted at intervals through the day, as the heat reached them, rendering them far from agreeable neighbors.

A number of deserters came in at various times, on the Howlett's Line, from some of whom valuable information was obtained. The 4th of July passed away very quietly, the position in front of Bermuda Hundreds not being attacked, as many of the men supposed it would have been. The month of July glided past, causing no change whatever in our position. The regular picket guard was daily sent forward, the men remained at their posts, and extraordinary quiet reigned. The pickets often exchanged newspapers, and conversed with each other across the lines, portions of which were only a short distance apart. Being on such good terms, there was, of course, no firing indulged in; occasionally, a cannon shot was fired, or the guns on the river bank opened on the fleet; with these exceptions, the days were Sunday-like in their dullness, while the men were not at all injured by extra duty.

An attack was expected on the night of the 29th, which did not take place. About 4 o'clock on the morning of the 30th, General Grant's long-talked of *Mine,* was sprung. The explosion took place on the line around Petersburg, under a battery posted at Elliott's salient, and about one and a half miles from the city. The breastwork was demolished, and the earth, for a space of about 250 feet in circumference, violently thrown out, leaving a hole about 40 feet deep. The battery, (men and guns,) with three companies of infantry, (who occupied the redoubt as a support to the battery,) were thrown high into the air, and shared a most heart-rending death. Before the smoke had cleared away, a heavy force of the enemy, massed for the purpose, were hurried forward and occupied the breach made in our fortifications; their guns from all sides opened, and a general hubbub ensued.

The Confederate troops on either side of the breach, were, at first, thrown into much confusion, but soon rallied, and closing upon the enemy, fought with desperation; but it was quite impossible for so small a force to battle with successful results against about one-third of General Grant's army; consequently, they were compelled to fall back, though but a short distance. The enemy, pushing his men through the breach, occupied about 300 yards of our line. General Mahone arrived just about this time, and, encouraging our men by his presence, succeeded in forcing back a large portion of the enemy, capturing great numbers of prisoners, and occupying a part of the works.

Later in the day, another attack was made upon him, and he was entirely driven out, leaving numbers of his dead on the field, 855 men, 74 officers, (including one Brigadier General and his staff,) 12 stands of colors, and 4 pieces of artillery, in our possession.

Their loss in killed and wounded was unquestionably heavy, judging from the numbers of their white and negro soldiers left on the field. Our loss was small; the enemy gained nothing by this great event, from which their people had seemed to anticipate so much, the time at which it was expected to transpire having been announced by their newspapers.

On the same day, (30th,) one of our Brigade, belonging to the Thirtieth Virginia, was shot for desertion to the enemy; having been caught with a party of Federal raiders, he was recognized, tried, and condemned; his execution took place at 12 o'clock, M.

On the 1st of August, 1864, a flag of truce was sent in by General Grant, asking the privilege of burying his dead. It was granted, causing, for the first time in months that had passed, a general quiet, for five hours, on the lines around Petersburg. At the expiration of the truce, the guns and mortars of the Federals re-opened. On the 5th of August, the enemy opened a "Masked Battery," and the night was made hideous with the shot and shells spluttering around; the gunboats and land batteries also opened, and the uproar was prolonged for hours. At this time, the wells, which had been ordered to be dug in rear of each regiment on the Howlett's Line, had been completed, resulting in supplies of excellent water

About this time, a law creating an Invalid Corps having been passed, Colonel M. Marye asked to be transferred to it, so that his Regiment might have a full compliment of field officers, and Lieutenant Colonel A. Herbert might be promoted to the rank of Colonel, the duties of which office he was filling so acceptably to all. His request was complied with by the War Department, and Lieutenant Colonel Herbert promoted to the Colonelcy. Captain Grayson Tyler, who had been acting Major of the Regiment since the fall of Major R. H. Simpson, was promoted to the Lieutenant Colonelcy.

The troops fared well, though all merchantable articles, especially edibles, were at exorbitant prices: Potatoes, $4 per quart. Onions, cymlings, and tomatoes, from 75 cents to $1 each. Pies from $2.50 to $3 apiece, according to size. Cider, $1 per quart. Apples, from $2 to $3 per dozen. Our soldiers' pay was $16 per month.

On the night of the 5th of August, the small mine, completed under the enemy's picket line and a sap that they were working in front of Gracie's salient, on the Petersburg side of the Appomattox, was sprung by our troops, blowing up the Federal skirmish line, and completely demolishing the work under the sap, thus entirely frustrating their purpose. Their troops, for a while, were thrown into great confusion, thinking, perhaps, that we were about to attack them, but as no such thing had been intended by our army, the scene closed with a fierce artillery duel.

General Lee, in company with General Pickett, inspected the Howlett's Line on the 10th of August. They were also present at the shelling of the enemy's camps and batteries near Dutch Gap, from our batteries at Howlett's, on the 12th; we had one man killed and six men wounded in the fight.

About the 14th, General Grant moved a considerable part of his army to the north side of the James river, and, for several days, the air was filled with the thunderings of artillery from that direction. Several divisions from the Petersburg line, and three regiments from ours, were sent over, and hard fighting took place; but as the Federals gained nothing, by the 19th most of their troops had returned to the south side.

Heavy fighting took place on our extreme right, near the Weldon Railroad, during the 19th, 20th, and 21st instants, when the enemy succeeded in gaining a foothold and fortifying himself. They lost heavily in both killed and captured, but with forces so numerically superior to our own, an immense depletion in their rank and file would have been necessary before they could have had cause to feel that they had sustained serious loss.

Not long before daylight on the 25th, the men of our Regiment were awakened by the discharge of musketry on their right; tumbling out and forming into line was but a minute's work; we soon discovered that our skirmishers were charging the enemy's pickets, in order to get possession of a ridge in front of Generals Barton's and Hunton's brigades.

The right advanced first, then the left; the latter was repulsed by the enemy, and our loss was considerable. The right, consisting of Generals Barton's and Hunton's brigades, drove the Federals from their rifle-pits, killing and wounding some, and capturing 59 prisoners. Soon after, however, the enemy having received reinforcements, drove back General Hunton's men, but General Barton retained the position captured in front of his line. Our Regiment had five wounded and one captured; after about two hours' fighting, quiet was again restored and time passed off as usual.

The following day, (26th,) a heavy battle occurred on our extreme right, in the vicinity of Rheim's Station. The Federal cavalry were employing themselves in tearing up the track of the Weldon Railroad, and, whilst thus engaged, General Hampton, with his cavalry, overhauled them, driving them back beyond their infantry supports, and then, dismounting his men, he fought their infantry, driving them back upon their strong works, and capturing some 800 prisoners.

At this time, General A. P. Hill's Corps advanced, made a vigorous attack upon their strong position, and, completely routing them, succeeded in capturing their breastworks, together with a large number of prisoners, 9 pieces of artillery, and 7 stands of colors.

During this period, prayer meetings, morning and evening, were held in our Brigade camp, and many determined to relinquish the fleeting pleasures of worldly enjoyment, and become followers of that Saviour who bids all: "Take my yoke upon you, and learn of me; for I am meek and lowly in heart, and ye shall find rest for your souls, for my yoke is easy and my burden is light." A Christian Association had also been formed, of which Colonel Herbert was President. Such meetings and associations served greatly to lighten the toils, trials, and monotonies of camp life.

The fever and ague having broken out amongst the men, spread to an alarming extent; more than half the men of one of our regiments were confined with them, and among the members of one battery, near us, there was not a sufficiency of men well enough to work their guns.

The Dutch Gap sappers and miners, furnished by Butler, were very frequently much annoyed by our mortar shelling, and their work progressed slowly. The Gap is a narrow neck of land running out towards, and not very far from, the Howlett House, but on the opposite side of the river. This neck making a great curve in the James River, Butler expected, by ditching, or canal making, to pass our obstructions and batteries without trouble; as disappointment comes least to those who expect least, he found this road a hard one to travel.

On the 10th of September, one of our Regiment, Cologne, Co. K, was captured whilst on post beyond the pickets.

September was a quiet month for our Regiment, there being but little fighting, and our duty not being at all heavy. During the latter part of the month, General Longstreet, having recovered from his wound, returned to his Corps, and, on the 28th, in company with Generals Pickett and Corse, he appeared along our line; had not the fear of drawing upon the party a fire from the enemy restrained them, the boys would have given "Old Pete," as many of them called him, a rousing cheer of satisfaction.

Fort Harrison, on the north side of the James, was attacked at an early hour on the morning of the 29th, and captured. One regiment from each brigade of our Division was ordered to the scene of conflict, and, on the following day, our forces attacked the enemy, making two attempts to recapture the Fort, both of which were unsuccessful. In the afternoon of the same day, a terrific cannonading, coupled with heavy picket firing, was indulged in on the Petersburg line; the noise was continued, without intermission, until late in the night.

It is only those who have witnessed such rifle and mortar shelling as frequently took place upon the above mentioned line, from over 500 guns and mortars at a time, can comprehend the grandeur of the scene; words are inadequate to describe the feelings of the beholder, as myriads of shells and shot, rising, falling, crossing, curving, and bursting, in awful splendor, in the front, to the right, left, and rear of his position; illumining the heavens with their glare, for miles.

The ditching of Butler's famous Dutch Gap Canal continued, and, during September, numerous attempts were made by our forces, with heavy land batteries, in conjunction with the James river fleet, to break up the work, but, like a ground hog, he continued his burrowing, and the stronger the endeavor to unearth him, the more obstinately he persisted in his work.

The many hard fought battles that had transpired on different parts of the line, the diminished fare issued to the troops, and the monotonous life led by them in the trenches, were begining to shew their effects very plainly in the spirit of depression to which many of the men were succumbing. For over three years they had battled in defence of all that was dear to them in life, with gallantry and zeal well nigh unexampled in the annals of the history of any nation. The results of the sacrifices they had so cheerfully endured were disheartening in the extreme; hemmed in on all sides by an invading host, whose majority was composed of the refuse population from every point of the compass, afforded but little prospect for the establishment of that liberty, in the defence of which, so many noble Southern hearts, passed from the tumult of the battle field, to the Court of their God.

Notwithstanding this depression, notwithstanding the fact that they had scarcely space allowed them for necessary bodily exercise, their escutcheon remained untarnished. Battles were yet to be fought in which that energy, the most powerful capacity of which is the offspring of trial and suffering, and the instigator to unparalelled exertion, must shew itself equal to the emergency. There were but few, if any, delinquents from duty, in these trying scenes, among those enrolled as members of the Seventeenth Vi—————

The history of a regiment, in contrast with that of an army, is seemingly but a small affair, yet, in the hearts of the relatives and friends of the members of a single company, the record of the entire outside world is insignificant indeed, in comparison with that which chronicles the chivalrous deeds and unblemished reputation of the atom, as it were, with whose honor is identified that of their own and their neighbor's households.

THE WINTER OF '64 AND '65.

THE month of October, 1864, opened with a heavy rain; the water pouring down in torrents, rendered camp life in the trenches, not altogether as agreeable as it might have been, under other circumstances.

General Forrest was busy in the rear of Sherman's army in the West, destroying the railroads and cutting off his supplies; General Beauregard had been sent from the army of Northern Virginia, to the command of two departments in the South, embracing General Hood's army, and those of our forces in Florida and around Charleston, South Carolina; the latter named place was in command of General Hardee; Butler was still engaged in digging at Dutch Gap, under severe artillery shelling, whilst General Lee and his men, were in and around Richmond and Petersburg, defending the Capitol of the Nation. The position of our army remained unaltered, while the daily crack of the sharpshooter's rifle and the quick report of the bursting shells, resounded from the hills around, as of yore.

No new attempt at a "grand flank movement" had been indulged in by General Grant, with his hordes of well-fed soldiers, consequently, time passed in the ordinary routine of duties, varied at times by heavy artillery duels, conducted between the land batteries of the enemy near Dutch Gap, and our own guns at

the Howlett House. Our terribly thinned line of
half famished men, held their own before the swarm-
ing ranks of the army of the Potomac, which were on
both sides of the James and Appomattox rivers; the
bulk of its forces had been withdrawn from the North
to the South side, and resting near City Point from
their toils and losses in the battles near Fort Harrison,
were busily concocting new movements.

On the 7th of the month, at an early hour, a brigade
of our cavalry supported by infantry, made an attack
upon the enemy, posted, with their right wing resting
on the Charles city road, and their main infantry force
near Fort Harrison, and drove them from two lines
of intrenchments, forcing them back upon the New
Market road, upon a third line of heavy works. We
captured ten pieces of artillery, with their caisons and
horses, and a number of prisoners; our loss was but
slight. General Gregg fell in this battle, at the head
of his Brigade, nobly doing his duty.

During the first of this month, the men on the
Howlett's Line were kept busy arranging for winter
quarters; log huts covered with boards, were erected
near the line, and the rifle-pits in front were also
covered to protect the pickets from the weather.

This line had become so quiet, and the picket firing
so unfrequent, that it was no longer necessary for the
troops to shelter themselves behind the earthworks,
hence, they could sleep once more above ground, with
a feeling of security.

On the 13th, the enemy made another effort to advance his position on the North side, but his attempts were all fruitless. His final effort for that day, was made in the afternoon, when he brought a superior force against that portion of our fortifications (on the North side); this, however, though more gigantic than his former operations, was equally unavailing, for he was handsomely repulsed, losing heavily, after which he withdrew his forces within his own entrenchments.

On the 17th, one hundred and eight of our Regiment, volunteered to assist in building a church, in which the Brigade might hold its meetings, and worship in spirit and in truth the " Father of light, from whom cometh down, every good and every perfect gift, with whom is no variableness, neither shadow of turning." The work was commenced on the same day; the men were regularly detailed to assist in its erection. The members of Parker's Battery, occupying a redoubt between our Regiment, and the Fifteenth Virginia, also lent their assistance.

The guns from the enemy's land batteries on the North side, kept up a brisk fire for about two hours, on the 22d, to which there was prompt response from our gunboats lying in the stream; the result, however, amounted to nothing.

The ranks of our army were greatly augmented in consequence of an order, recalling all able-bodied men on detached service, back to their regiments, and, during the beautiful weather with which we were favoured in October, the troops having regained their former buoyancy, looked forward with the eagerness of yore to an encounter with the enemy.

When the church was completed, it was at once put in requisition for our daily prayer meetings, which were usually conducted by the Chaplain of our Regiment, Mr. Baker; they were always well attended by the men. A spirit of grace seemed to pervade a greater portion of the army; numbers came forward, avowing a lively hope of an inheritance in that better land reserved for the faithful followers of Christ. It was truly heart-thrilling to hear the songs of praise ascending upon the twilight air from that band of warriors, ready to obey the first summons to the field of battle, where, perhaps, they were to meet death at the onset; and, while the heart thus thrilled with the melody of human voices, joy unspeakable was born of the knowledge that many in those ranks were doubly soldiers. Those who had enrolled under the Heavenly banner, resolved to "fight the good fight of faith," viewed with an eye of calmness the approach of any ordeal through which they might be called to pass, trusting in the Omnipotent for a happy result.

Had the remainder of our army and our people been equally trustful in Him, our highest anticipations might have been fully realized.

On the 27th, General Mahone attacked the enemy on our right, about seven miles from Petersburg; captured 400 prisoners, 3 stands of colors, and 6 pieces of artillery, with but a very small loss on our side. The enemy, in turn, attacked him, when three of their lines were broken; at night they fell back, leaving their wounded and upwards of 250 dead on the field. We were also successful in the battle on the north side, General Fields capturing 500 prisoners and 7 stands of colors.

The rations issued to the troops on the Howlett's Line, at this time, consisted of a third of a pound of bacon, one pound of flour, and a tablespoonfull of rice, per diem.

The new church was first occupied for Division service on the 30th, when a sermon from Rev. Mr. Baker was listened to with interest by a large assemblage of soldiers.

The Regiment was, at this time, making a daily detail of forty men for picket, and, at night, fifteen men for guard duty on the parapet; the number of men present for duty in the Regiment did not exceed 250.

On the night of the 30th, General Mahone, with a part of his Division, penetrated the enemy's picket line in his front, and captured 230 men and officers, without losing a man.

On the 1st of November, General Lee, in person, accompanied by his staff, inspected the Howlett's Line.

As some of our men had deserted to the enemy, during the recent trials and sufferings in the trenches, General Pickett issued an order, offering 20 days furlough to each one who should arrest a soldier attempting to desert, or 30 days to each one who should fire upon and thus secure the body of a deserter. The adoption of this method was productive, beyond doubt,

Everything remained unusally quiet on the Howlett's Line during the first half of the month of
November; the daily morning and evening Prayer
meetings were never neglected in our Regiment; th e
men employed themselves in a variety of ways, when
not on duty; game abounded, affording sport as well
as luxury to our huntsmen; snares were placed, and
many a rabbit paid the forfeit for meddling with them.
The huts were well attended to and kept in the state of
cleanliness, so in conformity with gentlemanly taste.
The position was somewhat strengthened by a second
abatis in front.

On the night of the 17th November, the pickets in
front of Generals Hunton's and Stewart's Brigades,
attacked the enemy's pickets, and forced them back
upon their reserves; we captured one hundred and
twenty prisoners, including one Colonel, two Captains,
and two Lieutenants. In front of General Hunton's
line, our pickets were only about fifty yards in advance, so by occupying the posts vacated by the enemy
we were enabled to straighten our picket line, and
while so doing, place it at a greater distance from our
main trenches. Our injuries in this little fight, (mostly
to General Hunton's Brigade,) were one killed and
nine wounded.

It was expected by the troops on our side, that the
enemy would atttempt to re-capture the position on
the following night, but they were disappointed, though
not disagreeably so, as they were not disturbed, except
by occasional picket firing; the 19th was not so quiet,

cannonading and picket firing continuing throughout the day.

The nights of the 20th, 21st, and 22d, were very trying upon the pickets in front; heavy rains filled the rifle-pits, and as the enemy kept up a continual fire from videttes stationed at the various points, the troops were subjected to great danger from inability to screen themselves therefrom, in consequence of the water in the ditches.

It was ascertained on the 22d, that the skirmish line in front of our Regiment, was composed entirely of negro troops; many of the boys were in favor of a charge upon them, but there were no orders to that effect and the negroes remained.

The Regiment received orders on the 24th, to prepare two days rations, and to keep in readiness to move at a moment's notice, which was obeyed, but the cause which prompted this was probably removed, as we heard nothing further in connection with it.

A negro deserter came in on the Howlett's Line, on the night of the 26th, and gave quite a sad account of the ill treatment received by those of his complexion from their emancipation champions. During the latter part of the month, orders were received for us to maintain a sharp picket fire upon the negroes, so long as they remained in our front, whilst our batteries were to shell them at intervals.

The continued activity and frequent conflicts between the lines, did not prevent the men from attending daily worship in their comfortable chapel. The

Rev. Dr. Stiles spent a week in our camps and preached daily to attentive congregations. The spirit was moving in the midst of the camp fires and many precious souls were brought into His service.

Several engagements had taken place on the river, between the land batteries and the gunboats, by which very little was accomplished on either side, except a a great waste of powder and iron, attended with unmusical sounds.

The negroes were withdrawn from in front of the Howlett's Line, in the early part of December, thus restoring quiet again to the pickets.

Several demonstrations were made on the 10th of December; one of which was by General Longstreet, on the North side; he moved forward his troops, and finding only a line of pickets in his front, he forced them back to the New Market road, where encountering a heavy force well entrenched, he at once withdrew and occupied his former position; the purpose of the movement having been to ascertain as far as practicable, the enemy's strength.

Another was made by the enemy on our extreme right; they moved in a large body in direction of Weldon. Our cavalry pickets on the Vaughn road were driven in, and the Federals advanced towards Dinwiddie Court House. Our cavalry, reinforced by infantry, attacked and drove them back, after which, our lines were re-established; we then pursued the enemy into their own intrenchments.

On the 12th, Bishop Johns visited our Brigade, and

held regular service in the new chapel; sixteen soldiers
were confirmed by him; he had performed the same
rites for many in the other brigades of our Division,
but a few days previous; it was indeed encouraging
to the lovers of God, thus to see the manifestations of
His spirit at work upon the hearts of their comrades
in arms; men who, above all others, needed the con-
soling power of His precious promises, as unfolded in
the Gospel.

Christmas day passed very quietly. There were
neither fine dinners nor jovial parties to be found
among the troops on the Howlett's Line; some apple-
dumplings were enjoyed in camp, and several invita-
tions were extended by the Yanks for our pickets "to
step over and drink with them," but these were
declined.

An elegant dinner of the "good things of life" was
received by our Regiment, on the 29th, from the citizens living in the vicinity of Flat Creek, in token of
their appreciation of our successes in defending the
bridges near that point in May, 1864. The substantials and delicacies were alike acceptable, and received
unequivocal attention from each recipient, as the following announcement will show:

[FROM THE RICHMOND PAPERS.]

"The following is nobly conceived and beautifully said; and it
comes from a regiment that, from the 18th of July, 1861, to this
day, has signalized its courage on as many battle-fields, and won
as proud a name, as any that marches under the banners of our
beloved Confederacy. '

"We take much pleasure in complying with the request to
publish it:

"CAMP SEVENTEENTH VIRGINIA INFANTRY, ⎱
"January 1, 1865. ⎰

" *To the Citizens of Amelia county, Va.:*

"With much gratitude and pleasure, we acknowledge the receipt of your liberal donation of a Christmas dinner, through the hands of Rev. Mr. Littleton—a donation all the more appreciated from its being unexpected."

"We accept it as a spontaneous overflow of kind sympathy for soldiers unknown to you, and whose only claim upon your notice was a simple act of duty. As refugees, we appreciate the donation highly, and still more the motive that prompted it. It adds another incentive to nerve us for coming trials and dangers in a cause so sacred and dear to us all, and we will ever look back upon it as a pleasant episode in our history as a Regiment."

"May a kind Providence ever protect the homes and hearth-stones of such friendly and sympathetic hearts."

"We send you our greetings for the New Year: May it be a happy and prosperous one, and may you ever have as willing hearts to defend you, in your need, as beat in the breasts of your friends,"

"THE OFFICERS AND SOLDIERS OF THE

"SEVENTEENTH VIRGINIA INFANTRY."

The people of Richmond, and of other parts of the State, attempted to raise, by contribution, a grand New Year's dinner for General Lee's army, and after a great flourish of trumpets through the mouths of the daily papers, for at least some ten days previous to the time—it came.

It was certainly a large donation, and spoke well for the generosity of its donors, but there was bad management in its distribution; consequently, great waste. Our Regiment received 42 pounds of meat, 20 loaves of bread, and 1 peck of vegetables—a quantity insufficient for more than one company, hence, the different companies concluded to draw lots for it, and Co. B was the winner.

The soldiers in the trenches having heard of this prospective *feast*, as a natural consequence, had their mouths watering in anticipation; and had pictured for their own special enjoyment, smoking turkeys, with gravy sauce and stuffing, mince pies, and currant tarts, while some, no doubt, had visions of " plum-pudding;" but, alas! for such expectations! they toiled on, poor fellows! without realizing any nearer enjoyment of tempting viands than was afforded by their daily rations.

The New Year opened with cold, piercing weather, and the ground covered with snow; the pickets of both armies hugged their little fires closely, and there was *almost* quiet along the lines.   The frequent shelling at Petersburg afforded remunerative employment to the soldiers of our army, who gathered in many a dollar from the sale of shells, (whole or in pieces,) bullets, and balls.   They were disposed of to their Brigade Ordnance Officer, who had instructions to pay a stipulated amount, per pound, for all that should be delivered to him.

On the night of the 4th of January, 1865, after a sojourn of nearly seven months on the Howlett's Line, in front of Bermuda Hundreds, orders were received for our Regiment to move out from the trenches. About 9 o'clock, Hunton's Brigade passed down and occupied our position; after which, our Regiment, in company with the Brigade, marched in direction of

Chaffin's Bluff.   The night was intensely cold; to men who had been seven long months cooped up, it was pleasure indeed to be at liberty to stretch their limbs once more upon a march.   Arriving at the river, the pontoon bridge was crossed, and our destination, (Fort Gilmer, a large structure situated about one and a half miles from the river,) reached about half-past two o'clock in the morning.   The brigade on duty was relieved, and the men who were disengaged turned in to sleep in the tents vacated by the troops recently quartered there.   The camp was miserably constructed, rendering the change from the pleasant houses on the Howlett's Line far from an inviting one.   Our Regiment was posted on the left of the Brigade, and between Forts, Gilmer and Gregg.

The Federal picket line was about half a mile in front, where they were clearly visible, as were their fortifications, about 400 yards in their rear.   Fuel was so scarce that the men suffered terribly from the heavy rains, being unable to build sufficient fire to warm themselves.   The rations issued to us, while on the North side, were less in quantity and inferior in quality, especially the meal, which, at times, was so musty as to render it far from palatable.   But the men, most of whom were reared in affluence, rarely uttered a complaint, being perfectly aware of the condition to which the Commissary Department was reduced in regard to stores.   Our camp, too, was in horrid condition, being over shoe-top in mud and water.

In front of the lines on the North side, where we

were stationed, torpedoes had been placed, which were so arranged as to require but the weight of seven pounds to cause their explosion; they were made of thirty-two pound shells, having attached to them sensitive primers, which when stepped upon would produce a sudden upheaval of the earth, from which damage was likely to ensue to the trespasser.

The Brigade remained in this position until the latter part of February. Many of our men were without overcoats, and during the cold, raw, freezing nights of January and February, picket duty was no child's play.

Somewhere about the 20th of February, the Brigade was withdrawn, and marched back to its old position on the Howlett's Line; really glad were the officers and men to re-occupy their former quarters.

It was during this month that General R. E. Lee, was made Commander-in-Chief of the Armies of the Confederate States, and the appointment was hailed with expressions of delight by every soldier in his army. But, too late came the appointment, and as we draw near to the closing scenes of this four years struggle through which the army of Northern Virginia remained unwavering in their allegiance, and prompt in the performance of duty, from first to last, affectionate admiration for this great military Chieftain, will rise pre-eminent in the mind of the Southern reader; the mildew of time will never mar the brightness of his escutcheon, nor blot from our hearts the cherished image of our Military Father, for as such

From his kind indulgence and ever watchful care, for the welfare of his men—from his every act which marks him *"a chevalier sans peur, sans reproche,"* arises that unquenchable love which will survive in the bosoms of remote generations and quicken into being again as we shall gather in the land of love, where "time shall be no more."

The following is a partial list of Casualities in our Regiment, while occupying the Howlett's Line:

Private W. Fara, Company B, wounded; Private H. Garner, Company C, killed; Privates P. Gooding and G. S. Millan, Company D, wounded; Sergeant B. F. Fields and Private John Allison, Company E, wounded, the latter mortally; and Privates A. Harris and J. O. Pemberton, Company K, wounded.

THE LAST MONTH'S CAMPAIGN.

THE dark days were casting their mantle around us, as the month of March, 1865, with its thawing ice and swollen streams, opened its first dawn upon the Howlett's Line. Despondency, occasioned by late reverses to the Confederate arms, was leaving its impress, too plainly to be misunderstood, and, yet, the men of our Division determined to stand unfalteringly by the Confederacy to its latest breath, be the result what it might.

On the 4th of the month, orders were received by the Division for active field service, and, about daylight on the following morning, General Mahone's Division arrived; our command moved to the rear about three-quarters of a mile, and stacked arms in a large field.

Soon after, the wagons came up, and three days' rations were issued; the troops were then moved into a piece of woods near the turnpike and went into camp.

On the morning of the 7th, at 9 o'clock, a review of the Division was made; this exhibition of the men was a fine sight, after a winter of trench duty; 6,400 muskets were in line. Soon after, Generals Hunton's and Stewart's brigades were ordered off, and took the road to Richmond.

The residue of our Division remained near the Howlett's Line, until the night of the 9th, when, about 8 o'clock, it marched to Manchester, arriving there about 3 o'clock in the morning, after a muddy, and, consequently, a heavy march. It rained all night; about daylight it commenced snowing, and, during the day, continued to rain, snow, and hail, rendering the camp anything but pleasant.

The Federal raiders, at this time, were making havoc along the canal, and on the railroads above Richmond; the object in our Division's moving was to counteract these manœuvres as much as possible, and render such assistance as was in its power to our exhausted, decimated cavalry. Early on the morning of the 12th, the two brigades moved across Mayo's bridge, and marched up Main street, and taking the Brooke Turnpike, moved onward to the outer line of defences, where they formed in line of battle, anticipating an attack from a body of the enemy's cavalry, near the city.

The alarm bells in the city had been rung the preceding night, and the local troops were out in strong force to help repel the invasion. A brigade of Mahone's Division also arrived, and took position in the line. About 3 o'clock, P. M., our Regiment marched down the Military road to the Nine Mile road, distant about five miles, it being supposed that the enemy's infantry would advance from that direction as a support to their cavalry.

At daylight on the following morning, we again changed position, and marched to a point on the "Works" between the Meadow Bridge and the Mechanicsville road, when the Regiment was posted at different points on the line.

The next day, (14th,) the Brigade again marched, followed by the Division, (Generals Hunton's and Stewart's brigades having returned,) taking the Brooke Turnpike. General Longstreet was in command. After dark, the Division halted about twelve miles from Richmond, and formed in battle array on the crest of a hill overlooking Totopotamy Creek. Artillery and cavalry composed a part of the command; the object of the move was to intercept the raiders.

On the 15th, at an early hour, we again started, the Fifteenth and Seventeenth Virginia Regiments in advance, deployed as skirmishers; after marching about one and a half miles, the skirmishers of the Fifteenth came upon the enemy, when some little firing ensued, by which the latter were easily driven back. The Fifteenth had one man killed and three men wounded. We then passed on in direction of Ashland, hoping to overtake the main body of our foes, but, before our arrival, it had taken its departure.

The following morning, we moved to the neighborhood of Peake's Station, on the Virginia Central Railroad, where we prepared our rations. Taking up the march, we reached Hanover Court House the same evening, where a part of our Regiment was left to guard the pontoons, which had just arrived from Richmond for the purpose of bridging the Pamunkey. Several days after, the command returned to the vicinity of Richmond, and encamped on the Nine Mile road. On the 21st, a review of our troops took place at the Fairfield Race Course. Everything remained comparatively quiet on all the lines, until the morning of the 25th.

Just before daylight, the skirmishers in front of Generals Gordon's and Johnson's Divisions, posted in front of Petersburg, and embracing Colquet's Salient advanced, capturing the enemy's pickets, without firing a gun; upwards of five hundred prisoners, including one Brigadier General, fell into our hands; afterwards our forces drove the enemy out of two lines of his entrenchments, and took possession of the large fort on Hare's hill, known as Fort Steadman, containing nine guns and eight mortars.

The Federals were taken so completely by surprise, that they fell back in great confusion. After having these lines in possession, it was found by our Generals that the capture of the strong works in rear of, and commanding their main line, would occasion too great a loss in making the necessary assault, so it was decided to withdraw the troops to our old position.

By this time, our antagonists had entirely recovered from their surprise, and opened a terrific fire of shot, canister and grape, upon our troops in the fort; for some hours the battle raged furiously; our men holding their position until ordered to fall back. Many on our side were killed and wounded; the nature of the ground would not allow the removal of the heavy guns, which in consequence were spiked, and then abandoned.

Our troops had never fought with greater gallantry, but the overpowering numbers of the opposing army

proved too many for them, in their enclosed position.
Our Division had been ordered over, but on reaching the cars in Richmond, the order was countermanded, and we returned to our camp on the Nine
Mile road; before night, however, orders again arrived, when we took possesion of the cars, were carried
to the vicinity of Swift Creek, and encamped, ready
for removal to any point where we could render assistance in case of stringent need.

On the 29th of March, our camp near Swift Creek
was broken up, and we marched to the Southside Railroad, about one mile above the city of Petersburg,
where the Division was being rapidly collected, and
sent off on cars awaiting to transport it. Just before
dark our Regiment left on a train, and arriving at
Southerland Station, disembarked, and marched about
two miles, where we laid down to sleep until the arrival of the residue of the Division.

Sheridan, with a host of cavalry and infantry, was
at this time moving against the railroad, where sharp
work and bloody deeds were expected by the troops
under General Pickett.

The rain fell in torrents upon the weary forms
sleeping in silence near Southerland Station; about two
o'clock the following morning, we were aroused from
our slumbers, and forming into line, moved off in the
storm as rapidly as the darkness would allow us, in
direction of the extreme right of General Lee's lines.
About eight o'clock A. M., after a wearisome march,
we reached our destination, and formed for battle,

just outside of the fortifications, and near to where General Wise's command and the enemy had had a severe fight, a short time previous.

Soon after halting, Generals Lee and Pendleton arrived; from their movements, it was inferred by many of us, that preparation for a great battle was in progress.

In the afternoon, about two o'clock, we again changed our position; we marched forward in direction of Five Forks, but had not advanced more than two miles, when skirmishing commenced in our front; halting, the men began to remove the fences and convert them into rude rifle-pits, or breastworks; but before this was accomplished, the firing grew heavier and extended to the left, upon which we were ordered in that direction; ere reaching the spot whence the sounds of fighting proceeded, they ceased altogether, and we learned that they had been caused by the enemy's cavalry having charged our troops, who opened fire upon, and repulsed them.

During the firing, some ladies and children were noticed by our men in a field some hundred yards or more in our front, running about in great alarm, not knowing what to do, or where to seek refuge from the balls whizzing through the air. Their house was not far distant in front, and they had deserted it, hoping to find shelter elsewhere. One of the members of Company A, of our Regiment, called the attention of General Corse to the state of affairs, who sent a courier to tell them to plunge into the woods on their right and come into our lines, which was soon accomplished, and they were thus rescued from their perilous situation.

After the firing ceased, the command moved on to Five Forks, where General Payne and his cavalry had been skirmishing with the enemy during the day ; the firing on this portion of the line, which had ceased for some hours, was again renewed upon the approach of our command, but the enemy were soon driven back, when we passed to the rear a short distance, formed in line of battle, stacked arms, and remained for the night, during which the rain poured without intermission, and continued until after the dawn of the morning of the 31st day of March.

Early upon that morning, (March 31st,) a new line of skirmishers was formed, but in an hour or so after, they were ordered back to the Regiment; a scouting party sent out had returned, after ascertaining that the Federal forces were moving in direction of Dinwiddie Court House. We immediately marched off with the Division, upon another road than that taken by the enemy, for the purpose of intercepting them, and soon after, the battle of Dinwiddie Court House, opened

After a short march, the Regiment reached its destination, and found that the cavalry were already engaged with the enemy, and had been successful in driving them back beyond a stream, near thereto. Our men were then moved across the stream, a line of battle formed, and skirmishers thrown forward, after which, they advanced rapidly towards the enemy's position, driving in his pickets, until the crest of a hill was reached, distant about four hundred yards from his main body; at this point, our skirmishers halted and awaited the arrival of our Division, which was advancing; after its arrival, a line was formed between a fence and a heavy growth of young pines.

Whilst we were getting into position the enemy charged, driving back the Thirty-second Virginia Regiment, which was on our right, and his skirmishers bore down upon our flank and rear, capturing Capt. James Steuart and some few men on the extreme right of our Regiment, but our position was held. At first the men were slightly confused, but immediately thereafter rallied, and forced the enemy back, not however, until about thirty-five of our men were killed and wounded, and some, though not many, taken prisoners.

The members of Company A, (Seventeenth Virginia,) with other companies of the Division, were then detailed to act as skirmishers; they moved forward, and after passing through a piece of woods came in sight of the Federals, about three quarters of a mile distant, beyond an open field, with skirmishers in front, protected behind a breastwork of rails. As our skirmishers became visible, our enemies opened upon them with artillery, but did no damage. Up to this time, our Division had remained in the woods, but being informed of the existing state of affairs in front, it immediately marched forward, while the skirmishers were ordered to continue to advance, which they did

18*

under a heavy fire, driving those of the Federals in upon their main body.

Our line of battle now appearing, the enemy retired about a mile, to a ridge in his rear. Night now closed in upon the scene; the troops halted, were ordered to stack arms, and to sleep near them. Company A was relieved from duty in front, after which, the members returned to the battle field in quest of their wounded, five of whom had fallen in the morning, during the advance. After midnight, they came in to the Regiment, having conveyed to the field Hopital, all their wounded except one man, whom they did not succeed in finding; this done, they gladly laid themselves down, to rest from the exertions of the day.

Though the Federals had been driven several miles in this battle, the injuries inflicted upon them was but slight, and the advantage derived by ourselves little more than nominal.

The folowing incident transpired a very short while before this engagement, and is worthy a place upon our record.—It is entitled:

"HOW THE CONFEDERATES MISSED A FEAST AT DINWIDDIE."

On the morning of the battle of Dinwiddie Court House, Sergeant J. P. Jordan, Company H, Seventeenth Virginia, Private F. Beach, Company D, Seventeenth Virginia and three others, members of the Brigade, whose names we have been unsuccessful in recalling, were sent by General Corse in direction

of the enemy's position, with instructions to capture
one of the pickets, if posible, in order to ascertain
the strength and location of the army to which he be-
longed.

The party proceeded at once in direction of the
enemy, taking the straight road, trusting to circumstances and sharp eyes to show them the Yankees
whereabouts. They had not marched far when a
volley advised them of the situation of the Federals;
without waiting, they plunged into the dense pines on
their right, and making a detour of some half a mile,
struck the main road again, this time in rear of their
foe.

In their front, and extending for several miles
down the road, appeared a large wagon train; a glorious spectacle, in the eyes of our half starved Confeds,
was this same train, 'no doubt, well laden with provisions.

Our hungry Sergeant immediately detaching one of
his command, sent him, by a circuitous route back
again to the Brigade, with a message to Colonel Herbert: "To bring, if possible, the Seventeenth Virginia
and capture the train."

The party then "treed," to await the result. Some
time elapsed; and no signs of the Regiment were
forthcoming. A few minutes more, and a mounted
Federal officer appeared, riding directly towards them
from the wagon train. To prevent an alarm, the officer
must necessarily be captured—but how was this to be
accomplished? It would not be expedient to halt

him, for his comrades were in close proximity and would hear the challenge.

Without giving notice to his companions, a plan of capture was soon matured in the mind of the quick-witted Sergeant; dropping quietly to the ground, followed by his command, the quartette faced the enemy, single file, and marched forward, keeping a *large oak tree* between themselves and the officer.

On reaching the tree, the Quartermaster, for such he proved to be, was politely requested to continue his ride, in which he was escorted by two of the party and delivered over to the Brigade.

But one man now remained to the Sergeant; yet, still hopeful that the Regiment would come, they kept their position. Not a great while after, a party of the enemy, having missed their Captain, entered the woods in search of him, when, as a matter in course, the Sergeant and his command were compelled to fall quietly back, which was done successfully; they reached the Regiment as it was on the eve of moving out to the battle-field.

The receipt of marching orders had prevented the Seventeenth Virginia from *capturing that train*; the gallant Colonel Herbert having made application to General Pickett, for permission to do so.

It was thus, that the Yankees saved their train, and the "Rebels" missed a feast at their expense.

The record of the last "month's campaign" is finished; but the heart-rending trials of the ten days which succeeded would beggar the descriptive powers of the most gifted, and yet the half would remain untold.

As the few members left of the Seventeenth Virginia Regiment, were quietly sleeping during the last night of the last month, visions of home and friends were probably adding their charms to the refreshments of slumber, but the startling dream of culminating events haunted them not.

THE CLOSING SCENES.

THOSE of the Seventeenth Virginia Regiment, whom we had left in temporary repose at the close of the preceding chapter, were aroused about daylight on the morning of the 1st day of April, 1865, with orders to withdraw from the vicinity of Dinwiddie Court House to Five Forks.

The forces of the enemy followed, so soon as they found the Confederates were falling back, and were very near capturing a part of the wounded as they arrived within a few yards of the hospital, when the last of the men were being borne away upon the shoulders of comrades.

Upon reaching the extreme right of the infantry line of our army, near Five Forks, the troops halted, and were allowed to prepare their breakfast, which was not sufficiently luxurious to necessitate a bill of fare.

About an hour after, the Regiment proceeded to a road, along which it formed in line of battle, when they went promptly to work to throw down the fencing, and convert it into breastworks.

The artillery was also brought up and placed in position; scarcely had these preparations been completed when the cavalry of the enemy made their appearance, and began skirmishing with our cavalry on the right. The artillery opened upon and forced them to retire, but they soon advanced again, when one squadron charged to within · about two hundred yards of our position, wheeled and disappeared in the woods.

For several hours thereafter quiet reigned, except occasional skirmishing on the left. Late in the afternoon heavy firing commenced on the left, and increased until it extended along the entire line, except in front of the Seventeenth Virginia, where all remained undisturbed. Although it was ·noticed that the firing extended to the rear, there was but little attention paid to it at this time, the men of our Regiment being impressed with the idea that our line continued in that direction, and consequently that all was right.

Soon after, the enemy made demonstrations in our front; a battery of horse artillery and two regiments of infantry were dispatched to the left to reinforce the troops at that point; in a few moments, however, the men of the battery returned, reporting that just as their guns were placed in position, the enemy had penetrated and captured them.

Affairs were now assuming a startling aspect, especially for the members of the Seventeenth Virginia, who saw no resource other than to be ever on the alert ready to meet the emergency.

Not very long after the artillerymen returned, the men of those regiments which had been driven from their position on the left, were approaching in disorderly retreat through the woods. Our Regiment being

under pressure from three sides, had necessarily to fall
back on the Brigade ; an effort was made to rally the
fleeing men, and form in position at right angles with
the line of works, but this it was impossible to accomplish, as the retreating column, hotly pressed by the
enemy, was too thoroughly disorganized.

Three times our Regiment rallied and fought the
enemy with the tenacity of bull dogs, but it was unavailing ; a handful of men could effect nought in conflict against the powerful wing of an army gigantic in
numbers ; most unwillingly this knowledge was allowed entrance into the minds of our veterans, but
there was no refuting it ; then came the order for the
men to take care of themselves. Thus closed the battle of Five Forks.

It was just at this time, when the capture of the entire force engaged was almost a certainty, that Sergeant
Ira Deavers, a member of Co. H, tore the old tattered
" Flag " of our Regiment from its staff, and secreting
it in his bosom, safely retained it, notwithstanding the
perils and trials consequent upon the "blue days" that
preceded and followed the surrender of our army.

The color-guard having been entirely annihilated, it
was the gallant Deavers who volunteered to take
charge of the flag ; and nobly he performed it, thus
saving us the mortification of having it fall into the
hands of the enemy. It is to this day, and will ever
be, valued by its fortunate possessors, as one of the
most precious mementos of those loved comrades, who,
in acting "well their part," poured out their life's

blood in its defence, recognizing it as emblematic of a noble part of our national escutcheon.

After the close of the war it was divided, and each of its remaining defenders cherished the fragment of plain discolored bunting which fell to his lot, with feelings of sad affection, which language is inadequate to describe. But to Deavers belongs the glory of having saved it.

The enemy had possession of our artillery, and we expected every moment to have it turned upon us, but such was not the case; when darkness closed upon the frightful scene the Confederates were moving rapidly in retreat along the road.

It must be said here in justice to the cavalry, that they fought valliantly under the circumstances, even more so than the infantry, when the knowledge of defeat insinuated itself along the line.

After the battle, General Pickett's Division, for the first time since it had been organized, was much demoralized; the men were scattered everywhere through the country. The loss in General Corse's Brigade is estimated at somewhere near forty men; from the Division there were a great many missing.

After the retreat, many of the command struck for the railroad, where they formed again, but it was impossible to conjecture how many were absent. About three o'clock on the morning of the 2d of April, we moved off to a ferry on the Appomatox, where we laid down to rest, and slept until daylight. Throughout the night, heavy cannonading was progressing in the direction of Petersburg, but we at the ferry could only imagine what was transpiring at that point; soon after daylight, General Pickett gave orders for a march, hoping to reach Southerland Station, but after advancing about one mile, wagons and some of the wounded were met, when the news of the evacuation of the lines around Petersburg, then in progress, was announced for the first time.

The enemy having broken through the scant line of men at Burgess' Mills, four miles to the right of the city, thus cutting us off, the order was given us to return to the ferry. After reaching there, an attempt was made to cross, but finding the stream too swift and deep to ford, and as the boat would consume too much time in ferrying all over, it was decided to to avail ourselves of a bridge some fifteen miles further up the stream.

Before leaving, the wounded and sick were sent over, and then the Division moved off; Gen. Corse's Brigade acting as rear guard. As the enemy in squads of various dimensions were assiduously scouring the country, it became necessary for the command to move in as solid a body as possible; this being ordered, the men formed, and marched in heavy column, ready for duty should an attack from any source be made upon them. We were without anything to eat and nearly exhausted from heat, hunger, and fatigue, yet, we marched rapidly, until about four o'clock P. M., when we halted to rest; in about half an hour afterwards, greatly to the surprise of all, the Division wagon train drove up, having escaped the enemy the day previous, when the line was broken.

As soon as they arrived, General Corse's Brigade was ordered forward to take possession of the bridge in anticipation of the coming of the enemy's cavalry, which was moving in that direction by another road. After marching until late at night, the plan was again changed, and our Brigade, (General Corse's,) quartered in a pine woods, there to rest from the toils of the day and to find in sleep, temporary oblivion to the heart-scathing reality of our situation.

When Monday morning, (3d April,) arrived we were aroused for the march, whereupon, it was discovered that nearly all the wagon trains from the army around Petersburg, had arrived during the night, by which arrangement the Division had a train from eight to ten miles long to protect. The time necessarily consumed in getting it into motion was considerable, greater than one unfamiliar with military life would imagine; it was started at last, however, and the troops took up the line of march as rear guard.

Not many miles had been traveled, when it was noticed that our cavalry were deploying as skirmishers on the right, in the wood; a short distance further on, we fell into position for the protection of the wagons as they passed over Deep Creek. This was a precautionary move, as the enemy was near. When they had passed over in safety, General Hunton's Brigade and the cavalry, were left to fight the Federals, while the other portion of the command, hurried quickly

forward to a bridge higher up the stream, which the
enemy were attempting to repair, in order to cross
upon it.

Upon our arrival, skirmishing immediately commenced; notwithstanding, a detail of men were dispatched to burn the bridge, but owing to its being
wet, they succeeded in affecting only its partial
destruction. We remained at this point during the
night, being in readiness to repulse any assault that
might be made upon us.

Early the following morning, another detail was
sent to complete the annihilation of the bridge, while
our Regiment, with the residue of the troops, moved
about five miles higher up, formed in line of battle
and constructed a breastwork of trees, felled by us for
the purpose.

When this operation was nearly accomplished, firing
commenced on the right, occasioned by the cavalry of
the enemy charging that part of the line, and being
repulsed, they very soon after withdrew.

During the night, at this point, a number of large,
bright fires were built along our position, after which
we quietly decamped, taking the direction of Amelia
Court House.

Soon after the dawn of day on the 5th of April,
our Division, with its long wagon train in charge,
reached the Danville Railroad, about three miles below
Amelia Court House, where, for a good length of time
it halted, allowing the troops with their cortege of
ladies, children, and their attendants, in every con-

ceivable form of conveyance, from Richmond and Petersburg, to pass on. Here, and for the first time the news was received of the evacuation of Richmond, and our lines in that vicinity. It had occurred during Sunday night, leaving the city to the merciful hands of the Federals, who entered, and occupied it on Monday morning.

The column again moved on, passing through Amelia Court House; but in consequence of the road in our front being effectually blockaded by the wagon train captured, and burned by the enemy that morning, thus destroying all our stores, medical, commissary and ordnance, we were compelled to select another route, and proceeded, with General Mahone's Division in advance.

Not long after, it was ascertained that the enemy were again in front in considerable force, consequently, they had to be whipped off, before the column could proceed. Marching had now become a perilous operation; the cavalry of the enemy were numerous on all sides, and every now and then, would dash in upon the wagon train, capture, burn, and be off before our infantry could get near them, then occupy the roads in front, and harrass us in every way possible.

The troops marched, almost exhausted from excessive fatigue and lack of food, throughout Wednesday night, (the 5th,) with the exception of about one hour, in a severe rain storm. On the next morning, a halt for an hour was allowed in which to rest and breakfast the latter consisting of parched corn and coffee for some, whilst many had not a mouthful of anything.

The suffering of every one was, indeed, great; men were so overcome as to slumber soundly in line, and as our Regiment passed along, numbers of the army were fast asleep in the fence corners, temporarily indifferent to whatever might be transpiring. From the time our Regiment left the neighborhood of Petersburg on the 29th of March, the members of it had been permitted but one entire night's rest; having been either march-ing or fighting, and had lived principally on parched corn during the period.

When the halt and breakfast were concluded, the Division again marched, moving near to Sailor's Creek, where it again halted, while the wagons were passing. We had not been long at a stand-still, when skirmish-ing commenced with the cavalry; a force of infantry detailed from the command was thrown out to the front, Company A, of our Regiment, being among the number. This squad of skirmishers had not been long in line, some few hundred yards in advance of the main body of our troops, when the rattle of musketry arose in a piece of woods on the right, through which the wagon train had passed, and almost immediately the teamsters and stragglers were seen rushing there-from; the enemy's cavalry, taking advantage of a gap in the column, had made another charge upon the train, and captured a number of pieces of artillery that were moving in line with the wagons, which they turned upon our skirmishers. At this time the Division was ordered up, and very quickly it drove the enemy back, recapturing two of the guns; but the Federals having received reinforcements of infantry, the battle became general and very severe.

The divisions of Generals Lee and Anderson were then brought forward; the booming of artillery, and the loud rattle of musketry, resounded on all sides. One shell exploded in front of our Regiment and killed the first sergeant of Company A, Addison Saunders, as gallant a soldier as ever faced the enemy, and wounded several others; Geo. Pickett, of Company F, another fine specimen of a brave man, being among the number.

Late in the day, the enemy, with an overpowering force, broke through our position on the left, and getting into the rear, opened a cross fire with artillery. Heavy masses of the Federals now swept down the line, disorganizing and capturing a large number of the brigades, very few of which came out in organized bodies; those that effected their escape did so under a most terrific fire; many fell, and from necessity, were left to the mercy of the victorious enemy.

The battle was prolonged until night, and it is known as the battle of Sailor's Creek. During the day, the wagons traveled off to the High Bridge, and many of the soldiers, in disorganized bodies, followed in their rear; cavalry, at different points, dashed into the train, damaging it considerably; artillery also poured shot and shell into it as it moved off hastily.

Upon reaching the bridge, which was crowded with

troops, a panic was raised, which would have resulted in fatality to many had it not been for the presence of mind and exertions of a portion of them.

Sleeping in the fence corners, old cars, wagons, or whatever afforded shelter, the night of the 6th of April was passed by the scattered troops along the route between the High Bridge and Farmville.

Everything on the succeeding morning, (the 7th,) was in utter confusion in and around Farmville. Car loads of flour and bacon had been dispatched from Lynchburg, with which the wagons, as they passed, had been loaded and sent on, so that rations could be issued to the starving men in the ranks, then arriving on their way through. None, however, were issued to them, so it was decided among the poor-fellows, who were very hungry, to charge the commissary stores and help themselves; this was done in gallant style, and many a one went on his way rejoicing in the trophy of a ham or a haversack of bread.

An attempt was made by the Federals to cross the river, near Farmville, later in the day, but they were beaten back, and a number of them captured by the infantry and cavalry bringing up the rear.

The following is taken from the diary of one of our Regiment, who, with another of his company, were the only two who escaped from the Sailor's Creek battle. It was written on the 7th, and runs thus:

"During the past ten days our losses have been very heavy, and we are now sadly straitened for food and forage, while we are pressed on every side by a large army that is abundantly supplied with everything. Still, I am willing to follow as long as 'Uncle Bob' leads. I only hope the Yank's may not get him, whatever befalls the rest of us."

The night of the 7th, was passed by a large portion of our command near the New Store, Buckingham county, and the march resumed the next day at an early hour. Flour and bacon, in small quantities, were issued to the troops on that Friday night, the first they had received since the previous Sunday evening; a great trouble was experienced in the effort to find suitable means to bake the bread, the utensils for the purpose having been thrown away some days previously.

At this time the horses and mules were unfitted, in most instances, for the draught of even the empty wagons, and numbers of them sank down in the road and died, utterly incapable of proceeding another step. Those that could move were hitched to the guns to assist in dragging them a little further; the wagons were destroyed, the caissons having been either destroyed or captured prior to this time.

On the afternoon of the 8th, a halt was made within about two miles of Appomatox Court House, in order to rest the animals, while the commissary officers were sent out to forage for the broken down teams. Up to a late hour in the afternoon, the march had not been molested by the enemy, but just before darkness set in, they dashed into the artillery, parked near Concord Station, some three miles from the Court House, and capturing the trains laden with provisions sent from Lynchburg for the sustenance of the army, set fire to, and destroyed them.

Our troops were forced back and their guns captured; the fighting continued until after night commenced, the Federals gradually gaining ground, until our line of battle was within a quarter of a mile of the Court House. Quoting from the before mentioned diary, we are told: " We are now in a pretty bad fix and I cannot imagine how ' Uncle Bob' is to get out, as the Yanks are now in our front and rear and a column moving up from Farmville on our flanks."

"Commissary came in with a little corn and beef; two cars of the former and about a pound of the latter were issued to each man. Went to a farmhouse and traded my *neck-tie* for a piece of *corn bread.*"

During the night, the trains moved, (such as could do so,) and by seven o'clock on the following morning, (9th,) they had parked on the side of the hill, about one and a half miles from the C. H.

The captured prisoners were also marched up, and placed in a ravine near by. The day had now arrived for the surrender of General Lee's army, but the troops at the hour mentioned were not aware of it. They thought strange of the movement; *i. e.*, parking so early, without a days march; but not much time elapsed before the air was rife with the rumor, that our soldier life was rapidly approaching its last sad scenes.

About seven o'clock, (the hour mentioned,) fighting along the lines was renewed, and continued until between nine and ten o'clock, when all firing ceased. The cavalry under General Fitz. Lee's command made its escape through a gap in the Federal line, but this opening was soon closed, and thus all channel of escape cut off.

We were now, completely surrounded on all sides, and not long after nine o'clock, General Custer of the Federal army, entered our line, under flag of truce, and proceeding to General Longstreet's headquarters, arranged for a meeting between Generals Lee and Grant. The meeting took place in the house of Mr. McLean, where terms were agreed upon for the surrender of General Lee's army.

In the afternoon, a great jubilee took place among the Federal forces present, but the hearts of the irreproachable Lee and his veterns, were bowed with that sorrow whose depth neither tongue nor pen may describe.

On the 10th, the officers busied themselves in making out property returns, having wagons parked, guns stacked and other necessary arrangements made. On this day, rations of one pound of beef to each man, were issued by the United States authorities, to the Confederate troops. The following order was then issued, and the hour of parting drew near.

HEADQUARTERS ARMY NORTHERN VIRGINIA, }
April, 10th, 1865. }

General Order No. 9:

After four years of arduous service, marked by unsurpassed courage and fortitude, the Army of Northern Virginia has been compelled to yield to over-whelming numbers and resources.

I need not tell the brave survivors of so many hard fought battles who have remained steadfast to the last, that I have consented to this result from no distrust of them. But feeling that valor and devotion could accomplish nothing that would compensate for the loss that must have attended the continuance of the contest, I determined to avoid the useless sacrifice of those whose past services have endeared them to their countrymen.

By the terms of agreement, officers and men can return to their homes and remain until exchanged. You will take with you the satisfaction that proceeds from a consciousness of duty faithfully performed, and I earnestly pray that a merciful God will extend to you his blessing and protection.

With an unceasing admiration of your constancy and devotion to your country, and a grateful remembrance of your kind and generous considerations for myself, I bid you all an affectionate farewell.

(Signed)   R. E. LEE, General.

MEMENTOS.

——:o:——

JOHN Q. MARR.

The lamented *John Q. Marr* was a whole-souled
gentleman, an honorable, upright citizen, and a good
soldier.   He was born on the 27th day of May, 1825,
in the town of Warrenton, Fauquier County, Va.

His great-grandfather left France at the time of the
Revocation of the Edict of Nantes, and was among the
first settlers of the above-named section of our old
State.   He was the second son of John Marr, whose
labors as Commissioner in Chancery in the Superior
and County Courts, and in other offices of trust con-
fided to him by his neighbors and fellow-citizens, are
still fresh in the minds of many now surviving him.
His mother, (a daughter of Dr. Gustavus B. Horner,
an eminent physician in his day,) still survives, at the
advanced age of seventy-two years.

Marr entered the Virginia Military Institute in
July, 1843, as a cadet, and in 1846, he graduated with
the second distinguished honor of his class; as a member of the first class, he was one of the cadet captains.

Immediately after graduating, he received the appointment of Assistant Professor of Mathematics and
Tactics in the Institute, and filled the position with
great credit, until called home by the death of his father.

Though young Marr held a post of preferment, received heartfelt praise for his progress in science, and was flattered with the hope of future advancement by the teachers of the Institute, if he would remain, he still saw and felt that duty called him home to his widowed mother and fatherless sisters; banishing, therefore, from his mind these bright anticipations of future eminence, he obeyed the dictates of his noble nature.

By extraordinary exertion, he succeeded in placing his mother and family above want. The first tribute of trust conferred upon him was his appointment to the position vacated by the death of his father. To this he also added, as his father had done, the gratuitous services of a justice of the peace.

His attainments were such (having studied, but never practised, law) that, upon the death of the lamented Hunton, the magistrates of the county appointed him the presiding justice of the court. This, when we remember his youth at the time, must be acknowledged as a high demonstration of respect and trust, called forth by his superior intelligence and dignity of deportment.

The next token of confidence was from the people, who elected him Sheriff of the large and opulent county of Fauquier. After performing its arduous and responsible duties for two years, a full term, he was again unanimously elected. Upon a full, calm survey of its troubles and responsibilities, he declined the office; his past ample experience in its anxieties and heart-harrowing scenes determined him to forego its pecuniary gains and patronage so coveted by many.

The grandest and most decisive proof of the estimation in which his judgment and ability to serve were held, was clearly manifested in 1861, when an election for delegates to the convention was held.

The following extracts from his response to calls made upon him by his fellow-citizens, to permit his name to be used as a candidate for the convention, will show truly his position in regard to his State and the welfare of her vital interests. He closes his address in these words:

"If, therefore, you think proper to confide such great trust to my judgment and discretion, I shall be grateful for your suffrages. If, on the contrary, there should be other gentlemen before you in connection with this trust, on whose judgment, discretion and patriotism you would feel safer to rely, vote for them—your interest and your duty demand it.

"As for myself, whether in a representative capacity, or as a private citizen, my fortunes are indissolubly connected with Virginia, the land of my birth, and by whom I have been nurtured with more than a parent's care, and on whose bosom I shall repose when time, with me, shall be no more. 'She shall know no peril but that it shall be my peril, no conflict but that it shall be my conflict, and there is no abyss of ruin to which she may sink, so low, but that I shall share her fall.'"

It is needless to say, that John Q. Marr received the largest vote ever polled in the county, and was made

In April, 1861, Marr entered military service as captain of Virginia volunteers. It appears that he had heard, from other than military sources, of his appointment to a lieutenant colonelcy in the volunteer forces, as not long before his death he had inquired of a member of his family whether his commission had reached home. The promotion had been made, but by some fatality his commission had miscarried and remained in the dead-letter office for months after his death. It was post-marked "Richmond, May 9, 1861," and read as follows:

" *The Commonwealth of Virginia to John Q. Marr, greeting :—*

" Know you, that from special trust and confidence reposed in your fidelity, courage and good conduct, our Governor, in pursuance of the authority vested in him by an Ordinance of the Convention of the State of Virginia, doth commission you a LIEUTENANT COLONEL in the active volunteer forces of the State, to rank as such from the second day of May, 1861.

" In testimony whereof, I have hereunto signed my name as Governor, and caused the Seal of the Commonwealth to be affixed, this 5th day of May, 1861.
(Signed)   " JOHN LETCHER."

When the sad news of his death reached the town of Warrenton, the hearts of old and young were bowed in mourning. The Confederate flag was lowered to half-mast, and tokens of sorrow for the fall of a loved and truly great man were visible on all sides. His remains reached Warrenton on Saturday evening, when they were met and escorted into the town by the Lee Guard and a large concourse of citizens. On the following day, all that was left of the gallant soldier, was de-

STEALING A GRAVE.

While encamped near Guinea's Station, on the Richmond and Fredericksburg Railroad, during the winter of 1862, quite an amusing incident occurred between two of General Hood's regiments, one from Arkansas and the other from Texas, which were encamped a short distance from us, near Massaponax Church. It appears that the Texas regiment was detailed to go on picket duty, just below Fredericksburg, to watch the enemy and prevent him from throwing a pontoon across the river. While engaged on this duty, the Arkansas regiment made "a raid" on the deserted camp, and captured nearly all the cooking utensils, (articles then very scarce and much in demand.) A short time afterwards the Arkansas regiment was called on to perform the same duty, and, while absent, the Texas boys paid its camp a visit, recaptured their cooking utensils, and carried off almost everything they could lay their hands on. The Arkansas boys, seeing the state of affairs on their return, determined to watch their opportunity for revenge.

About ten days after this, one of the Texas regiment died, and a party of his comrades started out to prepare a grave. After having completed their sad task, they returned to camp for the body. In the meantime, a small party from the Arkansas regiment, came out to perform the same solemn duty, bearing the remains of their dead comrade with them. Finding a grave already dug, they quietly buried the body and returned to camp.

The Texas party, upon their return to the grave, comprehended the situation at a glance, and ever after "yielded the palm" for stealing to the Arkansas boys.

LITTLE LULY.

(Written by LIEUT. COL. WM. MUNFORD)

She sits in her chair in her chamber,
  A miniken, moody and mild,
And old people seemed to be puzzled,
  At seeing our curious child.
She rocks to the hymns she is humming,
  And gloomily fixes her gaze
On figures that flash in the firelight
  And float in the fanciful blaze.

To birds in the parlor she prattles,—
  The painted birds up on the wall,—
And spreads for them daily such dainties
  As berries and water for all ;
Then closing the door very gently,
  She stops at the key-hole to peep,
She says they are eating and drinking—
  She saw them so once in her sleep.

She lolls on the floor by the fender,
  And gives the old Lion a hug,
The old Lion woven in worsted
  That lies on the new parlor rug ;
She pats him and calls him ‘‘Old Fellow,’’
  And tells us she saw him on guard,
At the gate for the bug-a-booz coming,
  One night when 'twas snowing so hard.

She cuts up her calico pieces,
  And sews on her curious things,
And working her whimsical patterns,

She dresses them up every day,
And each has its place and its plaything,
  And each a particular play.

Now, sometimes she gives them a party,
  The Chess men are bid to the " Hall "—
The Kings and the Queens and the Bishops
  Are brought to the Baby-house Ball.
The Knight never goes in the parlor,
  But stands on the outside, of course,
The ladies expressing—says Luly—
  Regret that he can't leave his horse.

When supper comes on in the evening,
  She works with a farcical zest,
And keeps up the party quite gaily,
  By talking for hostess and guest;
The King at the head of the table,
  The Queen at the opposite place,
All standing in stateliest order,
  She makes the Old Bishop say grace.

My Luly had lost a young playmate,
  The last of a lingering race,
We carried her down to the cedars,
  The bosky old burial place;
She clung to me closer that evening,
  Said : " Father, when Luly shall die,
Don't cover her up in the grave yard,
  To keep her away from the sky."

I told her the grave was God's garden,
  To plant out His prettiest flowers,
That thence they are moved in His mercy
  To bloom in His beautiful bowers—
The blossoms He buries in winter,
  And covers in snow from the cold,
So like the shroud wrapped around Cary,
  The sunlight of Spring will unfold,

That even the loveliest lily
  That lolls on the laziest wave,
In winter time buries its beauty
  And blooms again blanched in the grave.
A smile through her pretty eyes played then,
  A moment forgetting her pain,
The tears seemed to sparkle with gladness,
  Like sunshine when streaming through rain.

She said she was dreaming so sweetly
  Last night in her nice little bed,
That standing on clouds in the starlight,
  The Heavens were touching her head ;
That then came the dear little Cary,
  But only to kiss through the blue,
As oft as the pane in the window
  Your Luly plays kissing with you.

I asked her "how Cary had entered ? "
  She said with her serious air :
" The moon I suppose did just open
  And God carried Cary through there."
Oh ! Luly, my dear little angel,
  God grant that we both may be blest,
That the moon which has opened for Cary,
  May soon roll away for the rest.

I thank thee, O ! Father in Heaven !
  Because from the prudent and wise
Thou hidest those things thou revealist
  To babes, with their Heavenly guise !
Him, who is invisible, seeing
  They walk in the glorious light ;
And even so let it be Father !
  For so it seems good in thy sight.

"THE WARRIOR'S GRAVE."

Sleeping, sleeping 'neath the shadows
  Of Virginia's mountain peaks—
Where the "Valley" streams are wending,
Where the aged oaks are bending,
  Sighing 'midst the tempest's freaks—
Rests the mortal part of Jackson,
Resting 'till the trumpet speaks.

Waiting, waiting for the summons
  Of Jehovah's final call—
Lies this mortal dust in keeping.
Loving hearts are sadly weeping
  O'er a country's hero's fall—
Moaning for the soldier, Jackson,
Loved and honored by us all.

Fragrant, fragrant o'er the grave-sod,
  Blooms the yellow-mountain rose—
With the robing red-breast singing,
And the rippling water ringing
  Forth its echos as it flows—
Rests the mortal part of Jackson,
Resting from its earthly woes.

Happy, happy, and imortal
  Is the Christian's soul in bliss—
Sainted, and in sweet communion—
Looking for the last reunion—
  Smiling 'neath a Saviour's kiss,
Dwells the lofty part of Jackson,
Goodness, that a people miss.

S. W. PRESTMAN.

Capt. S. W. Prestman, of Company I, Seventeenth Virginia Regiment, who was wounded at the battle of Bull Run, July 18, 1861, is remembered by the surviving members of that band of soldiers with feelings of fond regard. As an officer and social companion, he was without exception, beloved and honored. His untimely end, after such a bright and goodly record, will not be out of place in the annals of his first command.

In May, 1862, he was ordered to report to General Beauregard at Corinth, Mississippi, and served with distinction as Engineer in the Western army. Upon the arrival of the army at Chattanooga, he was appointed Chief Engineer of General Hardee's Corps, and as such, served faithfully during the Kentucky campaign. Upon the return of the army, he received the appointment of Chief Engineer of the army of Tennessee, with a position on General Bragg's staff. He afterwards served under General Johnston, and ever carried with him a knowledge of having done his duty as a soldier.

In January, 1864, his health gave way, and upon application, he received a furlough to visit his native State to recruit it. Whilst enroute to his home, and upon arrival near Danville, Va., the accident which deprived him of life, occurred. He had stepped out of the cars to warm, during the stoppage, and in crossing the track, (the engine having been detached for water,) he slipped and fell; he was too weak to regain his feet in time, and the engine returning, struck him, killing him instantly.

Colonel Prestman was a most gallant officer, and from his conduct in the many battles and army movements in which he was a conspicuous actor, he was frequently mentioned, with well deserved praise, in official reports.

He was universally beloved by all who came in contact with him, and his sudden death, when so near a reunion with his family and friends, cast a deep gloom over the hearts of many who served with him, both in the Virginia and Western armies.

———:0:———

IN MEMORIAM.

Died.—In Washington City, on Tuesday, the 5th day of October, 1869, of Erysipelas, Mr. John A. Divine, only surviving son of James F. and H. Elizabeth Divine, of Leesburg, aged 26 years and five days:

[From the Leesburg Mirror.]

Death of John A. Divine.—Our obituary column this morning records the announcement of the death of John A. Divine. Aware that after death the obituary column, no less than the "sculptured urn" too often records, not what the deceased was, but "what he should have been," we nevertheless feel that justice demands something more than a passing notice to the memory of one who gave the morning of his "brief, brave young life," to a cause whose only recognition of his services is now found in the enduring sympathy of its friends.

But a few short weeks ago, the subject of this notice left Leesburg in the bloom and vigor of youthful manhood—the very picture of health, full of life, and energy and hope, with every indication of many long years before him. To-day his body rests in the bosom of mother earth, and his spirit has winged its flight to the God who gave it—a fearful admonition of the immutability of that solemn decree, that "in the midst of life we are in death."

Eight years ago, when the dim speck of war was first seen upon the horizon, though a mere boy, he returned to this town, the home of his childhood, and joined his fortunes with those of his kindred and friends, and for four weary years struggled with and for them in a fruitless effort to beat back the dark wave of wrong and injustice that threatened to submerge them. As a member of the Loudoun Guard, Seventeenth Virginia Regiment, he participated in the first battle of Manassas, on the 18th of July, 1861, and the records of his Company attest that, in every march, skirmish, or regular fight, in which that gallant Regiment bore a part, either on the soil of Virginia, Maryland, or Pennsylvania, John A. Divine followed the flag of the Confederacy, until that symbol of his early, ardent love was lowered in defeat upon the memorable plains of Appomattox. Quiet and unobtrusive in his manner, but animated by a soul that knew no fear and shrunk from no danger—impelled by a conscientious sense of duty—with nothing to contend for but the sacred love he bore his mother,

Virginia, he regarded the post of danger the post of honor, and wherever the conflict raged fiercest his manly form was ever seen. Many will be the tears shed o'er his memory, that one so generous, so genial, so happy in his disposition, and withal so brave and so esteemed by those who knew him, and who for four years had faced death in a thousand forms without a scar, should fall so suddenly and so young.

He died on Tuesday evening, after a brief but malignant illness, of only six day's duration. His remains were brought to this town on Wednesday, and deposited in the M. E. Church, South. At 4 o'clock, a brief but impressive discourse was delivered by the Rev. Dr. Head, after which, attended by Laurel Division, Sons of Temperance, of which organization he was a member, and an unusually large concourse of citizens, his body was borne to Union Cemetery, and as the sun sank to rest on that beautiful October evening, 'mid falling leaves and withering flowers, all that was mortal of our young friend was consigned to his narrow bed, overcome by the last great enemy of his race—Death.

And now, while the flowers of Autumn, placed upon his early grave by the hands of affection, are still green, and the fresh earth yet presses lightly upon his bosom, we suggest that a subscription be started for the purpose of erecting o'er his grave a suitable tomb, that will attest the gratitude of friends and mark for all time the last resting place of the gallant dead. He has given his body to the worms, and his spirit to

God—his memory alone remains with the living; let us cherish it as we would a brother's. Any contributions left at this office for the purpose indicated, will be faithfully applied.

[FROM THE LEESBURG WASHINGTONIAN.]

Death of John A. Divine, a member of the Seventeenth Virginia Regiment.—The intelligence of the death of this young man, cut down in the very dawn of manhood, which occurred in Washington, on Tuesday last, will be received with painful regret by all his old comrades in arms, and by a large circle of acquaintances. He shared the fortunes of the entire war, most of the time as Orderly Sergeant of Company C, (known as the Loudoun Guard,) Seventeenth Virginia Regiment. Of him can it be said, that the name of a truer, braver and more constant defender of the cause of the South, at the time "which tried men's souls," cannot be found upon the muster rolls of the Confederate Army.

In the history of his Regiment, prepared a short time before the close of the war, by order of the Division Commander, his name appears as having participated in every battle, fight, skirmish and march in which his Regiment was engaged—an honor of which but few can boast. He was beloved and respected by all who knew him, and his memory will be long cherished by his companions and associates.

Peace to his soul. A nobler type of brave
And generous manhood ne'er wore the grey.
Though Death has cast him in the dark, cold grave,
His life, unstained, shall have an endless day.

LIEUT. THOS. V. FITZHUGH.

Dear Tom Fitzhugh! who does not remember him? The life of the "Old Dominions" when in Alexandria; of the companies when in barracks at Manassas Junction; and of the "Old Seventeenth" when at Manassas, Centreville, Fairfax Court House, on the Peninsula, and around Richmond; always bright and amusing; in battle, brave as a lion; on the march, cheerful; around the camp-fire, irresistable.

What a favorite the old Sergeant was with officers and men! and what a gallant Lieutenant he was as he "went in" with the "Old Dominions" at Williamsburg and Seven Pines!

We will all ever remember dear old Tom, with his warm, true heart, his winning smile, and droll stories. His was an earnest, Christian heart; his soul is, we trust and believe, with Jesus; and many were the hearts that sorrowed, and still sorrow, over the Christian warrior's fall, when duty, without regard to danger, called him to the defence of Richmond.

MUSTER ROLL

OF THE

SEVENTEENTH VIRGINIA.

(Based upon the Rolls of September, 1861.)

————————

FIELD AND STAFF.

(Those marked thus: * distinguished on the field for gallantry.)

*M. D. Corse, Colonel, wounded at Second Manassas, Boonsboro', and Sharpsburg; made Brigadier General, November, 1862; wounded at Drury's Bluff.

*William Munford, Lieutenant Colonel, with the Regiment until reorganization.

*Geo. W. Brent, Major, assigned to duty with the Army of the West, March, 1862.

*A. J. Humphreys, Adjutant, made Captain Company A, April, 1862.

*M. M. Lewis, Surgeon, Made Medical Director of Brigade.

*H. Snowden, Assistant Surgeon, made Surgeon upon the promotion of M. M. Lewis.

Wm. B. Richards, Jr., Captain and Assistant Quartermaster, made Major and Assistant Quartermaster, and assigned to duty at Gordonsville.

Victor M. Brown, Captain and Assistant Commissary, made Major and Assistant Commissary of Brigade, 1862.

22*

Rev. John L. Johnston, Chaplain, served with Regiment until 1862.

*Jos. F. Francis, Sergeant Major, killed in the battle of Seven Pines.

*Geo. C. Adie, Quartermaster Sergeant, elected Lieutenant Company I, April, 1862.

Jas. H. Brown, Commissary Sergeant, transferred to Brigade Commissary Department, 1862.

MEMBERS OF FIELD AND STAFF AFTER SEPTEMBER 1, 1861.

*Morton Marye, Colonel, unfit for field service on account of wound received at Second Manassas; transferred to Invalid Corps, August, 1864.

*Arthur Herbert, Colonel, Acting Colonel of Regiment until date of commission, August, 1864.

*Morton Marye, Lieutenant Colonel, made Colonel, November, 1862; lost a leg at Second Manassas.

*Arthur Herbert, Lieutenant Colonel, made Colonel, August, 1864; wounded at Drury's Bluff.

*Grayson Tyler, Lieutenant Colonel, Acting Major of Regiment from May to August, 1864.

*Arthur Herbert, Major, wounded at Seven Pines; made Lieutenant Colonel, November, 1862.

*R. H. Simpson, Major, severely wounded at Drury's Bluff; died from effects of wound, in Richmond, June 9, 1864.

*J. H. Bryant, Adjutant, appointed Captain and Aide-de-Camp to Brigadier General Corse, November, 1862; wounded at Boonsboro'.

*W. W. Zimmerman, Adjutant, served with distinction till close of war.

*H. Snowden, Surgeon, elected to House of Delegates; assigned to Examination Board, 1864.

J. W. Leftwich, Assistant Surgeon, made Surgeon, *vice* H. Snowden.

J. W. Leftwich, Surgeon, served with Regiment till close of war.

Dr. —— Boswell, Assistant Surgeon, transferred to Artillery.

R. H. Turner, Captain and Assistant Quartermaster, made Major and Assistant Quartermaster of Brigade, January, 1863.

C. W. Green, Captain and Assistant Quartermaster, served until transferred to Artillery by General Orders No. —, 1864.

H. B. Taliaferro, Captain and Assistant Commissary, assigned to duty with Brigade, 1864.

Rev. G. H. Norton, Chaplain, served faithfully with Regiment till August, 1862.

Rev. —— Baker, Chaplain, served faithfully with Regiment till ————.

*T. G. Hart, Sergeant Major, badly wounded at Drury's Bluff; died from effects of wound.

*D. A. Marks, Sergeant Major, wounded at Williamsburg; served till close of the war.

C. J. Wise, Quartermaster Sergeant, served throughout the war.

T. L. Chase, Commissary Sergeant, served throughout the war.

F. M. Henderson, Ordnance Sergeant, made Brigade Ordnance Officer, November, 1862.

Geo. Wise, Ordnance Sergeant, assigned to Company G, First Regiment Engineer Troops, November, 1863.

E. C. King, Ordnance Sergeant, served with Regiment till close of the war.

COMPANY A.

("ALEXANDRIA RIFLEMEN.")

*Morton Marye, Captain, elected Lieutenant Colonel, April, 1862.

*A. J. Humphries, First Lieutenant, Adjutant of Regiment till reorganization; then made Captain Company A; killed at Williamsburg.

*W. W. Smith, Second Lieutenant, made First Lieutenant Company A, April, 1862; wounded at Frazier's Farm; captured at Manassas Gap and held prisoner till close of the war.

*P. B. Hooe, Second Lieutenant, declined re-election on account of ill health; afterwards made Captain and Acting Adjutant General to Brigadier General Corse.

C. J. Wise, First Sergeant, appointed Quartermaster Sergeant 17th Virginia, April, 1862.

*John Addison, Second Sergeant, elected Second Lieutenant Company A, April, 1862; wounded at Williamsburg and Second Manassas.

*Thomas Perry, Third Sergeant, elected Second Lieutenant Company A, April, 1862; with Regiment in fourteen battles.

C. W. Green, Fourth Sergeant, made First Sergeant Company A, April, 1862; Second Lieutenant in May, 1862; Captain and Assistant Quartermaster, January, 1863.

*Addison Saunders, First Corporal, made Second Sergeant, April, 1862; First Sergeant, May, 1862; killed at Sailor's Creek by a shell.

*W. E. H. Clagett, Second Corporal, made Third Sergeant, April, 1862; Second Sergeant, May, 1862; severely wounded at Seven Pines.

Wm. Murray, Third Corporal, made Fourth Sergeant, April, 1862; discharged, 1862; over age.

*Wm. E. Gray, Fourth Corporal, made First Lieutenant Company G, April, 1862; killed at Seven Pines.

Privates.

Adam, John G., transferred to Second Virginia Cavalry, November, 1862.

Addison, W. D., with Company A until close of the war; wounded at Dinwiddie Court House.

Avery, R. W., wounded at Seven Pines; detached at General Pickett's Headquarters, November, 1862.

Ashby, W. W.

*Addison, John F., elected Second Lieutenant Company G, April, 1862; killed at Williamsburg.

*Abbott, Frank H., Killed at Williamsburg.

Adams, Francis, transferred to Maryland Line, May, 1862.

Burke, Jourdan M., detached with Signal Corps, June, 1862.

Bryant, John Y. Jr., discharged on account of ill health, May, 1862.

Crockford, W. H., transferred to Twelfth Virginia Infantry, January, 1863.

Carter, Meriwether, discharged on account of ill health, in winter, 1861.

Chase, T. L., wounded at Frazier's Farm; made Commissary Sergeant of Regiment, July, 1863.

Cawood, Chas. H., made Sergeant in Signal Corps, June, 1862.

Cadle, James R., transferred to Maryland Line, May, 1862.

Dyer, F. Baker, discharged on account of ill health.

Douglass, Thos. U., transferred to Second Virginia Cavalry

Davidson, Francis J., discharged on account of ill health.

Dunn, John W., transferred to Second Virginia Cavalry, in fall, 1861.

Fairfax, A. C., severely wounded at Seven Pines.

Foard, E. Norval, discharged on account of ill health, in winter, 1861.

Grady, Frank T., discharged on account of ill health.

Gwinn, Thos. T., transferred to Triplett's Battery.

Gunnel, Henry L., made a Lieutenant in First Virginia Battalion, October, 1864.

Green, Rob't H., died of disease in Charlottesville, June, 1862.

Gwinn, Geo. E., transferred to Maryland Line, May, 1862.

Hunt, Albert L., on detached service; in January, 1864, made Captain and Assistant Commissary of Fifth Virginia Cavalry.

*Hite, Hugh S., killed at Williamsburg; a good soldier.

*Hite, Kidder M., made First Corporal Company A, January, 1864.

Hicks, Geo. L., discharged on account of lameness.

Harmon, William, discharged—being a Marylander—and entered Tenth Virginia Cavalry.

Hartley, Ephraim W., died of disease at Staunton, July 22, 1862.

*Hunter, Alexander, wounded at Second Manassas; transferred to Fourth Virginia Cavalry, July, 1863.

Hyde, Reginald F., transferred to First Regiment Engineer Troops.

Hutchison, Ludwell L., on detached service with Signal Corps; killed at Spottsylvania Court House, May, 1864.

Hoxton, William W., transferred to Stewart's Horse Artillery, 1861, and made a Lieutenant.

Harmon, Chas. P., discharged—being a Marylander—and joined Imboden's Cavalry.

Jamieson, Geo. W., discharged on account of ill health, fall, 1861.

*Johnson, Rob't C., wounded at Williamsburg; killed at Frazier's Farm.

Jackson, And. J., discharged in summer, 1862; entered Quartermaster's Department.

Kelley, E. F., on detached service during the war with Medical Department.

Lambert, B. F., on detached service in Commissary Department

*Lee, Daniel M., killed in the charge at Frazier's Farm.

Mills, John, discharged—being a Marylander—in May, 1862.

Mason, John S., wounded at Second Manassas; made Lieutenant in Signal Corps in fall, 1862.

Mason, Landon R., discharged on account ill-health.

Marshall, E. C., Jr., transferred to Stribling's Battery, July, 1862.

McVeigh, James H. Jr., made Sergeant Company A, May, 1862; wounded badly at Williamsburg; transferred to Fourth Virginia cavalry, May, 1863.

*Morrill, Wm. T., made Color Sergeant of Regiment; killed at Seven Pines.

Milburn, W. C., on detached service during the war with Medical Department.

Murray, Jesse, with his Company until close of war.

Marye, Charles B., transferred to Braxton's Battery, 1862.

*McMurran, Samuel, in thirteen battles with his Company; wounded at Drury's Bluff; killed at Sailor's creek.

McKnight, C. H., badly wounded at Williamsburg; right

Mason, J. T., made midshipman, 1861.

*Malone, Edward, made Lieutenant in Third Regiment Engineer Troops, April, 1864.

*Perry, William, in seventeen battles with his Company; made Corporal, April, 1862; wounded at second Manassas; made Sergeant, January, 1864; present at surrender.

Potter, George F.

*Partlow, Theodore A., struck by a grape shot and three bullets at battle of Frazier's Farm, and died the following day.

Paul, Wm. J., wounded at Sharpsburg; transferred to Cavalry, 1862.

*Paul, Samuel B., made Sergeant, April, 1862; wounded at Williamsburg; made Lieutenant Company G, Nov. 1863; killed at Dinwiddie Court House.

Powell, R. C., made Assistant Surgeon in Navy Department, October, 1862.

Powell, Alfred H., transferred to Sixth Virginia Cavalry, fall, 1861.

Price, Mark L., with his Company until close of war; wounded at Seven Pines.

Purcell, Wm. F., discharged May, 1862, being a Marylander.

Robinson, R. H. P., discharged on account ill-health.

Slater, Joseph, discharged on account of injured foot, 1862.

Sangster, J. H. L., made Corporal Company A, August, 1862; mortally wounded at second Manassas.

Sully, Robert M., on detached service with Engineer Corps; made a Lieutenant therein.

*Stickley, James, made Corporal Company A, April, 1862; Sergeant, May, 1862.

*Swann, John N., mortally wounded at Williamsburg; died at Fortress Monroe.

Smith, Charles A., with his Company during the war; wounded at second Manassas.

Savage, John H., transferred to Maryland Line, May, 1862.

Thompson, John E., transferred to Maryland Line, May, 1862.

Taliaferro, Ed. T., wounded at Williamsburg; discharged, winter, 1862.

Thomas, Joshua, on detached service at Headquarters Army Northern Virginia.

Turner, Thomas B., wounded at Williamsburg; transferred to Scott's P. Rangers, August, 1862; made a Lieutenant thereof; killed in a skirmish.

Taliaferro, H. B., detached in Commissary Department until made Captain and Assistant Commissary, December, 1863.

Warfield, Abel D., discharged; over age; fall 1861; afterwards Foragemaster for La. Brigade.

Wright, Wm. D., transferred to Second Virginia Cavalry, fall, 1861.

White, Thomas M., on detached service at Headquarters Army Northern Virginia.

Wise, Edwin N., on detached service with Engineer Corps; made First Lieutenant Engineers, and assigned to First Regiment Engineer Troops.

Withers, Littleton, detached with Medical Department on account of bad health.

*Zimmerman, John R., in thirteen battles; with his Company during the war.

NAMES OF MEN WHO JOINED COMPANY A, AFTER SEPTEMBER 1st, 1861.

Ashby, Vernon W., wounded at Frazier's Farm; transferred to Cavalry, 1862.

*Bryant, J. Herbert, appointed Adjutant Seventeenth Virginia, April, 1862; badly wounded at Boonsboro'; made A. D. C. to General Corse, November, 1862.

Buford, P. S., detached with Pioneer Corps till October, 1864.

Bowers, D., exchanged to Twenty-ninth Virginia for Sam'l Loggans.

Cary, Clarence, made midshipman C. S. Navy, 1861.

Chase, J. E., on detached service as Division Dentist.

Eaches, H. B., severely wounded at Frazier's Farm; thereafter detached.

Eaches, J. M., transferred from First Missouri Infantry, February, 1864.

Edwards, B. C., wounded at Dinwiddie Court House.

*Fairfax, E. V., killed in the charge at Williamsburg.

Ford, H.

Foster, George R., on detached service.

*Hart, John S., made First Sergeant Company I; killed at Frazier's Farm.

Hough, Harrie, detached at General Pickett's Headquarters, November 10, 1862.

Hancock, J. D.

Hillsman, A. S.

Hancock, William, discharged; over age; February, 1864.

Haskins, D. H.

Jones, S. J., wounded at Dinwiddie Court House.

Johns, E. F., wounded at Drury's Bluff; discharged—ill-
health, December, 1864.

Kerr, George.

Laughlan, W. C.

Landreth, Thomas.

Loggans Samuel.

May, Reuben, on detached service.

McCawley, A. S. B.

Nannie, B. W., died of consumption in Petersburg, December, 1863.

*Paul, R. C., made Second Lieutenant, Company I.

Pulliam, T. A.

Ramsay, George W., with his Company during the war;
present at surrender.

Rowland, Abner.

Stoots, John.

Sutherland, John.

Turner, Wilson, transferred to Stewart's Horse Artillery;
killed at second Manassas.

COMPANY B.

("WARREN RIFLES.")

*Robert H. Simpson, Captain, made Major Seventeenth Vir-
ginia, November, 1862; mortally wounded at Drury's
Bluff.

Newton W. Snyder, First Lieutenant; not re-elected at
reorganization; since dead.

Thomas W. Petty, Second Lieutenant; not re-elected at
reorganization; served in Twelfth Virginia Cavalry.

Victor M. Brown, Second Lieutenant; made Captain and Regimental Commissary, 1861; Major and Brigade Commissary, November, 1862; served till close of war; since dead.

*Francis W. Lehew, First Sergeant, made First Lieutenant Company B, April, 1862; Captain Company B, November, 1862; served till close of war.

Richard L. Timberlake, Second Sergeant, entered Twelfth Virginia Cavalry, 1862; mortally wounded at ———

*Richard B. Buck, Third Sergeant, made First Sergeant Company B, April, 1862; Lieutenant in 1862; served till close of war; wounded at Dinwiddie Court House.

*William A. Rust, Fourth Sergeant, made Third Sergeant Company B, April, 1862; badly wounded at Williamsburg, and detailed in Quartermaster's Department thereafter.

John W. Boone, First Corporal, exchanged to Twelfth Virginia Cavalry, 1862.

Henry Walter, Second Corporal.

George Groves, Third Corporal, detailed in 1863 as Regimental shoemaker.

*Thomas N. Garrison, Fourth Corporal; badly wounded and disabled in the battle of Sharpsburg.

Privates.

Ashby, B. A.

Bowen, Thomas A., discharged in 1862.

Buck, Charles N., disabled by accidental wound, April, 1862.

Brown, David.

Brown, James E.

Balthis, William H.

Brown, Jesse.

Cornwall, Lebius, served with his Company till close of war.
Chapman, S. F.
*Carder, Stephen, mortally wounded at Seven Pines.
Chuning, Walter.
Cooley Samuel C., transferred to Seventh Virginia Cavalry in 1862.

Copp, Leonard, died, May 2d, 1862.
Castelow, George W.
Cline, Wm. R., made Sergeant of Company B; transferred to Seventh Virginia Cavalry, 1863.
*Darr, Marcus D., killed in the battle of Boonsboro'.
*Darr, Philip C., killed in the battle of Frazier's Farm.
Derflinger, Jonas J., served with his Company till close of war.

Duke, George, served with his Company till close of war.
Earle, Baalis.
Eckardt, Charles, killed in the battle of Five Forks.
Farra, Walton, wounded while on the Howlett's Line.
*Fristoe, Scott, served with his Company till close of war.
Forsythe, William.
*Forsythe Milton, killed in the battle of Five Forks.
Fox, Charles W.
Fox, Lemuel F.
Grove, Amos, discharged in 1862; over age.
Garrett, Newton, served with his Company till close of war.
Gordon, James W., died, April, 1862.
Grubbs, Franklin, died—date not known.
Harry, James P.
Hopper, James, died—date not known.
Johnston John J., transferred to Seventh Virginia Cavalry; killed.

23*

Kenner, William B., served with his Company till close of war.

Kidwell, John T.

Kendrick, James W.

Lehew, Charles E., served with his Company till close of war.

Lake, John H.

Littleton, E. S., served with his Company till close of war.

Miller, Joseph W., served with his Company till close of war; wounded in the battle of Flat creek.

Mitchell, Robert B.

Miller, David.

Myers, Gasper, served with his Company till close of war.

McDonald, William H., served with his Company till close of war.

McKay, Thomas B., put in a substitute in 1862.

Nail, James J.

Oliver, James A., on detailed service during war in Quartermaster's Department.

Painter, John R.

Painter, William H.

Peterson, Elijah.

*Petty, James T., served with his Company till close of war; wounded at Dinwiddie Court House.

Pipher, De Kalb, made Corporal, then Sergeant Company B; transferred to Seventh Virginia Cavalry, 1863; afterwards killed.

Peterson, J. W.

Petty, George N., exchanged to Twelfth Virginia Cavalry, October, 1862.

Richardson, C. W., transferred to Seventh Virginia Cavalry, 1862.

*Richardson, William, made Lieutenant Company B, April, 1862; mortally wounded at Williamsburg.

*Roy, Walter S., made Sergeant Company B, 1862; Lieutenant Company B, November, 1862; served with distinction till close of war.

Rinker, Romanus, served with his Company till close of war; wounded at Dinwiddie Court House.

*Roberts, Marcus, killed in the battle of Flat creek.

Reed, Peter, served with his Company till close of war.

Ritenour, Isaac.

*Scroggin, Peyton, killed in the battle of Williamsburg.

Spengler, D. H.

*Spengler, S. F., mortally wounded in the battle of second Manassas.

*Steel, John W., killed in the battle of Frazier's Farm.

Santmyers, Thomas W., served with his Company till close of war.

Settle, George W.

Seemers, John.

Spicer, Charles W.

Saffell, Ed. M.

*Steed, C. J., killed in the battle of second Manassas.

Triplett, William B.

Triplett, Leonidas.

Tyler, Gustavus, made Corporal Company B; served till close of war.

Turner, R. H., made Captain and Regimental Quartermaster, April, 1862; Major and Brigade Quartermaster, November, 1862.

Turner, James H.

Thompson, E. D., served with his Company till close of war.

Turner, William B., made Corporal Company B; served
till close of war.

Thompson, Gilbert.

Walter, William.

Williams, George N., discharged in 1862; over age.

Williams, William.

Willy, Atwell T.

Watkins, Samuel A., served with his Company till close of
war.

Weaver, Robert L.

Buck, Alvin D., on detached service at Army Headquarters.

Buck, Irvin A., went, as clerk to Gen. Beauregard's office, to
the West; made Captain and A. A. Gen. to Maj. Gen.
P. R. Cleburn, December, 1861.

Brown, James H., served with his Company till close of
war.

Campbell, Thomas R.

Hope George H., detached service during the war.

*Roy, Thomas B., went, as clerk to Gen. Beauregard's
office, to the West; made A. A. Gen. to Gen. Hardee at
battle of Shiloh; Major in August, 1862; Lieutenant
Colonel, in March, 1863.

Scroggin, Lewis A., detailed as teamster in Quartermaster's
Department.

Stickley, Philip, served with his Company till close of war.

NAMES OF MEN WHO JOINED COMPANY B, AFTER SEPTEMBER 1st, 1861.

*Turner, Smith S., made Second Lieutenant Company B,
April, 1862; First Lieutenant, November, 1862; served
with distinction till close of war.

Williams, George A., made Captain and A. A. General to Brigadier General Liddell, in June, 1862.

Petty, Bertrand W., made First Sergeant Company B; served till close of war.

Cook, Giles, Jr., made Sergeant Company B; transferred to Seventh Virginia Cavalry in 1863.

*Brown, John N., killed in the battle of Drury's Bluff.

*Broy, Elias, killed in the battle of Seven Pines.

Broy, William.

Brown, George W.

Brown, Joseph, died—date not known.

Brown, Joseph.

Cooper, Edward, served with his Company till close of war.

*Chrisman, John W., killed in the battle of Williamsburg.

Elbon, Joseph, on detached service.

Hopper, Harrison, served with his Company till close of war.

*Hickson, William, killed at Cold Harbor in 1864.

*Keller, Joseph, killed in the battle of Flat creek.

Parmer, Edward.

Petty, Henry S., served with his Company till close of war.

*Reager, Lewis, killed in the battle of Flat creek.

Steed, Charles B., killed accidently, April, 1864.

*Simpson, John W., killed in the battle of second Manassas.

Simmons, Charles, died—date not known.

*Stokes, Joseph, killed in the battle of Dinwiddie Court House.

Venable, James.

Willey, Achillis, discharged—date not known.

Willey, Jacob, served with his Company till close of war.

COMPANY C.

("LOUDOUN GUARDS.")

George R. Head, Captain, re-elected Captain at reorganization, but resigned.

William B. Lynch, First Lieutenant; elected Captain upon resignation of Geo. R. Head.

Charles B. Wildman, Second Lieutenant.

Jesse J. Stansbury, Second Lieutenant.

*W. W. Athey, First Sergeant, promoted First Lieutenant Company C, April 28, 1862.

A. J. Bradfield, Second Sergeant, on detached service in Commissary Department.

F. M. Henderson, Third Sergeant, promoted to First Lieutenant and Ordnance officer, Corse's Brigade, October, 1862.

Charles E. Evard, Fourth Sergeant.

William D. Easterday, First Corporal.

William S. Pickett, Second Corporal.

Benjamin F. Head, Third Corporal, promoted to Sergeant, April, 1862.

Edgar Littleton, Fourth Corporal, served through the war.

Privates.

Anker, Moses, discharged, August 10, 1862.

*Adie, George C., promoted Lieutenant of Company I, April, 1862; killed at Frazier's Farm.

Athey, John M.

*Atwell, Luther L., killed at Sharpsburg, and buried on battle field.

Bender, William.

Birkby, Charles T.

Birkby, Henry O.

Bopp, William G.

Brenner, John E., captured at Manassas Gap, and a prisoner till end of war.

Brown, Felding, discharged, July, 1862.

*Bradfield, C. H., very badly wounded May 31, 1862; Seven Pines.

Burke, Richard, promoted to Sergeant Company C, September, 1862; served during the war; wounded at Williamsburg.

*Brown, John C., killed at Sharpsburg.

Clagett, Thomas H., Jr., promoted Captain in Signal Corps, May, 1862.

Cockran, William J., with his Company during the war.

Cocklin, Michael,

Coury, David H.

Chamberlin, A. M.

Chamberlin, John, discharged, June 15, 1862.

Dailey, John T.

Donnelly, Edward.

*Divine, John A., promoted to First Sergeant Company C, September, 1862; was in every battle and skirmish his Company engaged in; since dead.

*Edwards, Chas. G., badly wounded in battle of Blackburn's Ford; promoted Orderly Sergeant Eighth Virginia, May, 1862.

Edwards, Chas. E., discharged May 16, 1862.

Fox, Erasmus H., discharged.

*Francis, Joseph F., Sergeant Major Seventeenth Virginia; killed at Seven Pines.

*Garner, H., promoted to Corporal Company C; killed on

Hamilton, Charles.

Hardy, Wm H., badly wounded at Sharpsburg.

Harris, Spencer M.

*Hatcher, Mahlon G., Color Sergeant Seventeenth Virginia;
   badly wounded at Williamsburg, and thereafter detailed
   in Quartermaster's Department.

Hammerly, John U.

Hurst, Samuel N., promoted to Corporal Company C; served
   during the war.

Insor, John, served with Company during the war.

Johanas, Martin.

Johnson, Wm. H.

Kelly, John W.

King, Edgar C., appointed Ordnance Sergeant Seventeenth
   Virginia, November, 1863; served till end of the war.

Kephart, Jasper C.

*Lambden, Geo. T., promoted to Lieutenant Company C,
   April, 1862; killed at Frazier's Farm.

Lauman, John H.

*Littleton, Francis B., promoted to Lieutenant, April, 1862;
   killed at Sharpsburg.

Linkins, Henry B.

Loughlin, Michael.

McCue, Patrick.

Manning, Jacob H., promoted Captain Signal Corps, June,
   1862.

*Murphy, John, promoted Color Corporal Seventeenth Vir-
   ginia.

Muse, James H., discharged in 1862, (July 16th.)

Mitchell, E. H., died in hospital at Manassas, January,
   1862.

Moley, James.

*Murphy, John L. A., lost a leg at Williamsburg; died in Old Capitol prison, June 30, 1862.

Norris, Thos. B., discharged July, 1862.

Orr, John M.

Orrison, Samuel.

Parker, Lafayette.

Quigley, John.

*Raney, Geo. W., killed May 19, 1862, by shell, while near Howlett's Line.

Ran, Charles H.

Rogers, Milton M., promoted to Lieutenant in Loudoun Artillery, May, 1862.

Rheim, James J., discharged May 15, 1862.

Rheim, Wm. G., discharged May 15, 1862.

Sexton, John W., wounded badly at Blackburn's Ford; discharged July 16, 1862.

*Sibbett, James H., killed at Williamsburg.

Sinclair, Chas. W., discharged July 16, 1862.

Skinner, Edgar, discharged.

Small, John C.

Steadman, Marshall B., discharged July 16, 1862.

Smart, Fayette, died March 24, 1863.

Thomas, Joseph B.

Thomas, Wm. H.

Thompson, John E.

Taylor, John M.

Vandevanter, O.

Wallace, David M., wounded at Seven Pines.

Wallace, James W.

*Wallace, Francis M., promoted to Sergeant Company C, April, 1862; killed at Boonsboro'.

*Wallace, James M. Jr., killed in battle Frazier's Farm.

Woodard, John W., died January, 1862.
Wright, John E.
Zealort, John, transferred to Maryland Line.
Adams, William, Regimental drummer.

NAMES OF MEN WHO JOINED COMPANY C AFTER SEPTEMBER 1, 1861.

Adams, Wm. F., discharged in 1862.
*Brightwell, Jas. T., killed at Drury's Bluff.
*Cherry, Benj. R., killed at Dinwiddie Court House.
Donnelly, Patrick.
Dove, D., Wounded in battle of Second Manassas.
East, Jos. H.
Ford, Sephton.
Hays, Edward.
Harris, Chas. T., with his Company through the war.
Hollingsworth, Thos. J., with his Company through the war.
Lefever, Henry, with his Company through the war.
*Lawhorn, Wm., lost a leg in battle at Dinwiddie Court House.
Massie, Z. P., served with Company during the war.
McCraw, Richard, died in hospital, August, 1864.
McCraw, Robert, died in hospital, July 25, 1864.
Mechols, Samuel, served through the war.
Morris, Nicholas, served through the war.
*Mechols, Rosemary, killed at Drury's Bluff, May 16, 1864.
Parker, John W. B., on detached service.
Reynolds, John, Served through the war.
Sewell, James W., died in hospital, North Carolina, April, 1864.

*Wright, Chas. E., killed in battle of Williamsburg.
Witt, Adam H., discharged July 9, 1864.

COMPANY D.

("FAIRFAX RIFLES.")

Wm. H. Dulaney, Captain, badly wounded at Blackburn's
Ford.

*Wm. A. Barnes, First Lieutenant, promoted to Captain
Company D, upon death of J. T. Burke; wounded at
Boonsboro'.

Francis G. Fox, Second Lieutenant.

*John T. Burke, Second Lieutenant, elected Captain Com-
pany D, April, 1862; wounded at Seven Pines; killed in
battle of Sharpsburg.

Alexander C. Williams, First Sergeant.

George W. Gains, Second Sergeant.

John D. Newnan, Third Sergeant.

John R. Steel, Fourth Sergeant, promoted Sergeant Company D.

William H. Steel, First Corporal.

James R. Steel, Second Corporal.

Richard H. Butler, Third Corporal.

John H. Barnes, Fourth Corporal.

Privates.

Ashford, Charles C.

Ashford, Francis A; made Lieutenant Company D.

Ashford, John A.

*Barnes, Samuel L., killed in the battle of Dinwiddie Court

*Beach, Ferdinand.
Beach, James.
Brown, William H.
Beak, Thomas.
Beach, Richard.
Caton, John C.
Cash, Patrick.
Chichester, Daniel Mc.
Coon, Solyman.
*Corbit, Robert E., killed in the battle of Drury's Bluff.
Cornell, Charles.
Cornell, Alexander.
Cockerville, Joseph.
Cockerville, John H.
Cook, Israel, wounded in the battle of Williamsburg.
Crowley, Michael.
Davis, John H.
Davis, James F.
Dulany, Winn T.
Dove, Armstead.
Firmacom, Geo. W.
*Ford, Walter S., killed in the battle of Dinwiddie Court
   House.
Freeman, Joseph N.
Fairfax, James W.
Fox, Wm. H.
Gooding, Wm. P.
Guard, Robert.
Gunnell, Charles A.
Gossam, James H.
Grigsby, A. S.
Hall, William,

Hixon, John, wounded at Boonsboro'.
Howard, Peter.
Harmon, Henry T.
Ish, Milton.
Jackson, Charles.
Kidwell, John T.
Kincheloe, Robert E.
Kidwell, Charles.
Lynn, Thos. W.
*Marks, David A., wounded in the battle of Williamsburg.
Millan, George S.
Monroe, Deskin.
Mills, S. D., wounded in the battle of Williamsburg.
Mayhugh, James.
Mayhugh, Richard.
Mayhugh, George.
Nalls, Benj. F.
*Newcomb, John W., promoted to Sergeant Company D;
    killed in front of Cold Harbor.
Newman, Charles.
Payne, Sanford.
Pettitt, John T.
Pettitt, Geo. W.
Pettitt, Chas. R.
Pearson, James.
*Richardson, Jas. W., killed in the battle of Dinwiddie
    Court House.
Richardson, Geo. H.
Ratcliffe, John R.
Simpson, Silas J.
Speaks, Everett.
Spindle, Spotsylvania.

Steel, Robert, promoted to Color Sergeant; wounded at Seven Pines.

Sutherland, A.

Sutherland, E.

Sutherland, J. W.

Stallians, Wm.

Steel, Peter C.

Taylor, Robert S., on detached service.

Thomas, Edgar.

Thomas, James A.

Thompson, Minor L.

Trumble, Martin.

Wrenn, Nelson H.

NAMES OF MEN WHO JOINED COMPANY D AFTER SEPTEMBER 1, 1861.

Coons, Lyman, wounded at Yorktown.

COMPANY E.

("MOUNT VERNON GUARDS.")

S. H. Devaughn, Captain.

*Steuart, Jas. M., Captain, elected Captain, April 29, 1862; vice W. H. Smith, resigned.

William H. Smith, First Lieutenant, re-elected Captain, April, 1862, and resigned the next day.

William W. Allen, Second Lieutenant.

Charles Javins, Second Lieutenant, severely wounded at
Blackburn's Ford, July 18, 1861.

John T. Devaughn, First Sergeant, discharged on account
of over age.

*A. M. Tubman, Second Sergeant, promoted to First Lieu-
tenant, April, 1862; badly wounded at Boonsboro', and
retired.

Joseph Hantzman, Third Sergeant.

*James A. Proctor, Fourth Sergeant, wounded at Frazier's
Farm, and died from effects of wound.

*James E. Molair, First Corporal, killed in the battle of
Seven Pines.

*William M. Simpson, Second Corporal, promoted Lieuten-
ant Company E, April, 1862.

William Hammerdinger, Third Corporal.

John A. Humphries, Fourth Corporal, on detailed service
at Lynchburg.

Privates.

*Allison, John, badly wounded on Howlett's Line, and died
from effects of wounds; distinguished for bravery.

Allison, Richard F., wounded at Seven Pines.

Arrington, Charles H.

Allison, John H.

Allison, George W., on detailed service with Brigade Ordnance.

Biggs, Henry R., wounded at Yorktown.

Beach, Solomon.

*Bushby, Joseph, killed in the battle of Frazier's Farm.

Brown, Alexander H., on detached service with Medical

*Coleman, S. S., distinguished for gallantry; transferred to Navy Department, 1864.

Craven, George.

Conway, Albert.

*Colomus, Joseph, killed in the battle of Sharpsburg.

Clapdore, William H., transferred to Navy Department.

Chauncey, Thomas A.

Cook, John T., died of disease.

Cross, Thomas, with his Company during the war.

Davis, Thomas, on detached service with Quartermaster's Department.

Delphy, John, on detached service in Richmond.

Dudly, Joseph T.

Day, James, detached service in Lynchburg.

Duvall, James E., transferred to Maryland Line.

Donelly, John.

Davis, R. H., transferred to Cavalry service.

Davis, Arthur, on detached service with Quartermaster.

Darly, William.

Davis, Peter, on detached service with Ordnance Train.

*Emmerson, Benjamin F., wounded at Frazier's Farm, and died from effects of wounds.

Edwards, Ephriam, discharged—over age.

Field, Edgar H.

Field, Benjamin F., promoted First Sergeant, Company E.

Field, George W.

Fadely Charles W., wounded at Second Manassas, and discharged.

Flxhnor, William, discharged—over age.

Greenwood, Charles, promoted First Corporal Company E.

Gregg, Joseph, promoted Corporal Company E.

Gale, James, on detached service in Lynchburg.

Hudson, Thomas B., wounded at Frazier's Farm, and discharged.

Horseman, John.

Hicks, Albert, promoted to Second Sergeant Company E; .with Company till end of war.

*Harper, Washington M., promoted to Color Corporal; distinguished for gallantry; killed at Sharpsburg.

Harper, George G., discharged—over age.

Jones, Stephen.

Jenkins, William.

Kidwell, Hezekiah, died of disease.

Kraig, Godfred, procured a substitute.

Kirk, Harrison, discharged—over age.

Lyles, George W.

Lyles, Alexander.

Lewis, William L.

Lewis, Charles E., transferred to Cavalry service.

Lawler, John, transferred to Navy Department.

Myers, Abraham, furnished a substitute.

Murray, John W.

Mankin, Charles.

*McKnight, William P., elected Second Lieutenant, April, 1862; promoted to First Lieutenant Company E, July 26, 1864; received three wounds at Sharpsburg.

Ogden, George.

Ogden, Elijah, on detached service in Richmond.

Piles, Walter, discharged—over age.

Paff, Frederick.

Powers, Franklin, promoted Lieutenant Company G.

Proctor, John J.

Paine, John.

*Padgett, William T., killed in the battle of Williamsburg.

*Penn, Joseph B., killed at the battle of Williamsburg.

Rudd, Charles D., discharged—over age.

Richards, George H., on detached service in Commissary Department.

Roland, Richard, promoted Sergeant Company E; severely wounded at Seven Pines.

Rudd, Isaac W.

Rudd, Robert, on detached service in Lynchburg.

Robey, William, transferred to Maryland Line.

Sipple, Charles O.

Shinn, James W., on detached service in Quartermaster's Department.

Stephenson, Robert A., promoted to Sergeant Company E; afterwards Lieutenant in Twenty-fifth Battalion.

Schwartz, Isaac, furnished a substitute.

Summers, George L., promoted to Sergeant Company E.

Sullivan, John.

Snyder, George.

Swann, James.

*Skidmore, A. F., killed at Yorktown.

Turner, Albert, discharged—over age.

Underwood, William, with Company during the war.

Walker, James T., transferred to Navy Department.

*Warfield, George T., promoted Corporal Company E; killed at Frazier's Farm.

Walker, E. O.

Waters, John W., transferred to Navy Department.

Williams, Joseph, discharged—over age.

Warring, Edward, with Company during the war.

Warring, Basil.

*Wools, Albert, killed in the battle of Frazier's Farm.

White, Charles O., discharged.

Young, Daniel.

NAMES OF MEN WHO JOINED COMPANY E, AFTER SEPTEMBER 1st, 1861.

Greenwood, John, died of disease.
Rose, A. F., wounded at Boonsboro'.
Gardner, ———.
Kenly, ———.
Hanks, E.
Carrico, W.
Clarke, ———.
Glasscock, George, wounded at Dinwiddie Court House.
Abbot, George.
*Duncan, W., killed at Dinwiddie Court House.
Bransford, ———.
Cassel, ———.
Christian, ———, died from disease.
Shrakes, James P.,
Mankin, Samuel, } Alexandrians who joined about 1864.
Miffleton, Henry,

———

COMPANY F.

("PRINCE WILLIAM RIFLES.")

Geo. S. Hamilton, Captain, resigned at reorganization, April, 1862.

*Grayson Tyler, First Lieut., made Captain, April, 1862; acting Major from May, 1864; made Lt. Col. Aug., 1864.

*Winston L. Carter, Second Lieutenant, killed at Williamsburg, May 5, 1862.

John R. Jordan, First Sergeant, transferred to Navy Department.

*James E. Herrell, Second Sergeant, made First Lieutenant, April, 1862; Captain, August, 1864.

Lewis H. Hambrick, Third Sergeant, discharged.

*Joel N. Hulfish, Fourth Sergeant, made Second Lieutenant; killed at Frazier's Farm.

*James A. Pattie, First Corporal, made Sergeant Company F.

*Frederick Ebhardt, Second Corporal, lost left thumb at Williamsburg.

*Jessie S. Rogers, Third Corporal, made First Sergeant Company F; wounded at Seven Pines.

*Geo. S. Pickett, Fourth Corporal, severely wounded at Sailor's Creek.

Privates.

*Arnold, William.

*Brady, James D., killed in the battle of Seven Pines.

*Brady, Richard, died in Richmond.

*Brady, John W., died in prison.

*Basey, Edmond, made Sergeant Company F; killed at Seven Pines.

*Burgess, John R., killed in the battle of Frazier's Farm.

*Burgess, E. W., killed in the battle of Seven Pines.

Bristow, R. B., transferred to artillery.

*Baxter, Wm. H., wounded badly at Drury's Bluff; killed in the battle of Five Forks.

Cogan, Chas. E., wounded at Seven Pines.

Clowe, Thos. S., died at his home.

*Carter, A. J., wounded at Williamsburg.

*Clowe, E. W., wounded at Seven Pines, afterwards discharged.

*Cornwell, John W., wounded at Frazier's Farm.
Callehan, Patrick.
*Carter, James A.
Canty, Stephen.
Davis, Minor F., wounded at Seven Pines.
*Davis, Wm. E., wounded in the battle of Sharpsburg.
Duval, F. M.
Ellis, Thos. R., killed in the battle of Sailor's Creek.
Foley, A. R.
Foley, Richard A.
Foley, Willis F.
Flynn, John.
*Grayson, A. B., killed in the battle of Williamsburg.
*Galliher, M. W., wounded at Frazier's Farm, and discharged in consequence.
*Hutcherson, R. L.
Harrison, John C., transferred to ———.
*Hairless, James N.
*Hairless, Chas. S.
*Hurst, James R., killed at Petersburg by one of the Seventeenth Virginia.
*Hawley, A. B. D.
*Hixson, Felix G., killed in the battle of Frazier's Farm.
*Harrington, Daniel, discharged, over age.
*Hutcherson, F. M.
Kernard, Geo. W.
Keys, Rob't A.
*Lee, Reubin M., killed in the battle of Five Forks.
McDonaugh, Jas., discharged in 1862.
McIntosh, Wm. S., died in hospital—date not known.
*Moore, John A., supposed to have been killed at Five Forks.
Marshall, John G.

*Newman, M. R., wounded at Williamsburg; made Color Corporal.

*Nalls, Thos. W.

*O'Shea, Thomas, made Lieutenant Company I.

Polend, John T.

Polend, Chas. J.

Payne, James R.

Payne, Levi.

*Pierson, Geo. W.

Pierson, Rob't A.

*Rollins, James D., wounded in the battle of Frazier's Farm.

Riszin, John F., discharged while at Fairfax Court House.

Rennoe, John L., wounded at May's Head.

*Smith, Wm. R., made Sergeant Company F; killed at Seven Pines.

Sutler, William.

*Sherwood, W. W.

*Sullivan, Jas. R.

Sherwood, James B.

Turner, Thos. W., discharged on account of ill health.

Tillet, James F.

NAMES OF MEN WHO JOINED COMPANY F AFTER SEPTEMBER 1, 1861.

*Basey, Luther, died in hospital at Petersburg.

*Brawner, John A.

*Hite, George, supposed to have been killed at Sailor's Creek.

*Rollins, Geo. W., wounded at Five Forks.

COMPANY G.

("EMMETT GUARDS.")

J. E. Towson, Captain, entered artillery service.

W. H. Kemper, First Lieutenant, entered artillery service.

*Robert F. Knox, Second Lieutenant, promoted Captain Company G, April, 1862; wounded at Seven Pines, and Dinwiddie Court House.

Charles W. Wattles, Second Lieutenant, entered the War Department in Richmond.

*James W. Ivors, First Sergeant, wounded at Yorktown; died from effects of wound.

James Donohoe, Second Sergeant, record unknown.

Edmund Costigan, Third Sergeant, record unknown.

Michael Nugeant, Fourth Sergeant, record unknown.

*Patrick Doyle, First Corporal, promoted Sergeant, April, 1862; killed at Seven Pines.

Francis McEllier, Second Corporal; record unknown.

John Murphy, Third Corporal, record unknown.

James Brannon, Fourth Corporal, record unknown.

Privates.

Archibald, James, record unknown.

Butler, Thomas, record unknown.

Burke, Patrick, record unknown.

Bradley, James, record unknown.

Brennan, Thomas, record unknown,

Conner, Cornelius, record unknown.

Connelly, Francis, record unknown.

Carroll, Thomas, record unknown.

Cook, William, record unknown.

Delihunt, John, record unknown.

Dohoney, Daniel, killed at Boonsboro', Md.

Downey, Michael, record unknown.

Dohoney, John, record unknown.

Dyer, Michael, wounded at Williamsburg; discharged, 1862; over age.

Fitzgerald, Lawrence, record unknown.

Fitzgerald, Jerry, record unknown.

Farrell, Anthony, record unknown.

*Grace, John, with his Company during the war.

Griffin, Daniel, record unknown.

Harper, Charles.

Honigan, John, killed in the battle of Drury's Bluff.

Hayes, Thomas, promoted to Color Corporal; wounded at Sharpsburg.

Hassan, Patrick, record unknown.

Hart, Patrick, record unknown.

Hoar, Morris, record unknown.

Henry, Alexander.

*Harrington, Patrick, killed in the battle of Seven Pines.

*Johnson, James, with his Company during the war.

*Keating, James, killed in the battle of Boonsboro'.

Keating, Patrick, wounded at Williamsburg.

Lane, Patrick, record unknown.

Lynch, Morris, record unknown.

*Murphy, John, killed in the battle of Williamsburg.

Mack, Dennis, record unknown.

McSherry, Patrick, record unknown.

McSherry, Richard, record unknown.

Moore, Michael, record unknown.

McKeown, William, record unknown.

McCarty, Charles, record unknown.

Monahan, Lawrence, record unknown.

Mongoll, Frederick, discharged, 1862; over age.

Martin, James, record unknown.

*Manly, David, wounded at second Manassas.

Manly, Joseph, record unknown.

Nugent, John, record unknown.

Purcell, William, died in Richmond, 1863.

Quinn, James, record unknown.

*Riley, Patrick, promoted First Sergeant Company G; served with distinction during the war.

*Ready, John, with Company during the war—a good soldier.

*Smith, Hugh, record unknown.

Thompson, James, with his Company during the war.

Travers, Michael, record unknown.

NAMES OF MEN WHO JOINED COMPANY G, SINCE SEPTEMBER 1st 1861.

*James A. Fisher, promoted First Sergeant; badly wounded at Drury's Bluff.

*Paul, Samuel B., Lieutenant; formerly in Company A; killed at Dinwiddie Court House.

Robinson, ———, killed in the battle of Dinwiddie Court House.

Clark, G., record unknown.

*Haywood, William, killed in the battle of Drury's Bluff.

Elliott, Thomas, wounded at Drury's Bluff.

Looing, L., wounded at Drury's Bluff.

*Powers, F., First Lieutenant, wounded at Boonsboro', Md.

*Addison, J. F., Lieutenant; formerly in Company A; killed at Williamsburg.

*Gray, William E., Lieutenant; formerly in Company A; killed at Seven Pines.

Kennedy, Daniel, wounded at Dinwiddie Court House.

COMPANY H.

("OLD DOMINION RIFLES.")

*Arthur Herbert, Captain, elected Major, April, 1862; Lieutenant Colonel, November, 1862; Colonel, August, 1864.

*Wm. H. Fowle, Jr., First Lieutenant, promoted Captain, April, 1862; wounded at Seven Pines and Drury's Bluff.

*D. F. Forrest, Second Lieutenant, accepted a position on General Trimble's Staff, afterwards Paymaster in the Navy.

*W. W. Zimmerman, Second Lieutenant, promoted to First Lieutenant, April, 1862; served as Adjutant of the Seventeenth Virginia from November, 1862.

*A. C. Kell, First Sergeant, promoted to Second Lieutenant, April, 1862; wounded at Boonsboro'.

S. R. Shinn, Second Sergeant, promoted to Lieutenant of Heavy Battery, near Richmond; since dead.

*Thos. V. Fitzhugh, Third Sergeant, promoted to Lieutenant, April, 1862; wounded at Seven Pines, and died from effects of wound.

*Jas. E. Grimes, First Corporal, promoted to Sergeant; died from effects of wounds received at Williamsburg.

George Wise, Second Corporal, promoted to Sergeant Company H; appointed Ordnance Serg ant Seventeenth Virginia, November, 1862; assigned o duty with First Regiment Engineer Troc s, by ord of the War Department, December, 1863.

W. H. H. Smith, Third Corporal; since dead.

*Edwin G. Barbour, Fourth Corporal, a good soldier; died in prison from effects of wounds received at the battle of Williamsburg.

Privates.

Arnold, John, with his Company during the war.

Ashby, V. W., transferred to Company A while at Yorktown.

Adam, W. W., transferred to Cavalry while on Howlett's Line.

*Appich, Harrison, wounded at Seven Pines and at Sailor's Creek.

*Baldwin, Jonah W., died in Richmond from effects of wounds received at Seven Pines.

Baldwin, Ed. F., wounded at Seven Pines and at Sailor's Creek.

Beacham, Edwin S., died in Lynchburg from disease; a good soldier.

Bacon, Wm. H., with his Company during the war.

*Buchanan, Robert, promoted Color Corporal; died from effects of wound received at Manassas Gap.

*Bradley, Henry N., promoted to Color Corporal; wounded severely at Williamsburg, and afterwards on detached

*Burgess, Charles, killed at Frazier's Farm while gallantly fighting.

Berry, Douglass, on detached service in Lynchburg during the war.

Beach, John, with his Company during the war.

Brent, Virginius, severely wounded at Frazier's Farm.

*Boyer, Wm. H., promoted to Sergeant; wounded at Second Manassas; died from effects of wound received at Sailor's Creek.

*Ballenger, Clinton, killed in the battle of Williamsburg.

*Castleman, Wm. A., killed in the battle of Sharpsburg.

Collingsworth, Robert, with his Company during the war.

Calmus, August.

Carlin, J. E. F., on detached service during the war.

*Deavers, Ira, at Five Forks, when the Regiment was cut off, he secreted the " Colors " in his breast and saved them.

Duffey, John H.

Dozier, Melville, detached from Company as a courier for General ———.

Darley, Charles, lost his arm by an accident in Richmond.

Godwin, James, wounded at Seven Pines, and afterwards detailed on account of wounds.

Gardner, Wm. F., promoted Lieutenant Company H after battles around Richmond, 1862; wounded at Second Manassas; acting Adjutant of the Regiment at the time; detached as Adjutant, Post at Staunton, on account of wound, until appointed Chaplain of Twenty-fourth Virginia.

Howell, Emory, on detached service in Richmond.

Hough, Lewis E., on detached service at Post Office Depart-

Hough, Harrie, transferred to Company A while at Yorktown.

*Hall, Wm. J., wounded at Seven Pines; wounded in four
places at battle of Sharpsburg; on detached service thereafter.

*Higdon, Wm. J., on detailed service; voluntarily entered
battle of Seven Pines, and was killed.

Hurdle, A. U., detached in Richmond on account of ill
health; since dead.

Hunter, Chas. E., shot himself accidentally at battle of
Drury's Bluff.

Heiss, Fred. S., discharged in 1862 as an alien.

Holland, Wm. J., transferred to Maryland Line.

*Jordan, J. Pendleton, wounded in the battle of Frazier's
Farm in two places.

Kidwell, Wm. F., with his Company during the war.

Kidwell, Robert.

Kinsloe, Owen, on detached service with Quartermaster's
Department during the war.

Krouse, John E., disabled while cutting wood, and put on
detached service.

*Kelly, Thomas, with his Company during the war and in
all the battles.

*Lovelace, Wm. A., promoted to Sergeant Company H;
killed at Second Manassas.

*Lunt, Wm. H., killed in the battle of Seven Pines; a noble
soldier.

*Lannon, Patrick, killed at Williamsburg.

Latham, R. M., with Company until 1863; discharged on
account of injury.

*Mills, John T., killed at Drury's Bluff; distinguished for
bravery.

*Murray, John S., killed in the battle of Seven Pines.

Murray, Chas. H.

Miller, Fred. W., on detached service until 1864, with Company thereafter.

Murphy, James, entered Cavalry service.

McKeown, Nicholas, discharged 1862; over age.

Mankin, Oscar, wounded at Second Manassas, afterwards transferred to Cavalry.

Moore, Frederick, on detached service; since dead.

Plain, B. K., with his Company during the war.

Padgett, Benjamin, died at Culpeper Court House from disease, 1862.

Paul, Rob't C., transferred to Company A, at Yorktown.

Pattie, John H.

Pitts, Henry S., wounded at Williamsburg.

Riley, J. P., wounded at first Manassas, in hand.

Roxbury, Edward, with his Company during the war.

Simmons, Jos. F.

Summers, George W., wounded at Sailor's Creek.

Smith, S. D., wounded at Dinwiddie Court House.

Smith, James M., on detached service.

Suit, John, on detached service.

Summers, W., on detached service, with Ordnance Department, during the war.

Sutherland, Lee, transferred to Maryland Artillery, 1863.

Sowers, James K., entered Cavalry service; since killed.

Sedwick, William D., transferred to Cavalry.

Taylor, Robert J.

Taylor, George W.

Tatsapaugh, William H., discharged, 1862; over age.

*Terret, William, killed in front of Cold Harbor.

Travers, John, transferred to iron-clad at Kingston, 1864.

White, B. C., promoted Sergeant Company H; with his
  Company during the war.
Whiting, Charles, transferred to Cavalry.
Warfield, Edgar, on detached service with Medical Depart-
  ment; was at surrender
Wall, Augustus, with his Company during the war.
Withers, John B., entered the Cavalry service.
*Watkins, James H., wounded at Five Forks.
Wood, Francis, entered Artillery service.
Whitely, William, discharged, 1862; over age.
Williamson, James A., with his Company during the war.
Wise, Frank, on detached service; elected Captain of local
  defence Company, 1864.
Young, Robert, with his Company during the war; present
  at surrender; went down with ship Santee, December 30,
  1869.
Patrick, John H., transferred to Maryland Line.

NAMES OF MEN WHO JOINED COMPANY H, AFTER SEPTEMBER 1, 1861.

*Ballenger, Frank, killed in the battle of second Manassas.
Deavers, Barney, with his Company during the war.
Fewell, Rodie, with his Company during the war.
*Fewell, Haydon, killed in the battle of Frazier's Farm.
Howell, Asbury, joined Company in 1864; wounded at
  Five Forks.
Milburn, J. C., joined Company in 1862; was present at
  surrender.
Price, Charles.
Smith, James, on detached survice on on account of ill

Sedwick, Charles, discharged—under age.

Whittington, Rodie, killed at Seven Pines; joined Company day previous.

COMPANY I.

("O'CONNEL GUARDS.")

*S. W. Prestman, Captain, wounded at Blackburn's Ford; assigned to duty with Army of the West in May, 1862; accidently killed January, 1864.

*Raymond Fairfax, First Lieutenant; promoted Captain, April, 1862; in command of Division Pioneer Corps.

*H. S. Wallace, Second Lieutenant, promoted First Lieutenant, April 1862; in command of Company through the war; since dead.

James E. Green, Second Lieutenant, not re-elected at re-organization.

*John S. Hart, First Sergeant, killed at Frazier's Farm.

James Southerland, Second Sergeant.

R. C. Bell, Third Sergeant.

Michael Clune, Fourth Sergeant.

Patrick Creely, First Corporal.

Thomas Kelleher, Second Corporal.

J. W. King, Third Corporal.

J. Sulivan, Fourth Corporal.

Privates.

Bluit, William
Burmingham, Thomas.
Berry, John.

Boswell, James.
Cornell, Martin.
Cully, Michael.
Couda, John.
Carnell, W. A.
De Grave, Antoine.
Dougherty, Edward.
Goushur, Adam.
Heard, John L.
Hanriham, Michael.
Hanriham, Thomas.
Herring, Thomas.
Horan, Timothy.
Hurley, Cornelius.
Kennedy, Jeremiah.
Kinnery, William.
Kerby, Thomas.
Leary, John, record unkown.
McSherry, Michael.
McBride, Michael.
Murphy, Dennis, lost an arm in the battle of Blackburn's
    Ford; a good soldier.
McMahon, Michael, record unknown.
Murray, William, record unknown.
McCormic, Patrick, record unknown.
Mahar, Edward, record unknown.
McGuire, Owen, record unknown.
Noland, John, record unknown.
O'Hair, Michael, record unknown.
Phalin, James, record unknown.
Quigly, Patrick, record unknown.
Ryan, John, promoted Corporal Company I.

Ryan, Timothy, record unknown.
Rosa, Frederick, record unknown.
Slemmer, John, record unknown.
Slember, Benjamin, record unknown.
Shennessy, Simon, record unknown.
Tierney, Michael, record unknown
Townsend, George, record unknown.
Whalin, James, record unknown.
Connors, Owen, record unknown.

NAMES OF MEN WHO JOINED COMPANY I, AFTER SEPTEMBER 1st, 1861.

*R. C. Paul, Lieutenant, promoted Lieutenant Company I from Company A; wounded at Dinwiddie Court House.

*George C. Adie, Lieutenant, promoted Lieutenant Company I, April, 1862; wounded at Seven Pines; killed at Frazier's Farm.

Ryan, Patrick, wounded at Seven Pines.

*O'Shea, Thomas, made Lieutenant Company I, from Company F.

COMPANY K.

("WARRENTON RIFLES.")

B. H. Shackelford, Captain, discharged on account of wound received at Blackburn's Ford.

J. W. McGee, First Lieutenant, made Captain, vice B. H. Shackelford; served with distinction till April, 1862.

H. C. Withers, Second Lieutenant, honorably discharged in

S. C. Lindsay, Third Lieutenant, resigned September, 1861
—ill health.

David C. Graham, First Sergeant.

*A. M. Brodie, Second Sergeant, made Lieutenant Com-
pany K, April, 1862; wounded at Seven Pines.

J. H. F. Tompkins, Third Sergeant, made Lieutenant at
Fairfax Court House, afterwards honorably discharged.

John R. Turner, Fourth Sergeant, made Lieutenant at
Fairfax Court House, afterwards transferred.

Hugh T. Kemper, First Corporal.

William Lear, Second Corporal, transferred to another
service.

John Beckham, Third Corporal, made Sergeant Company
K, thereafter Lieutenant in Irish Battalion.

L. E. Hamme, Fourth Corporal, on detached service in
Medical Department.

Privates.

Allen, Henry, discharged—cause and date not known.

Allison, R. S.

Bragg, Wm. M., transferred to Mosby's command; died in
prison.

Bragg, Chas. P., transferred to ———; date not known.

Bennett, H. T., made Corporal Company K.

Brooks, Thos. D.

Brigges, Henry C., transferred to First Regiment Engineer
Troops; wounded at Drury's Bluff.

Cologne, J. A. C., made Sergeant Company K.

Cromwell, O.

Cole, Francis M., discharged—cause and date not known.

Cole, Jos. N., discharged—cause and date not known.

Carter, C. S., transferred to ———; date not known.

Digges, Geo. W., discharged on account of ill health.

*Digges, Chas. W. Jr., made Color Corporal Seventeenth Virginia; wounded at Seven Pines, thereafter transferred to Cavalry and made Lieutenant.

*Embrey, A. G., killed before second Cold Harbor.

Edmonds, Elias, wounded at ———, and discharged in consequence.

Fisher, James A., made First Sergeant Company G.

Fisher, John E., wounded at Seven Pines, thereafter unfit for duty.

Fletcher, Robert H.

Fletcher, Harrison.

Florance, Benj., made Corporal Company K.

Fletcher, Albert, on detached service with ———.

Francis, A. B., made Color Corporal; wounded at Dinwiddie Court House.

Fant, John E. P.

Field, W. H., died; date not known.

Frankland, W. E., transferred to Mosby's command; made a Captain.

Foster, Wm. G., made Sergeant of Company K; on detached service.

Fletcher, Edwin, wounded at the battle of Second Manassas.

Golway, Wm., discharged—cause and date not known.

Groves, R. H., made Corporal Company K; died from disease.

Hughlett, R. K., discharged—cause and date not known.

Hughes, Geo. N., made Sergeant Company K.

Harris, Albert, wounded at Howlett's house.

Hope, Jas. W., died; date not known.

Hoffman, O., wounded at Suffolk, thereafter discharged.

Hansbrough, P. C.

Hansbrough, John G.

Jeffries, Fred.

Jeffries, J. A., on detached service.

Jenkins, Geo. F., wounded at ———.

Jones, Elcon, transferred to Signal Corps; made a Captain.

Kemper, Geo. N.

Klœber, C. C.

*Kirby, James D., made Second Lieutenant Company K; at reorganization elected Captain; wounded at Dinwiddie Court House; present at surrender.

*Kane, Thos. F., killed in the battle of Seven Pines.

Leitz, George.

Lear, Alpheus, transferred to ———.

*Love, Robert, killed at Seven Pines.

McConchie, B. F., discharged; date not known.

McLearen, T. C., discharged; date not known.

McClanahan, Geo. W.

McIlhany, Hugh M., transferred to ———, and made a Lieutenant.

Moore, Jos. E., on detached service.

Mooney, N. R.

Mooney, G. T., wounded at Drury's Bluff.

McIntosh, C. R., wounded at ———.

Murray, Thomas J., made Sergeant Company K, afterwards Lieutenant of Irish Battalion.

Marshall, Robert T., transferred to Louisiana Artillery; killed.

Minter, William H., wounded at ———.

Nelson, Joseph H., transferred to Mosby's Command; made a Lieutenant.

Norris, W. C., Jr., on detached service with Ordnance Department.

Parkinson, John W., discharged—date not known.

26*

Pattie, James S.

*Pemberton, J. O., wounded at Williamsburg, and on Howlett's Line.

Payne, Richards, Jr., made Sergeant Company K, thereafter a Lieutenant in Irish Battalion.

Payne, Richard, killed at Williamsburg.

*Payne, Henry, wounded at Seven Pines.

Reynolds, L. H., discharged—cause and date not known.

Saunders, T. B., badly wounded at Suffolk, and discharged.

Sedwick, John F., transferred to ———.

Smith, Edwin, made Captain and Assistant Commissary Forty-ninth Virginia Regiment, September, 1861.

Smith, John J.

Smith, Norman E., transferred to Mosby's Command; made Lieutenant; killed.

Singleton, James A., wounded at Williamsburg, and captured.

Suddith, P. H., wounded at ———.

Sinclair, A. G., discharged on account of wound received at Blackburn's Ford.

Suddith, R. A.

Spilman, William M., badly wounded at Williamsburg.

*Slaughter, Lewis, elected Lieutenant Company K, April, 1862; served till close of war.

Smith, Albert, made Adjutant of the Thirty-eighth Virginia Regiment,

*Stanfield, H. A. R., made Sergeant Company K; killed at Drury's Bluff.

Stout, James H., assigned to light duty; ill health.

Tapp, H. J.

Thomas, J. P., made Corporal Company K.

White, Frank, transferred to ———.

Weaver, R. A., died—date not known.
Walden, R. E., wounded at ————.
Weaver, M. A.
Wall, William, transferred to ————.
Withers, A. F.
Whitescarrer, G. H., made Sergeant Company K; transferred to Mosby; made a Lieutenant; killed.
Washington, Mason.

————

NAMES OF MEN WHO JOINED COMPANY K, AFTER SEPTEMBER 1, 1861.

Day, Alexander, died—date not known.

NOTE.

The following Statement did not receive its proper place in the first pages of this record, because of ignorance of the subject. The writer takes pleasure in giving it space at this late day, (a number of pages of this work having been printed before his attention was called to it,) and hopes the readers of these pages will appreciate his feelings and join with him in regrets because of its omission.— " Better late than never."

STATEMENT.

The Loudoun Guards, (Company C,) and the Warren Rifles, (Company B,) were engaged with the Alexandria Battalion in the irksome duty of guarding the city of Alexandria previous to its evacuation. These companies were present when the Federal troops entered, and they marched out Duke street, with the Battalion, on the memorable 24th of May, 1861.

They were earnest, zealous co-workers in the cause, and are entitled to equal credit with the Alexandria companies.